PRISONER
ECHO'S WOLF #1
WEREWOLF MARINES

Lia Silver

Also by Lia Silver

Laura's Wolf (Werewolf Marines)

ISBN: 0692260226
ISBN-13: 978-0692260227

Table of Contents

Prisoner

ONE

DJ

We're Like Brothers

DJ Torres had broken a lot of rules in his life. But he'd never expected to break the most important rule of all, the rule he'd had drummed into his head since he was a little kid (and little pup), particularly since it was one of the few rules that he actually agreed with: "Never turn anyone into a werewolf."

It went on, at least the way DJ's pack elders had taught it to him, "Not even if they're your best friend. *Especially* not if they're your best friend. Not even if they're dying and it's the only way to save their life. *Especially* not if they're dying and it's the only way to save their life. They'll end up wishing you'd let them die. And so will you."

DJ looked down at Roy Farrell, his best friend, whose life he'd saved by turning him into a werewolf, and hoped to hell they weren't both going to end up wishing DJ had let him die.

The blazing Afghanistan sunlight glared off the white sand, making DJ's eyes water. Though they were shaded by a pair of boulders, the radiant heat made sweat trickle down his bare back.

The helicopter had mostly stopped burning, but it still sent up a plume of oily black smoke. On the bright side, it was a signal for medevac and rescue. On the dark side, it was also a signal for anyone in the vicinity who might want to kill or capture some Marines. DJ briefly released Roy's hand to pat his M-16 and Roy's SAW, just to reassure himself that he could snatch up either weapon in an instant.

The air was so bone-dry and still that DJ couldn't even smell the smoke. If he'd been a wolf, he could have. If he'd been a wolf, he could have detected not only the smoke, but also the twisted metal of the wrecked helo, the crushed weeds beneath them, and Roy's natural scent, a blend of charcoal, leather, damp earth, and dark chocolate.

As a man, all DJ could smell was Roy's blood. It had gotten all over him when he'd hoisted Roy over his shoulders and carried him from the helo. He could feel it drying in the sun, sticking his hair together in clumps and pulling at his skin.

Despite the heat and the shirt DJ had wrapped around him, Roy was shivering. DJ wondered if he should move Roy out of the shade, or if that would just give him a sunburn on top of the worst shrapnel wounds DJ had ever seen anyone take and not immediately drop dead.

Roy closed his eyes. His breath went out in a sticky-sounding exhale, leaving more blood on his lips. He didn't breathe in again.

DJ's heart lurched at the thought that after everything he'd done, Roy would die anyway, right now in his arms.

"Hey!" When that didn't get a response or an inhale, DJ slapped his cheek. "Wake up!"

Roy dragged in a labored breath, his eyes fluttering half-open. "I'm listening."

Which was another bad fucking sign, because DJ hadn't been talking. He'd talked so much in the last hour or however long it had been since their helicopter had been shot down, trying to keep Roy awake and tell him everything he needed to know about being a werewolf, that he'd had to stop for fear of losing his voice.

"What are you listening to?" DJ cleared his throat, but he still sounded like a rusty door when he spoke again. "What did I just tell you?"

"Uh…" Roy's gaze drifted into the distance. "Can't remember. Sorry. I'm a little… A little spacy."

Sorry, I'm a little spacy.

Meaning, *I'm in shock and bleeding inside and the only thing*

6

keeping me alive is my werewolf healing and I've probably got another half-hour or so before even that won't cut it any more.

And that was classic Roy. After all the time they'd spent together on their fire team, with Roy carrying the SAW and DJ carrying the SAW's extra ammunition, they'd gotten to be each other's universal translators.

I'm fine, DJ, stop bothering me.

Meaning, *I haven't slept in three days and I'm about to pass out, but don't worry, I can hold out till we get back to the base.*

I've got dust in my eyes, Roy, can you read this for me?

Meaning, *I'll lose my mind if I have to spend five minutes trying to read three words, and there's guys around who don't already know about me, and if they call me stupid I just might snap and punch them out and get another demerit.*

"It's okay, Roy." DJ squeezed his hands. "Just hang on, all right? You can't go to sleep till medevac gets here. Don't close your eyes."

Roy nodded, his face tightening like even that tiny movement required a huge effort. "I felt better as a wolf. Should I change again?"

DJ thought about it, remembering Roy's gigantic wolf sprawled panting on the sand, his thick white fur sodden with blood. "No. I don't think it would help enough to be worth it. You can only shift while you're conscious. If you turn into a wolf and then pass out, you won't be able to change back."

Roy actually managed to smile, which was more than DJ could do. "*You* could pester medevac into taking a wolf."

"Where the fuck *is* medevac?" DJ muttered, scanning the sky for the millionth time. It was a perfect, cloudless, brilliant blue, and absolutely empty.

Roy followed his gaze. Softly, he said, "It's a beautiful day."

DJ bit his lip and concentrated on the sharp pain until the prickling in his eyes subsided. "Do you remember any of what I told you about being a werewolf?"

Roy seemed to try hard to recall. Finally, he said, "My scent name is Guinness."

DJ surprised himself by laughing. Of all the useless, random things to stick in his mind! "Do you remember anything other than scent names?"

"They're an important cultural tradition."

DJ felt his eyebrows go up. "Now you're just fucking with me."

Roy didn't smile again— he probably didn't have the energy— but he admitted, "Yeah. That really is all I remember, though. Your scent name is Lechon. It means..." His voice trailed off, and he gave the smallest of shrugs.

DJ tried not to let his dismay show. Roy was drifting off again; he knew what lechon was.

"It's Filipino roast pork," DJ reminded him. "You had it last Christmas. Remember?"

Roy and nine other Marines who didn't have relatives nearby had come over to spend Christmas with DJ's family. While the guys sat around drinking beer and DJ's parents oversaw the roasting of the hog, the little kids formed a posse and moved in on Roy.

Their appointed leader said in awestruck tones, "You're so tall. Like a giant!"

"Only compared to DJ," Roy had remarked.

But agreeing at all was his downfall; next thing Roy knew, he was running around and around the backyard while the kids took turns riding on his shoulders, yelling stuff like, "Giddy-up, Midnight!" and "Activate the mecha-laser, Death Falcon!" and "Run, Hagrid! We're late for the Quidditch match!"

"*Remember?*" DJ repeated, when Roy didn't reply. "Christmas in San Diego? Pig on a spit? Getting commandeered to play horsie by a gang of sugar-crazed five-year-olds?"

Roy made a non-committal noise that DJ interpreted as, "Not really, but I'll say anything if it'll make you shut up and let me sleep."

"Okay!" DJ spoke loudly, before Roy could slip into unconsciousness. "I'll tell you everything again. Pay attention now."

"I am," Roy said, not very convincingly.

For the fourth time, DJ began, "I'm a born wolf. My pack is my family. You're a made wolf, and *you need a pack*. If you don't remember anything else, you have to remember that. I'll call my family and tell them I bit you and they need to adopt you into their pack, but you have to let them do it. If you don't bond with a pack, you'll lose your mind or commit suicide. *You need a pack.*"

"Can't you be my pack?" As Roy spoke, DJ felt him instinctively reaching out with his latent pack sense, trying to create a bond.

Startled, DJ didn't immediately raise his mental shields. There was no true bond yet, so the feelings he got from Roy were distant, something he understood rather than felt himself. He sensed Roy's determination to hold on, the steely willpower that had kept him going this long, his trust in DJ, his fear of dying, and his relief that at least he wouldn't die alone.

But most of what DJ perceived was physical sensation: an unbearable sense of drowning and a desperate hunger for air, tearing agony in his chest, overwhelming exhaustion and the near-irresistible desire to close his eyes and sleep, the coppery taste of the blood welling up into his mouth, and a bone-deep chill. And the one feeling that Roy clung to, the only one that wasn't terrible and frightening, which was the warmth of DJ's arms holding him.

DJ again bit down on his lip as he raised his shields, cutting Roy off. Roy flinched as if it had physically hurt him, though it couldn't have. But Roy had to have sensed DJ, as DJ had sensed Roy, and it must have felt as if he'd been pushed away and locked out.

DJ was probably doing the right thing, but he felt incredibly guilty. Not to mention scared that it was actually the wrong thing, and frustrated and angry at himself that he couldn't figure it out for sure. And that summed up this entire fucking nightmare of a deployment.

"I can't *now*," DJ said. "We'll be in a pack together later."

"My brother," Roy mumbled.

"Yeah, we'll be like brothers."

Roy shook his head, then spoke more clearly. "You're already my brother. We're brother Marines. So why not now?"

DJ tried to explain it in simple terms, hoping Roy was with it enough to understand. "Because we can't stay together after this. You'll be sent to a hospital, and I've got to stay with our unit. If we bonded as a pack and then we were cut off from each other, it would hurt you. It might even kill you. Born wolves can be separated from their pack for a long time, obviously, but made wolves can't."

DJ hesitated, eyeing Roy to see if he'd put two and two together: if he couldn't leave his pack and his pack was DJ's family, ten thousand miles away in San Diego, that would be the end of his career as a Marine.

They'll end up wishing you'd let them die. The remembered voice came to DJ so vividly that it was almost as if his grandmother had whispered in his ear.

He might have to leave anyway, because of his wounds, DJ argued with the memory of Grandma Steel. *And none of the other stuff you warned me about happened. He has the pack sense, so he won't be a lone wolf who can't bond and lose his mind from loneliness. If he doesn't have a power, that's no big deal. And if he has one that he can't control, it's obviously no big deal either or I'd have noticed by now.*

With an inner shudder, DJ recalled Grandma Steel's most horrifying story: the made wolf who couldn't control his power to create fire, and burned himself to death.

"You're going to be okay, Roy," DJ said, trying to convince himself as much as Roy. "Just stay with—"

"I'm sorry, DJ," Roy said abruptly. "I'm blacking out."

A second passed, and nothing happened. Then his eyes rolled back, his head tipped to the side, and his entire body went limp.

"Shit!" DJ tried to wake him up again, yelling at and even slapping him, but nothing worked. Roy lay across his lap, over two hundred pounds of dead weight, his face ashen. Red bubbles formed and broke at the corners of his lips. DJ told himself that at least that meant he was still breathing.

Then the most welcome sound DJ had ever heard filled the air, the steady whump-whump-whump of helicopter blades. As the medevac helo landed, while the Blackhawks that escorted it hovered above, such an intense wave of relief washed over him that he felt like he might black out too.

The Navy hospital corpsmen ran up. Half of them started examining Roy, while the others, to DJ's confusion, started prodding at *him.*

"Where are you hit?" one of them demanded.

"I scraped my leg. And I cut my arm. But it's not serious, don't bother with me."

A corpsman wiped a pad over DJ's bare chest. When the gauze

immediately turned red, DJ realized what the problem was.

"It's his blood," DJ explained. "I carried him out of the helo."

The corpsman glanced at DJ, then at Roy, who looked bigger than ever sprawled out on the ground. "You're strong."

"I'm a fucking Marine," DJ said, exasperated at himself for distracting the man when Roy was bleeding to death. "Just get him out of here, will you?"

To his relief, they were already loading Roy on to a stretcher.

DJ went with them, answering questions while leaving out the critical "I'm secretly a super-strong werewolf and I bit my buddy to give him werewolf healing powers" part: "Maybe a surface-to-air missile, but I'm really not sure;" "Yes, we were the only survivors;" "No, no one's fired on us here;" "No, we landed okay, he was wounded when the helo was hit;" "Oh, right, I forgot about his shoulder— yeah, that was from the crash, a piece of jagged metal wrapped around it;" "No, actually, he was conscious up until about fifteen minutes ago."

That last one got him some surprised stares, which to his relief seemed to distract them from the bite wounds on Roy's shoulder.

As he approached the helo, DJ let himself believe that everything would be all right. Roy would never do another tour of duty, but probably that was just as well. DJ would finish out his, and then he'd have to decide whether or not to re-enlist.

He was leaning toward not. More and more, he'd gotten tempted by the idea of spending time with his pack, of performing in clubs, of hunting in the mountains and the desert, of riding his Harley, and of doing it all without ever having to worry about getting blown up or shot or stress-injured, or having his friends get blown up or shot or stress-injured.

Maybe then he could meet a girl for more than a one-night stand. Being a Marine was a double-edged sword: he never had trouble finding a woman for a weekend fling, but he never found anyone he could take home and introduce to his family, either. Werewolf women sure as hell didn't want a man who was never around, civilian women mostly didn't either, and military women were never around themselves.

DJ thought about the kind of woman he'd want. After this fucking horrible deployment, what he wanted most was someone relaxing.

Someone sweet and gentle and accepting and calm.

Maybe a nurse or a doctor or a physical therapist: a caretaking type, but one who'd seen enough herself that his war stories wouldn't shock her and revealing that he was a werewolf, if she wasn't one herself, wouldn't send her running for the hills. His family would approve of a medical professional, and considering how much DJ had done to make them tear their fur out, it would be nice if he could do *something* they wouldn't hate.

She should be playful, too. Social. Energetic, or he'd drive her nuts. Uninhibited. They'd get off work and meet at a club, and he'd DJ and she'd dance, and then they'd go home together and have wild sex all night.

As he scrambled into the helo, he pictured the life he'd have when he got back home. He'd find a job in private security or law enforcement, he'd get to see his pack all the time, he and Roy could hang out all the time too since Roy would be in his pack, Roy would get better, DJ's pack would finally approve of what he was doing with his life, and DJ would find that gentle, sweet, playful, sexy, pack-acceptable woman of his dreams.

That pleasant daydream lasted exactly as long as it took for the helo to take off and for Roy to start gasping like he was choking to death.

The hospital corpsmen shoved DJ aside so they could cluster even closer around Roy.

"Tension pneumothorax," one of the corpsmen said. "Give me the fourteen-gauge needle."

As the corpsman drove the huge needle into his chest, Roy's eyes opened.

"It's all right," DJ called out, but he could see that Roy was in no condition to hear or understand. He started struggling wildly, but was pinned by the straps around the stretcher.

Roy abruptly stopped fighting, his blood-smeared face taut with rage and fear. All his muscles tensed at once.

Oh, shit, DJ thought.

The air shimmered over the stretcher, and a huge white wolf lay where Roy had been, panting and bloody, glistening fangs bared.

DJ threw himself forward, trying to block the view, yelling,

"Change back, change back!"

He opened himself to the pack sense and slapped his hand down on Roy's haunch, sending, *calm, safety, friends, pack.*

The air shimmered again, and the wolf was gone. And just in time, too: Roy's gray eyes looked into DJ's, confused and frightened, and then he passed out again.

The corpsmen were as still as if they were caught in a freeze-frame.

"What the *fuck* is going on back there?" yelled the pilot.

That seemed to set everyone in motion again.

"He's not breathing!" a corpsman called.

DJ could do nothing but watch, paralyzed with fear, as the corpsman shoved a tube down Roy's throat and attached it to some machine.

It wasn't until he saw Roy's chest rising and falling with mechanical regularity that he realized that even if Roy survived, he'd be royally fucked if he was revealed as a werewolf. DJ had to do something to distract the corpsmen so memorably that by the time they even recalled the wolf, they'd decide that they'd been so tired and stressed and sleep-deprived that they'd imagined it.

DJ was so tired and stressed and sleep-deprived himself that the only thing that came to mind was faking a combat stress reaction. He'd seen enough of those to do a convincing one. Unfortunately, they mostly weren't that dramatic. No one would notice if he talked too much or stared into space or got jumpy or became depressed or—

"Did you see—" one of the corpsmen began.

—or got extremely angry for no good reason.

"What the fuck is wrong with you motherfucking assholes?" DJ yelled at the top of his lungs.

That got the attention of the corpsmen.

"Cool it," one of them said. "We're doing the best we can for your buddy."

"Fuck your fucking best!" DJ shouted. He banged his fist on the floor, careful not to dent the metal. "It took you fucking hours to get here! My buddy could've fucking died! Fuck you all! Who needs terrorists when we've got dumb fucks like you? Fuck—"

A sharp pain stung his arm. He glanced over, and caught a corpsman withdrawing an empty syringe.

I guess I overdid it, DJ thought. *Sorry, Roy. I hope I didn't fuck things up for you* again.

"What was that?" He already felt dizzy.

"Just a mild sedative," the corpsman replied warily.

"Mild, my ass," said DJ, right before everything went black.

TWO

Echo

My Life Protects My Sister

Echo walked silently through the icy forest, toward the home of the man she'd been sent to kill.

It was a moonless night, and a thick layer of clouds hid the stars. Echo could see only the dim outlines of trees and, when she looked into the infrared, the red glow of a squirrel or owl's body heat. Ever since she'd parked off-road and started walking, flurries of snow had alternated with stinging sprays of hail, big as bullets.

Echo idly wondered if tonight would be the night she'd go down in a hail of actual bullets. She hadn't bothered to go to the dead drop and pick up her body armor, but wore the same clothes she'd arrived in: rock climbing shoes of thin leather so she could feel the ground almost as well as if she'd gone barefoot, an old pair of black jeans she could kick in, and a black tank top.

She'd gotten a few curious glances when she'd gotten off the plane, and when she'd used her cover ID to rent a car, the man behind the counter had said, "It's fifteen degrees below zero, honey. You might want to put on some layers before you go outside."

Echo, caught between impulse ("You don't say, *sugar-bunch,* I hadn't noticed,") and training (laugh, nod, say, "Me and my thermal everything are hitting the bathroom before I collect the car, don't worry,") had said nothing, but stared at him until he'd lowered his gaze and pushed her the keys.

As she came to the barbed wire-topped walls of her target's compound, snow swirling around her, she reminded herself to be cautious. Even the tiniest mistake could cost Echo her life.

And that would be bad, she reminded herself. *If I die, it will break Charlie's heart. If I die, they'll have no reason to keep Charlie alive.*

"So long as Charlie lives, I have to live," she said aloud, the fierce wind whipping the sound away. "My life protects my sister. I protect my sister with my life."

Maybe she'd said those words too often. They felt less compelling every time.

Echo made herself picture Charlie. Her sister, her twin, the other half of her soul— if Echo had a soul, which she doubted. Probably Charlie had gotten it all.

She thought of Charlie swimming in the heated pool, her fragile body at ease, supported by the water. Charlie in the cafeteria, stealthily tossing Skittles high into the air so no one could figure out where they were falling from. Charlie curled up in an armchair, happily reading a paperback whose cover showed a heaving-bosomed woman in a clinch with a billionaire or Viking or Navy SEAL. Once, to Echo's amusement, the cover had featured a time-traveling billionaire Viking Navy SEAL, wearing a three-piece suit, a horned helmet, and dog tags.

Charlie in a hospital bed with a needle in her arm and a tube down her throat, holding up a scrap of paper lettered shakily, *DON'T WORRY. I'LL BE OUT SOON.*

"So long as Charlie lives…" Echo whispered again.

Once Echo was certain that she wouldn't carelessly throw her life away, she made her move.

Echo took a pair of gloves from her pocket and put them on, then launched herself at the wall. Her powerful muscles sent her high into the air. For a split second, she enjoyed her own strength and the sense of flight. Then her fingers caught rough concrete, her soles braced against the wall, and she used her momentum to flip herself up and over the barbed wire.

Despite her promise to herself, she hadn't checked for guards. But nothing stirred as she landed lightly inside the compound. As the dossier had said, her target lived alone. The windows of his house were dark.

Echo inspected the house. Sure enough, it was booby-trapped. But she was supposed to make her target's death look like a misfired burglary or a revenge killing, not a stealthy assassination, so she didn't bother dismantling the traps. Instead, she pulled a large rock out of the frozen ground and threw it through the nearest window.

Glass shattered, and a small explosion lit the night. Echo dove through the smoking hole in the wall, landed in a darkened living room, and leaped to the top of a bookcase. She settled down in the narrow gap between the bookcase and the ceiling, waiting.

Semi-automatic fire raked the living room, first at waist level, then low to catch anyone who had dropped to the floor. Pages fluttered down from shredded books.

Echo's heart sped up until it reached its ideal rate, then continued to rise. She controlled it back to the ideal. She controlled her breathing, too, and ensured that her palms didn't sweat. Her body worked perfectly, giving her the exact amount of adrenaline release needed to maximize her for action and not a drop more.

The shooting stopped. The target stepped cautiously into the living room. Before he had a chance to glance up, Echo dropped from her perch.

He reacted quickly, but nowhere near quickly enough. He was still swinging his weapon in the direction where she had been when she sprang behind him, got her forearm around his throat, and snapped his neck.

Other than the tactile sensation of warm flesh compressing and hard bones cracking, Echo felt nothing. She let the corpse fall to the floor, trying to recall how long it had been since she'd experienced emotion when she killed. Two years? Three?

She couldn't remember. But it was good that she'd reached that point. Once she'd felt all kinds of things, so intensely that they'd nearly ripped her apart. But that had been years ago. Now, even when she was off-duty, she felt little. With any luck, one day she'd feel nothing at all.

Except love for Charlie, she amended. She had to keep that. It was the only reason her handlers had to put so much effort into keeping

Charlie alive. But Echo could lose every other feeling, as far as she was concerned. Feelings brought nothing but pain. Echo would be glad to be rid of them.

All the same, when she examined the less-shredded books, she was relieved to see that her target really was a white supremacist terrorist. Or, at least, he owned a lot of books that talked about exterminating "mud people" and "Jewish vermin."

Sometimes Echo suspected that her targets weren't the terrorists or criminals the dossiers claimed them to be, but merely people whom her handlers had decided were a threat to their secret projects. She didn't like to think that she might be murdering some journalist or crusading civilian whose only crime was getting too close to the truth.

Of course, the target who lay dead on the floor could be a racist but not a terrorist. It was even possible that her handlers had sent her to kill an obviously hateful person solely to make her feel better about being their pet assassin.

She took a step toward the doorway, thinking to search the house and see if she could find any evidence of bomb-making or violent conspiracies.

Police sirens keened in the distance. She slipped out of the house, leaped over the wall, and vanished into the woods.

In the short time it had taken her to complete her mission, the snow flurries had blown up into a blizzard. Echo walked through a world of white, and felt nothing. Not even cold.

Once Echo passed the entrance guards at Wildfire Base, she took the stairs down to the service level. It was a longer walk, but a quieter one. The unmarked corridors were deserted except for the automated vehicles trundling along by themselves, with their recorded voices chanting, "Robotic transport vehicles will not avoid you. Please step aside. Robotic transport vehicles will not avoid you. Please step aside."

She had her peaceful walk, then took an elevator to the apartment she shared with Charlie. Her handlers had been alerted the moment she'd returned, but she hoped they'd leave her alone for an hour or so before they came knocking, demanding a report. Obviously she'd executed her mission: she'd come back.

Echo stood by the retina scanner and opened her eyes wide. A light flashed, and the door slid open.

She froze on the threshold. Charlie was in the living room, but sitting stiffly erect in her chair, not curled up as she preferred, and she didn't smile when she saw Echo. Her paperback, featuring a heaving-bosomed woman clutching at a gladiator, lay bookmarked on the table. And Echo's least favorite handler, Mr. Dowling, sat across from Charlie in a chair dragged in from the dining room.

The sofa had been saved for Echo, but she didn't sit down. That might invite Mr. Dowling to stay longer. Instead, she stepped in front of it.

"I can deliver my mission report in your office," Echo said. "We don't have to bore Charlie with it."

Charlie made a face that Echo interpreted as fifty percent *Your missions don't bore me, what are you talking about* and fifty percent *God, yes, get this pompous asshole out of here so I can return to my beloved Maximus.*

"Momentarily," said Mr. Dowling. "Why didn't you collect your equipment from the dead drop?"

Echo shrugged. "I didn't need it."

Mr. Dowling's lips pursed. "We're concerned that you're becoming dangerously careless."

"I accomplished the mission," Echo said, annoyed. "Apart from not getting body armor that I didn't need and would've only weighed me down, I did it exactly as I was ordered."

"The dead drop also contained your weapon."

Oops. "I didn't need that, either. If it was important how I killed him, I should have been told in my briefing."

"The point is that you went into the compound of a dangerous terrorist completely unarmed and unprotected."

"The target is dead. What else matters?"

To Echo's surprise, the look of annoyance and frustration on Mr. Dowling's face was mirrored by one of anger and fear on Charlie's.

"What matters is that we have serious concerns about you," said Mr. Dowling. "You've taken completely unnecessary risks, and you've done so repeatedly and despite multiple warnings."

"I'll be more careful next time," Echo said, but she could hear the insincerity in her own voice, and knew the others could as well.

"Goddammit, Echo!" Charlie exclaimed, her pale face flushing pink. "Are you *trying* to get yourself killed?"

Unable to lie to her sister, Echo had to think about it before she replied.

"No," she said at last.

No, but I can't say that it would bother me if I did.

She looked inside herself for fear or sadness at the thought of her own death, and found none. Nor did she find anticipation or relief. She simply didn't care.

Charlie turned to Mr. Dowling. "I told you she was burned out. She needs a break. Give her a month off."

"She had last month off," Mr. Dowling pointed out.

"Well, it wasn't enough," snapped Charlie. "Give her another one."

"We're giving her a partner," said Mr. Dowling. "We think she'll do better if someone's there to keep an eye on her."

"I don't want a partner," Echo said, horrified. "I don't play well with others."

Mr. Dowling caught her gaze, then looked meaningfully at Charlie. "We think *everyone* will be better off if you have one."

A red haze settled over Echo's vision at the implied threat to her sister. If she snapped Mr. Dowling's neck, then picked up Charlie and bolted for the service corridors, she could probably make it to the vehicle bay before the alarm sounded…

"Echo!" Charlie said sharply, and banged her cane on the floor.

The haze faded. Echo folded her arms across her chest. "Who exactly do you think could keep up with me? You better not stick me with someone from your screwed-up pack of co-dependent made wolves."

A stifled giggle escaped Charlie's lips.

Mr. Dowling glared at both of them. "We're considering all our options for a suitable candidate. I merely wanted to inform you in advance, so it wouldn't come as a shock. And I didn't have to do that, so I hope you appreciate it."

Echo barely stopped herself from rolling her eyes. Probably what she disliked the most about Mr. Dowling was the way he made her feel and act like a sullen teenager. "You're too kind to me. I don't deserve it."

He shook his head in exasperation. "Come with me to my office and I'll take your mission report. After that, you're on leave till further notice."

Echo resignedly followed him out. As long as Charlie lived, Echo had no real power. She'd do anything to protect her last surviving sister, and her handlers knew it. If they wanted her to take a partner, she'd have to grit her teeth and accept it.

And when Charlie died and Echo had nothing left to live for, Echo would kill them all.

THREE

DJ

Wolf on the Run

DJ woke up feeling beat to hell. He didn't get a single second of peaceful amnesia, but instantly recalled everything. Roy's expression of mild surprise as he looked down at the blood pouring from his chest. DJ's fangs sinking into Roy's shoulder. Roy becoming a wolf in the medevac helo.

Once DJ opened his eyes, he'd find out if Roy had made it. As long as he pretended to be asleep, DJ could keep on believing that he had.

He'd never been good at keeping still. Or at letting curiosity go unsatisfied, even when he knew the news would be bad. He lay vibrating with suppressed energy, wondering where he was and what had happened to Roy, if he was alive and if DJ's ploy had worked and—

DJ opened his eyes and sat up, throwing off the covers. He was in a small, windowless room. The air that blew through the vents was cool and dry and smelled faintly of antiseptic. A private hospital room? There was no call button, though.

He wore white cotton pajamas, presumably hospital-issue, and the cuts on his leg and arm had healed to pink scars. DJ frowned at them. He'd been unconscious for at least a couple days, then. No wonder he was so stiff and sore. He had a caffeine withdrawal headache, too. Maybe the corpsman had accidentally overdosed him, or maybe he'd had a bad reaction to the sedative. It wouldn't be the first time meds hadn't worked on him the way they did on one-bodies.

There were two doors in the room. One wouldn't open, but the other was ajar and led to a bathroom. He considered knocking on the locked door, then decided to take advantage of the bathroom first. He used it, washed up, and then cupped some tap water in his hands and drank. It was completely tasteless, unlike the overly chlorinated water at his base in Afghanistan or the mineral-heavy water of Camp Pendleton. He drank again, wondering where he was. A different base in Afghanistan? A military hospital in Germany?

He reached out for the pack sense, but wasn't surprised when he felt nothing. Camp Pendleton was only forty miles from San Diego, but even that was too far for him to sense his pack. He smiled at the memory of how his sister Five would reach out to him every time she drove past the base on her way to or from Los Angeles, holding the contact until she finally faded out of range.

When he returned to the main room, a middle-aged woman was standing by the bed. She had shoulder-length hair the color of dust, and wore a doctor's coat without rank insignia. A civilian employee, probably.

"Dale Torres? I'm Dr. Semple." The woman offered her hand, which DJ automatically shook. In her other hand, she held a small black box— some medical device, DJ supposed.

"My buddy, Roy Farrell—" DJ, caught between "How is he?" and "Is he alive?" broke off without finishing the sentence.

"Please, sit down," the doctor said, indicating the bed.

DJ sat, then stood up. "How— Look, if he's dead, just tell me."

"He was taken to a shock-trauma unit," Dr. Semple said.

DJ sank back down on the bed. "So he's alive? How is he?"

"Let's talk about you for a moment. You seemed to experience some combat stress. Has that happened to you before?"

"Yeah, a couple times. How's Roy?"

The doctor didn't answer directly, which DJ hoped was because she didn't know rather than because she was trying to break the bad news in stages. "Does your combat stress always show up as outbursts of rage?"

"No." DJ wished he'd claimed he'd never gotten it before. He didn't want to discuss his fake rage or real stress. "How's Roy?"

"Let's not get off-track. We're talking about you now." Maybe it was DJ's paranoid imagination, but he could swear the doctor was enjoying herself. "Do you have nightmares? Or insomnia?"

Those last few months, Roy had barely slept. Sometimes Marco had to threaten to send him to the aid station unless he lay down and closed his eyes. Then Roy, who never disobeyed orders, would lie down and close his eyes. And Roy, who ran out under fire to rescue wounded men without a second's hesitation, would wake up shaking and drenched in sweat.

DJ forced his mind away from those memories. Answering the doctor's question was probably the quickest route to getting some answers himself. "If I drink too much coffee, sure I get insomnia. But not otherwise, and no nightmares. Speaking of coffee, would it be possible for me to get some? Like, right now?"

It was another cup poured into the ocean of DJ's frustration when the doctor ignored his request for a caffeine hit. "Do you ever have things that you can't stop thinking about, even if you want to?"

"Not the way you're thinking of."

"What way are you thinking of?"

"Song lyrics cluttering up my head. Tunes I don't even like. You know, earworms." DJ couldn't stand sitting still any longer, so he got up again. Then he remembered that he was trying to convince the doctor that he *wasn't* anxious, and stood awkwardly, forcing himself not to pace. "Do you even know what happened to Roy? Should I be asking someone else?"

Dr. Semple ignored his questions. "Tell me what combat stress feels like to you."

DJ was way too stressed out to keep track of complicated lies, so he stuck to the truth. "Like everything's going too fast."

"Such as?"

"My heartbeat. My thoughts. The rotation of the Earth."

"The rotation of the Earth?" Dr. Semple repeated, sounding fascinated.

"You asked. It doesn't happen very often, and it only lasts a couple hours. I don't get flashbacks. I don't get panic attacks. I don't have trouble eating." He caught himself pacing, and shoved his palm against the wall to make himself stop. "Losing my shit in the helicopter was a one-time incident because I was upset that my buddy *stopped breathing*, now will you please fucking tell me if he's still alive!"

Dr. Semple didn't reply for long enough that DJ knew what she'd say before she spoke. "I'm very sorry to inform you..."

But I saved him, DJ protested to himself. His thoughts were so loud that they drowned out whatever the doctor was saying. *I carried him out of the helo and I bit him and I got him through the change. He was breathing when I saw him last. I saved him.*

"How did he die?" DJ's own voice sounded as if it was coming from a long way away. "I mean, where? In the helo? In the hospital?"

The doctor tilted her head, as if considering how much to reveal. "In the hospital. His heart stopped after surgery."

"I didn't save him," DJ said numbly. "I did everything I could. And he still died."

"What did you do for him?" Dr. Semple asked.

For a brief, despairing moment, DJ didn't see any reason why he shouldn't tell the truth. Nothing mattered except that the best friend he'd ever had was dead. He couldn't imagine anything ever mattering to him again.

Except his pack. He still had to protect them. "I got him out of the helo. I bandaged his wounds."

"What else?"

I talked to him to keep him awake. I wrapped my shirt around him to keep him warm. I turned him on his side so he wouldn't choke on his own blood. I held him in my arms so he'd know he wasn't alone.

"What else?" Dr. Semple repeated.

DJ shook his head, unable to speak. The everlasting whirlwind of thoughts in his head had changed, not to the elegant simplicity of combat where they laid themselves out like beads on a string, but to a book he couldn't read and didn't want to.

He hoped Roy hadn't been left by himself in a bed, but had some nurse or medic to hold his hand at the end. Roy hated being alone.

"You did everything you could," the doctor said. "You even made him into a werewolf."

Automatically, DJ nodded.

"Was it the first time you'd done that?"

DJ's head jerked up, his mind abruptly spinning into gear again. He'd been set up! "I'm sorry, what were you saying? I wasn't paying attention."

"You heard me," Dr. Semple said. "And I saw you nod. You're a werewolf."

Adrenaline flooded DJ's veins, making his heart race and hands tingle.

I was so worried about Roy, I forgot to ask where I was, DJ thought. *I'm in one of* those *places. One of those evil secret labs they warned me about when I was a pup. I've been captured by people who lock up shifters and experiment on them— torture them— dissect* them!

Then a surge of hope nearly washed away his fear as he realized that *everything* might have been a set-up. Roy might still be alive, a prisoner like himself.

"What do you want from me?" DJ asked warily.

"What's your power?"

DJ wondered if that was a test to see if he'd lie. He lied anyway, giving the doctor his father's power. "Sometimes I dream of things happening in other countries. Every now and then I can get on the internet and find out more about what I saw, but usually it's not the sort of thing that makes the news."

"Like what?"

"Ordinary people's lives. Like, I'll dream of a Japanese schoolgirl taking a test. If I look up high schools in Japan, I'll see that it was a true dream, because all the details will be the same, and I didn't know them before. But I still won't know who she was or which school she was at, because I don't know Japanese."

If the situation hadn't been so dire, DJ would have laughed at the hilariously unimpressed look that crossed the doctor's face. Personally, though DJ wouldn't have traded his power for his father's, he'd always enjoyed hearing about Dad's dreams and thought it would be a fun power to have.

"Then let's start with a demo," said Dr. Semple. "I'd like to see your wolf."

Tempted as DJ was to agree and then immediately attack her, there had to be precautions in place to stop him from doing exactly that. The black box was probably a stun gun. If he sprang, he'd get dropped. The door must be locked and reinforced. Or else there were twenty guards outside. Or the room could be instantly flooded with knockout gas. Or all of the above.

"Let's make a deal," DJ suggested, trying not to visibly gauge the distance between him and the box. "I'll do it if you tell me what really happened to Roy."

Dr. Semple again tilted her head, then nodded. DJ figured she was getting the go-ahead from a tiny receiver in her ear. "He's alive."

DJ's knees went so weak that he had to sit down on the bed. It occurred to him that the doctor could be lying again, but DJ couldn't help believing her. Roy had endured wounds that should have killed him before he'd even made it out of the helo. He'd managed the intense effort and concentration that it took to become a wolf when he was bleeding out and on the verge of death. If he could do that, he could survive long enough to let his new healing powers work their magic.

"And? How is he?" DJ heard his voice shake with relief.

"He's in critical condition."

"What does that mean, exactly?"

"He's unconscious and on a ventilator. He can't breathe on his own. His vital signs are unstable." Dr. Semple eyed DJ as if she was waiting for him to cry or pray or something, then went on. "But his wounds are healing. His doctors believe that he'll recover."

"Where is he?" DJ demanded. "Is he here? I want to see him."

"He's at another facility, in a classified location."

"Where are we?"

"That's also a classified location."

"Oh, come on. You can at least tell me what country I'm in. Am I still in Afghanistan?"

"That information is classified." The doctor winced slightly, as if the voice in her ear was too loud. "If you cooperate, we could show you some video of your buddy."

Never leave anyone behind.

If Roy was in the same lab, DJ wouldn't try to escape until he could take Roy with him. But if he really was somewhere else, DJ needed to make an immediate break for it and go rescue him.

"I'll cooperate. Let's see the video."

"I don't have it yet, but I can get it for you after you shift."

"Right now?"

The doctor nodded. "That's the deal."

"All right."

DJ hesitated, uncomfortable and, bizarrely, shy. In his entire life, he'd only shifted with two people who weren't wolves, and they both might as well have been family. Becoming a wolf in front of a one-body stranger, and an evil doctor at that, felt halfway between committing a crime and stripping in public.

He felt silly turning his back, but it was the only way he could bring himself to do it. Let the doctor get a good look at his ass and tail. Facing the wall, DJ found his wolf.

The plain white walls didn't change, but the scents that filled the air were bright as paint. His hope and relief and fear and anger and embarrassment faded, as did his racing thoughts, replaced by a wolf's simple sense of purpose. He was no longer DJ Torres, whose natural scent of salt, oil, and burning wood had led his parents to give him the scent name Lechon, but a wolf who thought of himself by the scent alone.

Lechon turned toward the air vent and sniffed deeply, taking in the smell of antiseptic and air freshener and Dr. Semple's natural odor of candle wax. Then he closed his eyes and inhaled again, seeking out all the scents that floated in the air.

Lechon had always had an exceptionally good sense of smell. In an enclosed building with air that circulated around and around, he could pick up the scents of everyone inside. He let hundreds of people's scents drift by, seeking for Guinness's scent of dark chocolate, black leather, damp earth, and charcoal.

It wasn't there. Which meant Guinness wasn't there, either.

But he smelled something that intrigued him. A scent of green, of cut grass and new leaves. It was the scent of outside. If he tracked it, he'd get out, too.

Dr. Semple had the black box trained on him, ready to nail Lechon if he leaped at her. Instead, he leaped for the door.

He transformed in mid-air, slamming his entire body and his human power of strength into the heavy door. It ripped out of the wall. DJ was already lashing out with his fists and feet as he landed, sending several guards flying across the corridor. A few had already been knocked down by the door, but more were scrambling into position, raising their guns.

As the quickest guards fired, DJ dropped to the floor. He grabbed the fallen door and flipped it up, using it as a shield. Darts hissed through the air, then smacked into the door and clinked on the ground.

A movement from behind caught his eye. Dr. Semple was sneaking up on him with the black box. DJ snatched up a fallen dart gun and shot her in the chest. The doctor blinked, staggered, then crumpled to the floor.

DJ threw the door forward, hoping to clear the corridor. It slammed into four of the guards, and he used the dart gun to pick off the two who managed to dodge. Then he bolted down the hallway, lights flashing and sirens screaming in his wake.

He skidded round a corner, then ran into more guards. He was so close that he swung the gun rather than firing it, hitting two and forcing the others to duck, and kept on going.

DJ tore round another corner, hearing darts smack into the wall only inches behind him. More guards to the front. He fired a burst at them, then transformed as they started to fire back. Their darts struck the wall several feet above him, and they collapsed before they could try again.

Following the scent of green, he ran on as a wolf. He became a man to kick in a door and tear up a flight of stairs, then kicked his way out and became a wolf again. More guards tried to stop him, and more guards went down.

He had never used his full strength in battle before, nor had he ever fought as a wolf except in play. But it didn't feel like he was doing it for the first time. His Marine training melded with his wolf instincts, filling him with the fierce joy of combat and the hunt.

As Lechon came to another branching corridor, the scent of green became so strong that outside had to be just a door away. He became a man as he darted around the corner toward it.

The corridor ended in a closed door. A woman stood in front of it, blocking his way. Her hands were open and empty, and her blue jeans and red tank top were tight enough that it was obvious she wasn't concealing any weapons.

DJ skidded to a stop and looked her over again. This time he noticed that she was beautiful. She wasn't his type— too pale, too forbidding, too tall— but if you liked that sort of thing, she was perfect. Her short hair was white as frost, her cheekbones were sharp enough to cut, and her eyes, which she was using to give him an amazingly cold stare, were blue as an Arctic lake.

He'd had no qualms about taking down the female guards, not to mention Dr. Semple. An armed woman was a sister or an enemy, depending on what side she was on; he'd be an asshole or an idiot to treat her differently from a man in the same position. Bullets didn't turn into flowers just because they were fired from a woman's rifle.

But this woman had to be a civilian employee who had accidentally wandered into the crossfire. Her seemingly chilly stare was probably because she was shell-shocked and terrified.

DJ didn't want to scare her even more by yelling at her or shoving her out of his way. "Please step aside. Don't worry, I won't hurt you."

The woman laughed.

DJ undoubtedly looked more impressive in uniform than barefoot and in hospital pajamas, but even so, he was holding a weapon and was the obvious cause of the all-out alert. He briefly wondered if the evil secret lab doubled as an asylum, then decided that he'd already wasted too much time on the escaped lunatic or absent-minded scientist or lost supermodel or whatever she was.

He ran toward her, meaning to gently remove her from his path if she was too paralyzed with fright to get out of his way.

She darted forward to intercept him. Her movement was so fast that he'd barely even registered it before she grabbed his wrist, jerking him to a stop and wrenching his shoulder. Then she twisted his arm so quickly that he barely managed to catch her wrist before she would have broken his. The dart gun clattered to the floor.

I'm an idiot, DJ thought. *Taken in by a tank top. She's not a civilian, she's just out of uniform.*

He jerked his arm, but she managed to hold on. Her other hand swung out in a knife-hand strike, shockingly fast. He ducked, but she clipped him across the top of his head, hard enough to stagger him.

DJ swept her ankles, but he couldn't break her grip. She took him down with her. They hit the floor together, wrestling, each struggling to pin the other.

"You're a werewolf!" DJ gasped. "Fuck, you're strong."

The woman caught him with an elbow to the temple. The impact was as intense and dizzying as an electric shock.

"Werewolves are a dime a dozen." She didn't even sound out of breath. "I'm much more special than that."

He managed to lift his foot and stomp on her ankle, making her gasp in pain. But he still couldn't break free.

No one had ever given him this much of a fight. He was pretty sure he was stronger, but she was more flexible, lithe and slippery as a fucking eel. Just keeping her from head-butting him was taking all his strength. The scar on his side felt like it was splitting open every time he had to twist to force her down, making him wonder if the wetness there was sweat or blood.

DJ heard runners approaching, faint in the distance.

"Tell me what you are," he said, hoping to distract her.

She dug her sharp nails into his hand, drawing more blood, but he kept his grip tight on her wrists. The two of them were tangled up like a knotted string, with DJ on top. Her breath was warm on his face, and smelled like chocolate.

"Come on!" DJ yelled to cover up the footsteps. "I'm a wolf! What are you? A cobra? A— ow!— a leopard? A black widow spider? A duck-billed platypus?"

The woman's pale eyebrows rose incredulously, her ice-blue eyes fixing on his. "A *platypus?*"

"The cuteness is deceptive," said DJ solemnly. Out of the corner of his eye, he saw a guard peer round the corner, raise a dart gun, and take careful aim at his back. "Don't underestimate them. They're small, but fierce. Like me."

As the guard's finger tightened on the trigger, DJ flipped them over, landing on his back with her on top. The dart smacked into her shoulder.

"Son of a bitch!" the woman yelled.

"Fuck!" shouted the guard.

DJ laughed, giddy with adrenaline and success. "Taken in by the old platypus trick!"

With a final burst of strength, the woman freed her left hand and backfisted him across the mouth. DJ jerked his head aside, lessening the force of the blow, but his lips split in a bright flare of pain. Then her eyes closed, and she slumped down on top of him.

DJ levered her off and snatched up his fallen dart gun. The guard ducked back round the corner.

He hastily surveyed the area. There were no other guards in sight. The door was unmarked and seemed to open only by sensor, like the other doors DJ had gone through. So he opened it the same way he'd opened the rest, by kicking it in.

A blast of heat hit him in the face, staggering him. There was no green, no new leaves or cut grass, only white sunlight glaring off pale sand.

Afghanistan?

DJ had no time to waste wondering. He could run faster as a wolf, so he transformed and took off into the desert.

To his confusion, the scent of green rose up *behind* him. But this time he was close enough to catch an underlying tang of sweat. It wasn't a landscape, but the scent of the woman he'd fought.

That was strange. Normally people's scents were instantly recognizable as belonging to people, no matter how closely they resembled other smells. He'd never mistaken his grandmother's scent of sun-warmed steel for actual metal, or his brother's spicy scent for real nutmeg.

Lechon wondered if the mystery woman's odd scent had to do with what she was. A *plant* shifter?

He'd never heard of such a thing, but it could be possible. Grandma Steel said that there were hundreds, maybe thousands, of different types of shifters in the world, most much rarer than wolves. And like wolves, they kept to themselves. Lechon had only met two in his entire life, a coyote and a binturong.

He glanced backward. The secret lab was cleverly disguised as a rock formation, and seemed to be mostly underground. No one was chasing him— yet— but he probably didn't have much time before they did. Luckily, the air was so dry that scents would be hard to track, and the ground was either rock-hard clay or sand that fell in once his paws lifted, hiding his footprints.

The desert was marked by shallow canyons, low hills, and stark rock formations. He made for the canyons, where he wouldn't be visible from above. They intersected with each other, forming a maze where he could lose his pursuers. Lechon scrambled into the nearest one. It was narrow, lined with gravel and sand, and had walls of streaky stone.

He saw and scented dry weeds as he raced through the canyons, but never any water. The only animals were beetles that smelled oily or acidic, and the occasional lizard scuttling too high above his head to catch. The heat was intense. He panted to cool himself off, his tongue lolling, but it wasn't enough to make up for the sun beating down on his thick fur. This was no place for a wolf.

He became a man again. To his alarm, once he was on two feet, he staggered, his vision blurring. DJ felt so shaky and sick that he had to sit down and put his head between his knees. Pain flashed through his head in rhythm with his heartbeat. He was terribly thirsty.

"Heat exhaustion," he muttered. "Goddammit."

He'd run long and fast enough to evade pursuit, but he'd paid a price for it. All the fighting he'd done at full strength probably hadn't helped, either.

DJ had seen guys fall out from heat exhaustion, though he'd never done so himself, and knew the drill: get them out of the sun and have them rest, cool them off with wet cloths and cold packs, and give them water or Gatorade in small sips.

If he went back to the lab, they'd undoubtedly be happy to do all that for him, probably complete with interesting experimental drugs in the Gatorade.

He pressed himself into a scrap of shade. The dry heat seemed to suck the moisture from his body, as if he was sitting inside an oven. Lechon had burned his paws on the hot sand, so DJ's palms and soles were burned too. He examined them, then checked his side. His scar had opened up and bled, but only a little. He pulled his shirt down and put it out of his mind.

Without moving from the shade, DJ looked for a twig. There were none to be seen, but he found a stiff bit of weed that would work. He stuck it into sunlit sand and marked the end of its shadow with a pebble, then sat back to figure out his options while he waited for the shadow to move and tell him which way was west.

The landscape looked more like the American southwest than Afghanistan, with its thorny weeds, gnarled rock formations, and orange-pink stone. If he was near the coast and he headed west, he'd probably hit civilization, or at least a gas station, before too long. Or he could drop dead before he hit anything. It took three days to die of thirst, but heat stroke could kill you in a matter of hours.

Still, he'd rather chance the desert than turn around and go back. He'd never entirely believed in the stories of secret government labs that performed sadistic experiments on shifters, given that it was always a friend of a cousin's girlfriend's sister who'd escaped to tell the tale, but they'd scared the hell out him when he was a little kid. And now he knew they were real.

On the other hand, people *had* escaped. If he retraced his steps and let them re-capture him, maybe he'd get a better chance later. At the very least, he'd know to bring water and a hat. Shoes would be good, too.

While he waited, he tried to figure out what would be best for Roy. DJ couldn't help him if he was dead of heat stroke. But he couldn't help him if he was locked up, either. If he made it out of this desert, he could come back with help: werewolves, Marines, whistle-blowing journalists, *somebody*. This was way too big for him to handle on his own.

The shadow of the weed finally moved enough for him to get a direction. He put a pebble on the new end of the shadow. The first pebble marked west, and the second pebble marked east.

The dizziness had faded slightly, so DJ pulled out the stalk and brushed over the mark he'd made. He took off his shirt and tied it around his head, picked up the dart gun, and went on, heading west.

After a few more turns, he saw a huge rock formation within walking distance. He decided to hike to that, find a cave to sleep in for the rest of the day, then strike out again in the cool of the night.

As he walked, he played music in his mind. He didn't try to stumble through his most recent, hottest, coolest finds, but instead chose songs he knew so well that he didn't have to search for a single beat or rhyme. Tagalog or English, French or Punjabi, it didn't matter if he didn't understand the words so long as he felt the passion and the anger, the energy and wit.

DJ's lips moved soundlessly as he challenged himself to keep up with rappers who could fire out lyrics like bullets from a SAW. The rhythms gave him strength, the beat kept his feet moving, the music carried him forward, the voices urged him to never give up.

DJ woke up coughing. There was sand in his eyes— sand in his mouth and nose— sand halfway down his throat.

He rolled over, and white light nearly blinded him. He was lying in the middle of the canyon, in direct sunlight. Why would he have decided to take a nap there? His recent memories were hazy: walking and walking in that blast-furnace heat, his head throbbing, his feet sore...

DJ had never passed out in his life, but there was obviously a first time for everything. He hadn't even lost consciousness when he'd gotten third-degree burns, though he'd been in so much pain that he'd wished he would. Where the hell was he, with heat extreme enough to knock him out? He hoped he wasn't trying to walk to the coast of Utah.

Even sitting up required a tremendous effort. Every inch of him hurt. His head was splitting. His lips stung. His throat felt like sandpaper. His muscles were cramping, and so was his stomach. His soles were scraped raw. He was sunburned all over, and so exhausted that he felt crushed under the weight of his own weariness. DJ wanted nothing more than to curl up and go back to sleep.

If he did, he'd probably never wake up again.

He became a wolf and sniffed for water, mice, lizards, cactus, anything to give him a little moisture. He scented nothing but dust and weeds, minerals and dirt. A wolf could endure more than a man, so he went on in that form. But soon even Lechon was reeling, unable to bear the weight and heat of his fur.

When he became a man again, nausea hit him like a fist to the stomach. He doubled over, dry-heaving. Nothing came up. His mouth was too parched to even spit. When the spasms stopped, he wiped his face with a shaking hand. His hand came away dry, too. He'd stopped sweating. His body was shutting down.

That was the point where you didn't sit guys down in the shade with an ice pack and give them little sips of water; you called for medevac and airlifted them to the hospital, immediately. DJ could undoubtedly hold out for longer than the average guy, but even his werewolf healing couldn't magically produce water.

I am so fucked, DJ thought. *I'm going to die here, and no one will ever know to go rescue Roy. Everyone will think we were killed in the helo crash. My family will be heartbroken. God knows what it'll do to Alec and Marco if they lose both of us. I was a fucking idiot to keep running once it was obvious that there wasn't any water.*

But he couldn't stop moving now. There was no shade or water in the canyon. Maybe there'd be some in the rock formation. It wasn't like he had any better options. Even if he was willing to go back, he was much too far— and too far gone— to make it.

He forced himself to his feet, staggered, and fetched up against the rough granite wall. At least that provided some support. He made his way forward, leaning on the side of the canyon as he went, his eyes half-closed.

The memories that drifted through his mind felt more vivid and real than the sun that burned his skin and stung his eyes.

His pack sleeping in a pile on the living room floor after he'd returned from his first tour of duty, giving him the traditional traveler's welcome home. They might not approve of his career, but he'd never doubted their love. He was surrounded by fur and warmth and everyone's scents. The pack sense held him like he'd never left. His sister Five teased him that if he had a nightmare and bit her, she'd bite him back. But he'd slept like a pup.

The flash of the explosion. The impact of landing. Searing agony in his side. Roy picking him up as bullets hit the dirt all around them, his face dead white beneath the smears of dirt and blood. The smell of chemicals and soot and charred meat.

Staring at yet another incomprehensible set of marks on paper until he managed to decipher "rifleman." Crossing his fingers that the question was asking him to write out the Rifleman's Creed rather than explain the place of the rifleman in a fire team, DJ began to scrawl what he hoped would come out as, *This is my rifle. There are many like it, but this one is mine...*

The ice-blue eyes of the woman he'd fought, the astonishing strength of her grip, the silken brush of her hair against his cheek. Her scent of green.

When he fell again, the landing was surprisingly gentle. He must have made it through the desert, and collapsed on a bed of moss. He could smell cut grass and sticky new leaves.

FOUR

Echo

117 Degrees

Echo opened her eyes to the disconcerting sight of Mr. Dowling looming over her. She recoiled.

"You're awake," he informed her, as if he was briefing her on her own level of consciousness. "Your ankle is bruised and strained, but you can walk on it."

She was in one of the hospital's recovery rooms, but still dressed, lying on top of the sheets, and not hooked up to anything. Her ankle was wrapped in elastic bandages and elevated on a pillow, with a cold pack draped over it.

"What the hell happened?" she asked, sitting up. "Who was that guy?"

"That was Dale Torres, a Marine we captured."

"You *captured* a Marine? Couldn't you just have him transferred?"

Mr. Dowling gave her an irritated look. "It's not a simple matter to have a member of the armed forces transferred to a base that doesn't officially exist. Anyway, it was an independent decision made by an operative in Afghanistan. Born wolves rarely join the armed forces, so obtaining a born wolf Marine must have seemed like an unparalleled opportunity."

Echo read between the lines of Mr. Dowling's explanation: *Someone went way off-book in snatching a Marine, and we're all praying that this doesn't turn into a giant, career-ending clusterfuck.*

In the interest of getting on with it, Echo limited her inquiry. "How'd the operative spot him?"

"Torres was in a helicopter with Farrell, another Marine from his fire team. Their helicopter was shot down, and they were the only survivors. Farrell was severely wounded, and briefly transformed into a wolf during medevac. Torres clearly knew what was going on, and Farrell had bite wounds. We're still looking into their backgrounds, but we believe that Torres is a born wolf and bit Farrell to save his life."

"Where's Farrell?" Echo asked. "Was Torres trying to get to him?"

"Possibly. But Farrell's not here. It's unclear at this time whether he'll ever be fit for duty again. Though if not, we can still use him as a research subject." Mr. Dowling seemed to like that idea.

Severely wounded, bitten by a werewolf, and locked up for 'research,' Echo thought. *The poor guy probably wishes he was still getting shot at in Afghanistan.*

Mr. Dowling went on, "Torres, on the other hand, is an excellent candidate for recruitment."

"Good luck with that. If you think *I'm* a handful…" As much as Torres had clearly been surprised by her strength, she'd been surprised by his. She hadn't had that much fun fighting someone since Brava had died.

Mr. Dowling frowned. "Yes, I reviewed the tapes of Dr. Semple's session with him. Born wolves don't normally have such formidable powers. All the same, a ball was dropped."

"You mean, Dr. Semple dropped the ball."

Despite the long-standing feud between Mr. Dowling and Dr. Semple, Mr. Dowling didn't seem consoled by the thought of his rival getting in trouble. He ignored her cue and went on, "Torres injured fifteen guards and tranquilized seven, plus Dr. Semple and yourself. Not to mention doing thousands of dollars worth of property damage."

Echo enjoyed the description of how this Torres guy had wreaked havoc on the base. She'd have loved to do the same herself. "How long did it take you re-capture him?"

"We haven't."

"What? He escaped?" Echo was taken aback. No one ever escaped from Wildfire Base.

"*Yet.*" Mr. Dowling added quickly, "That is, we hadn't as of ten minutes ago. But he escaped on foot, so he won't get far."

"He just ran outside, with no supplies or water? And you still haven't gotten him? How long has he been out there?"

Mr. Dowling checked his watch. "Two hours, thirty-nine minutes. We sent four search teams, including the pack, but the air is too dry and still for them to pick up his scent. And it's too hot for them to spend much time outside their vehicles."

"How hot is it?"

"117 degrees."

Echo couldn't help admiring the nerve of a man who would venture into that killing heat, and the resourcefulness and endurance of one who could evade multiple search teams for hours. He couldn't escape, of course... Or could he? She smiled at the thought that he might. "No problem. I'll go fetch him."

Mr. Dowling gave her a warning look. "We want him alive and in one piece. Understand, Echo? If you harm him, there will be serious consequences. *Serious.*"

"I assumed you wanted him alive and unharmed," Echo said, baffled. "He's a recruit, not a target."

"Oh." Mr. Dowling looked abashed. "The way you smiled— and he did beat you in a fight— well, it was a natural assumption."

"I don't want to kill him. I smiled because..." She didn't want to admit that she'd been rooting for the fugitive. "I never get to do search and rescue. It'll be different. Fun."

Mr. Dowling seemed surprised by that. Was it that shocking for her to smile and say that she was looking forward to something? Apparently so.

They went to the vehicle bay, where he showed her to a Humvee with a medical kit and cooling-off materials, and reviewed first aid for heat illness.

"One last thing, Echo," he added.

She waited for him to again warn her not to kill Torres. Instead, he said, "If you help him escape, Charlie's pain meds will mysteriously stop working."

"I wouldn't dream of it." She slammed the door in his face.

Fucking asshole, Echo thought as she drove out. As if she'd risk Charlie for a stranger.

As if she'd risk Charlie for anyone.

Once she'd passed security and was out in the desert, she slowed, trying to see the landscape as a stranger would. As Dale Torres would.

She thought back to her encounter with him. The red alert and frantic yelling over the radio had given Echo the impression that the Terminator was on the loose. As she'd raced to intercept the prisoner, she'd pictured a hulking figure with steroid muscles, bulging veins, and a brutish face twisted in battle rage.

When she caught up with him, she thought, That's *the guy who's tearing up Wildfire Base?*

If she'd imagined the prisoner as handsome rather than monstrous, she'd have pictured one of the heroes from Charlie's books: dangerous, damaged, and domineering. He was handsome, in fact, but he also looked... nice. Sweet, even. Boyish. Not the Navy SEAL or billionaire hero, but maybe the billionaire's best friend or the heroine's brother. The one who didn't get his own book, due to being insufficiently screwed up and bossy.

Echo had dismissed those ridiculous fancies and examined her opponent objectively. Mid twenties— about her age. Asian, maybe Filipino. Medium height, muscular build, medium brown skin, dark eyes, black hair. In hospital pajamas and bare feet, his clipped hair was the most military thing about him.

In turn, he examined her. Echo usually wasn't much good at reading people, but he had a very expressive face. She caught surprise at her sudden appearance, followed by curiosity, a flash of admiration, dismissal of her as a threat, and finally, to Echo's confusion, sympathy.

His voice also startled her, first with its oddly pleasant scratchy quality, and then by the politeness with which he'd asked her to step aside, as if they were maneuvering on a crowded sidewalk. It was as incongruous as his promise not to hurt her. Armed with nothing but a tranquilizer gun, he looked so innocent that it was hard to imagine he was capable of hurting anyone. Certainly not her.

But he had. She was bruised all over, and every step sent a jolt of pain through her ankle. And he'd won, albeit by trickery. He'd *won.* Torres was the first person in Echo's adult life to ever defeat her in a fight.

The cuteness is deceptive, he'd said. *They're small, but fierce. Like me.*

He'd actually warned her that she was underestimating him, and she'd still done so. So had Dr. Semple. So had the entire base, apparently. That was something to start with: however far she thought Torres was likely to have gotten, she should probably double that distance.

Listening on the radio, she heard that the search parties had fanned out and were combing a ten-mile radius around the base, figuring he couldn't have gotten too far in the deadly heat.

He's twenty miles out, she thought. *Minimum. Wolves can run at thirty-five miles per hour.*

What else did she know about him?

From the trick he'd played on her, he was bright. Observant. Quick-witted. He'd undoubtedly gone into the canyons, where he couldn't be easily spotted. She wished she knew if he had any idea where he was, but she guessed that he'd at least figured out that he was somewhere in the southwest. If that was the case, he'd head west, for the coast. Echo turned the Humvee in that direction.

The pack had apparently come to the same conclusion; Echo spotted a parked Humvee with Guadalupe Cordero sitting in the passenger seat and listening to the radio, no doubt directing the pack's operations. Her crutches leaned against the seat, and the scarred side of her face, with its black eye patch, was turned toward Echo.

The rest of the pack was outside, investigating a small mesa of orange and red granite. It was split with fissures, some wide enough to crawl into, and pocked with caves. The alpha, Emmett Anderson, stood overseeing them, hunched under the brutal sun. His graying hair, the deep lines in his face, and his air of weariness made him look old, though he was only forty.

Loser, Echo thought. *Some alpha. The only thing he's good for is controlling the pack sense, and he fucks that up every other month.*

Every now and then, a pack member would get angry or depressed or stressed out, the emotion would be transmitted and amplified through the pack sense, Emmett would fail to shut it down, and one or more of the wolves would be overwhelmed by it. Usually they just had an embarrassing public breakdown, but Ty once punched out a guard. More seriously, last month Amber stole and crashed a base vehicle, though luckily she'd walked away with only a broken wrist.

Echo happened to know that one of the reasons Dr. Semple still kept an eye out for potential made wolf recruits was that she was hoping to turn up another alpha. She'd had high hopes for Guadalupe, but though she had the willpower and leadership capabilities that Emmett lacked, she couldn't control the pack sense. So far, none of the made wolves could.

No wonder Mr. Dowling was so excited at the prospect of recruiting a born wolf. Torres couldn't join the pack— he had to already have a pack of his own— but at least he wouldn't be afflicted with its problems.

As Echo pulled up, Push Malakar squirmed out of a narrow crack in the mesa, her strong brown arms scraped and her black hair hanging all over her sweaty face, and shook her head with a grin and a shrug.

"Nothing!" Push called. "But I'll do the next as a wolf. Maybe I'll pick up a scent."

Emmett's radio crackled, and Guadalupe's voice suggested, "Try a bigger cave. Remember, Torres has to be able to fit in."

The air shimmered, and Push became a sleek gray wolf. Her jaws gaped as if she was laughing. She leaped into the air, scrabbled for purchase at the mouth of a cave halfway up the low mesa, and vanished within.

Echo wasn't surprised to see that Push seemed to be enjoying herself. The more strenuous and dangerous a job was, the better she liked it. While the rest of the wolf pack had volunteered because they were dying anyway, Push had been a perfectly healthy adrenaline junkie who'd thought that a 50-50 chance of dying in agony and an additional chance of her transformation going horribly wrong was a reasonable trade-off for the possibility of becoming a super-powered werewolf.

Echo had to admit that Push had known herself well: she was the only member of the pack who showed no signs of regretting her decision. Of course, she'd also lucked out and gotten a useful power with no life-ruining side effects. Echo doubted Push would have been so chipper if she'd ended up like Amber or Match.

The other wolves seemed less enthusiastic about the search. Amber Killeen and Ty Roberts were poking around other caves, Ty with a flashlight and Amber in her tawny wolf form. Amber drooped, tail down, and sweat plastered Ty's white shirt to his dark skin. Match lay panting at the mouth of another cave, weighed down by his thick black fur.

The radio crackled, and Guadalupe's voice cut across the parched air. "Tell Match to get in the Humvee with me. He looks like he's overheating. Actually, you should all take a break."

Emmett became a heavyset brown wolf and nudged Match. The black wolf obediently loped to the Humvee and joined Guadalupe in the air-conditioned interior.

Echo rolled down her window. The heat was stunning; she instinctively pulled back.

Emmett became a man again. "Amber, transform; you'll get heat stroke."

The tawny wolf seemed not to hear. Ty gave her side a thump. "Come on, Amber. You heard him."

With a shimmer like a heat wave, the wolf became a woman. Amber had dressed for the weather, as much as she could: white jeans stuffed into boots, long-sleeved white turtleneck, white scarf tied around her head, and white leather gloves. Only her face and long blonde hair was exposed, but Ty still took a habitual, cautious step back.

"Did you catch his scent here?" Echo called out.

Emmett shook his head. "Too dry."

Amber added, "We think he's gone to ground. He'd feel sick, realize he can't go on, and find a shady place to hide in. And this is full of shady places."

It was a reasonable theory, if you hadn't fought Torres. And he'd probably do it eventually. But Echo bet he wouldn't have gotten to that point anywhere near that soon.

"But it's only a few degrees cooler in the caves," Amber went on.

"He'd pass out and never wake up."

"Speaking of which…" Emmett cupped his hands around his mouth: "Everyone, back to the Humvee! Rest and hydrate!"

Echo rolled up her window and drove on. With all the breaks the pack would have to take in this heat, they had no chance of catching Torres. Unless he gave up and turned back, Echo was the only person on the entire base who had a shot at finding him before he dropped dead.

She mentally replayed her fight with him as she drove, searching for more clues. Instead, she recalled his distinctive scratchy voice, and wondered if he'd been interrogated for so long that he'd worn it out or if he always sounded like that. Most men who fought her seemed angry or resentful at her strength, in the split second before they realized that she could kill them and got scared. Torres had sounded admiring when he'd called her strong, and he'd never seemed afraid.

Echo had been outraged when she'd realized that he'd been distracting her so he could use her as a human shield, but now it made her laugh to remember how he'd compared himself to a platypus. What sort of man would come up with *that* as a distraction, in the middle of a desperate fight?

She hoped she'd get to fight him again. No one wanted to spar with her any more. She was too fast and too strong, and she always ended up hitting someone too hard, either by accident or because she lost patience with holding herself back. But if she ever got a chance to spar Torres, she could go all-out. He could obviously take it.

Echo scanned the desert, looking for some landmark to the west that he might have headed toward. Basic desert survival was to find shade and stay in it during the day, but there was little shade to be found here. She settled on a striking rock formation. It was to the west, it looked like it would have caves, you could see it from the canyons, and it appeared to be close enough to walk to. She happened to know that it wasn't, but Torres probably didn't. If she searched all the canyons leading toward it, she should find him eventually.

She parked the Humvee and climbed into the back. Echo ignored the stunner in the holster on the wall. That was a tool for normals. She didn't need it. Instead, she pulled on a long-sleeved cotton shirt and a hat, loaded a rucksack with water and a cooler with cold packs, drank a bottle of water, and got out.

Despite her resistance to temperature extremes, the heat staggered her. By the time she'd finished searching the first canyon and its nearest offshoots, she'd drunk another two bottles. Even so, she had a slight dehydration headache. She checked her watch, and was alarmed to realize that Torres had been in the desert for nearly five hours.

She returned to the Humvee and checked the radio, hoping someone else had found him. No such luck. Push had gone down with heat exhaustion, and the entire pack had returned to the base. The remaining search parties were starting to talk about body recovery.

Echo replenished her water and entered the second canyon, determined to find Torres. Alive. She didn't like the thought of him dying alone in the desert, brought down by heat and thirst. A man who could fight like him ought to die in combat, like she would some day.

If I'm lucky.

Echo quickly cut off that train of thought. She hurried down the canyon, limping slightly. Halfway in, she found scuff-marks in the gravel, left in a winding, uneven trail. He'd been staggering, either unaware that he was leaving footprints or too weak to clear them away. Echo hastened on, past the place where he'd fallen and scrabbled in the sand to get up, past the shirt and dart gun he'd abandoned on the ground, and turned the corner at a near-run.

A ridiculous amount of relief filled her when she saw him, leaning against the canyon wall and stumbling forward, his head hanging down. She couldn't believe he was still on his feet.

"Torres!" she shouted. He didn't turn, either when she yelled or when she ran up to stand in front of him.

"Torres?" Echo put her hand on his shoulder, bringing him to a halt. "Dale?"

He lifted his head, as slowly as if it was a heavy weight, and gazed out with eyes so blank that she knew he didn't see her.

"I made it," he muttered, and collapsed into her arms.

His skin was dry and burning hot, and his breathing was rapid and shallow. She touched the side of his throat, feeling for a pulse. His heart was racing.

Heat stroke. As Mr. Dowling hadn't needed to remind her, that could kill a person in fifteen minutes. If she didn't cool him off first, he could be dead by the time she got him back to the Humvee.

Echo found an area shaded by an overhang and laid him down there. As she settled him down, she saw what appeared to be a gash in his side. She inspected it, concerned, then saw that it was a wound that had already healed. A mass of scar tissue stretched over his ribs, shiny and tight and discolored. A long red furrow cut through it, cracked and bleeding a little at one end. He'd been badly burned, and not all that long ago. She wondered how it had happened. A bomb?

She placed cold packs under his back and on his chest and thighs, then began pouring water over him. His brown skin was reddened and starting to blister, and the soles of his feet were bloody and raw. His lips were split with painful-looking cuts. Though that was the least of his problems, it made her feel more guilty than that negligible injury warranted. If she'd known he was going to tear out into the desert and nearly kill himself, maybe she wouldn't have hit him so hard.

His eyes opened slowly. They were very dark brown, almost black, set off by straight, thick eyebrows.

"I broke him," he mumbled. "I broke him and I couldn't fix him."

At least, she thought that was what he said. His voice was so hoarse that he was hard to understand.

"Here, have some water," she said. "Drink it slowly. Little sips."

She lifted his head and held a bottle to his swollen lips. His hair was cut so short that it looked bristly, but it was soft against her palm. He followed her directions, though she suspected it was from ingrained training rather than because he'd understood her.

By the time he was a third of the way through, all the moisture had evaporated from his body and clothes. She put down the bottle, picked up another, and drenched him again.

"Once you finish the bottle, I'll take you where it's cooler," she promised him.

Torres didn't seem to hear her. "I screwed everything up. Me and my big fucking mouth."

"What did you screw up?"

"My buddy. My brother. Best fucking Marine you'll ever see."

Echo remembered Mr. Dowling's briefing. "Farrell?"

Torres nodded. "I tried to fix him, but I only made it worse."

So that was what Mr. Dowling had meant about Farrell probably never being fit for duty again: something had gone wrong with his transformation. Echo hesitated, unwilling to say anything that could rebound on Charlie, then decided that she hadn't been forbidden from *talking* to Torres. And he'd sounded so sad and bitter that she felt an odd impulse to console him.

"You were trying to save his life," Echo reminded him. "You meant well."

His dark gaze drifted out of focus. "I pushed him too hard. Marco warned me, but I didn't listen. I'm such a fuck-up."

Drawn into the mystery, Echo asked, "Who's Marco?"

But Torres wasn't in any condition to hear her. He turned his head restlessly to the side. His cheek radiated heat against her fingers. "Where's my pack? I can't reach the pack sense."

Torres would probably never see his pack again. She wondered how he'd hold up without it. In theory, born wolves could survive indefinitely away from their pack. In practice, they needed some kind of contact sometimes, even if it was only a phone call every couple months and a visit once a year. If they were cut off completely, they grew reckless and self-destructive, and eventually got themselves killed.

A pang went through her chest, as if a fist had squeezed her heart. But maybe Torres would be different. Tougher. He'd smashed his way through the base— he'd defeated her— he'd survived the desert—

"Nanay...?" Torres called out hoarsely, and coughed. "Nanay, stay with me. I don't feel good."

Echo held the bottle to his lips. "Here, drink some more. It'll make you feel better."

He turned away, letting the water spill over his chin. "I'm fine. Give it to Alec, he needs to hydrate."

Echo spoke sharply. "Torres, drink. That's an order."

That got through to him. He swallowed obediently, in textbook slow little sips. As he did, she wondered exactly what the base planned to do with him.

Nothing terrible, Echo told herself. *He's a recruit, like the made wolves. They'll send him on missions, that's all.*

That's all...

Torres finished the bottle. His skin had dried up again, so Echo poured more water on him. The cold packs had gone lukewarm. But she could see that she'd done him some good. His breathing had slowed and steadied, as had his pulse, and he looked a little less dazed.

"All right," Echo said. "We can go to the Humvee now. It's air-conditioned."

"I think you'll have to help me walk." He sounded apologetic.

"You don't have to walk. I'll carry you."

She waited for his disbelieving look, but he simply said, "Thanks. I'm awfully tired."

Echo hefted him across her shoulders. He'd cooled down some, but his skin still felt hot. She set a brisk pace along the canyon, glad that she'd found him when she had. Werewolves were tough, but she doubted he'd have survived another hour in that canyon. Maybe not even another half-hour.

His breathing was steady in her ear, a comforting sound. When Echo was a child, all five of the sisters had sometimes slept in the same bed, the rhythm of their mingled breathing lulling them to sleep.

Not long after Althea died, the handlers decided that the four of them left were too big and too old to share a bed. But they did anyway, sneaking into a room after lights-out and squeezing in together.

After Della died, the handlers had decided it might be a good thing for the sisters to sleep close together, and offered them a king-sized bed. Echo and Charlie and Brava huddled together in it, holding each other tight and feeling the empty spaces on either side.

Then Brava died, and the sense of someone missing became overwhelming. Charlie and Echo asked to move to a smaller apartment with a double bed, where they'd be less likely to reach out for Brava every night.

Their handlers moved them, but it was never the same. Every night that Echo wasn't out on a mission or Charlie was off with her infatuation of the month, Charlie would fall asleep and Echo would lie awake beside her, waiting for her breathing to stop.

Once Echo thought of that, a familiar fear gripped her. What if Charlie was dying *right now*? Her imagination sped down a well-worn track, as she pictured herself returning to the base, Mr. Dowling waiting in her empty apartment, Echo shouting at him to go ahead and tell her—

Torres stirred, his fingers closing around her arm. "Are we there yet?"

Startled, Echo nearly lost her footing on the canyon's treacherous slope. "Almost."

When she laid him down in the back of the Humvee, his eyes were bright and alert. "You're the woman I fought."

"Yes."

"Were you carrying me just now?"

She nodded. "I found you in a canyon. Don't you remember?"

He looked at her like she was a lunatic. "I was unconscious."

"You woke up for a while. We had a whole conversation."

"We did?"

"Sort of. You were pretty out of it." Echo stepped around him to turn on the ignition and the air conditioning, then returned and opened the cooler. "Who's Marco?"

"He's the team leader of my fire team." Torres tried to sit up, wincing.

Echo put her hand on his chest. "Stay down. I'm getting ice."

"Oh, right." He lay still, watching her curiously.

She began laying ice packs on his body. "And who's Nanay?"

"It's 'mom' in Tagalog." He gave her a quizzical glance. "What in the world was I talking about that involved Marco *and* my mother?"

Echo opened her mouth to recite his words back to him, then closed it. His sharp gaze, quick speech, and confident air, even as he lay captive and helpless on the floor of the Humvee, betrayed nothing of the guilt and sorrow and vulnerability she'd seen before. She felt like she'd accidentally read his secret journal.

The best she could do was pretend it hadn't happened. And she certainly wasn't going to embarrass him by telling him he'd called out for his mother. "Got me. You weren't making much sense."

"I'm not surprised. I think I'm really sick. I should probably go to a hospital."

"As soon as I cool you off a bit more, I'll take you there," she promised.

"Oh, hey, do you know anything about my buddy?" Torres asked hopefully. "His name's Roy Farrell. He was badly hurt— maybe he's in the same hospital you're taking me to…?"

"He's alive. But he's not around here. I don't know where he is."

Torres looked both disappointed and relieved. "Where are we now? Please don't tell me that's classified."

"Why would I do that?"

"Dr. Semple did."

Echo put ice packs against either side of his neck. "Dr. Semple is into mind games. She'll say anything to fuck with you."

"I noticed. So where are we?"

"Death Valley."

His entire body jerked with surprise, nearly dislodging the ice pack she'd just laid on his stomach. "Fuck! Seriously?"

"Seriously. You tried to escape into the literal hottest place on Earth."

"Talk about out of the frying pan and into—" He caught himself. "I bet you're sick of that joke. Exactly how hot is it today?"

"117 degrees. You're lucky you survived."

His dark gaze met hers, all joking gone. "Am I?"

She knew exactly what he meant. Echo opened her mouth to assure him that he wouldn't be harmed, but he was still gazing earnestly into her eyes, as if he trusted her to tell the truth.

"I don't know," she said.

"What do they want with me?"

"You're a recruit. They'll send you on black ops missions."

"Assassinations?"

"Well, sometimes it's other things."

Torres closed his eyes, his battered face creasing with weariness. "I am so fucking in over my head."

Echo took the opportunity to pour water over him.

He sighed in relief. "Thanks. That feels good. What are you, a tree shifter?"

"A—" Echo was hard to surprise, but that threw her. She wondered if he was delirious again. "A what? A tree shifter? You mean, do I *turn into a tree*?"

Torres opened his eyes and actually smiled at her. "Well, I turn into a wolf."

"No, I'm not a— Do tree shifters even exist?"

He shrugged. "Got me. What are you, then?"

She was seized by an unexpected mischievous impulse. "I'm a platypus shifter."

Now it was his turn to be thrown. She watched his mobile face register a quick sequence of thoughts: disbelief, contemplation of the possibility that it might be true, amusement at the thought that it might be true, *hope* that it was true, then the rueful decision that she was teasing him. "You are not." Then back to hope. "*Are* you?"

Echo couldn't resist teasing him some more. His facial expressions were so entertaining. "Maybe."

"Come on, what are you really? I have to know. You don't want to go to all this trouble to save me, and then have me to die of curiosity."

"It'll be tough, but I think you'll make it."

"I might not. I'm a delicate flower." He eyed her hopefully again. "You're some kind of cat, right? You move like a cat. A mountain lion? A white tiger? A snow leopard? Am I close? Spill it."

"Or what, you'll turn into a precious little rose bush? Shut up and drink some more water." Echo opened a bottle. She started to slide her hand under his head, but he caught the bottle.

"I got it." He propped himself on one elbow and started drinking.

"Slowly," she cautioned. "Small sips, or it'll make you sick."

"I know." In between small sips, he said, "I went through boot camp in San Diego. Then I deployed to Afghanistan. I've seen a lot of heat exhaustion. So, what's it like being a platypus?"

Deadpan, she said, "*Awesome.*"

"I thought so."

He went on drinking, while Echo tried to figure out how the hell she'd gone from punching out the prisoner to bantering with him. The entire day had been bizarre. She didn't get knocked out. She didn't lose fights. She didn't save people's lives, or administer first aid, or claim to be a platypus. She didn't have conversations with strangers— She didn't feel sorry for strangers— She didn't *banter!*

"What's your name?" Torres asked.

"Echo."

"That's pretty. Got a last name?"

"No."

He paused with the bottle halfway to his lips. "You don't?"

"No."

"Are you famous?"

"Well, there aren't many platypus shifters."

Torres laughed. The cuts on his lips cracked open and bled. He dabbed at them with the back of his hand.

"Sorry about that," Echo said, though she'd only been doing her job.

"Fair's fair. I stomped on your ankle. What an introduction, huh? Let's try again. Hi, I'm DJ Torres."

He held out his hand. Just as she realized that he intended her to shake it, he yanked it back, wiped off the blood on his pants, and offered it again. Echo didn't understand why he cared about getting a little blood on her, especially when she was already covered with dust and sand and his sweat and her sweat. But she couldn't think of any good reason not to shake his hand, other than that prisoners didn't normally do formal introductions with their captors, so she gingerly took it. He was getting some strength back, squeezing her hand in a firm grip,

"What's the J stand for?" Echo asked.

"Jockey." DJ laughed again at her expression, sending another trickle of blood down his chin. He wiped it away. "The D is for disc, not Dale. I DJ at clubs. I mean, when I'm not fighting in Afghanistan. What do you do when you're not rescuing people from Death Valley?"

The question hit her like a blow. She didn't feel herself move, but something about her must have changed, because all the cheer fell from DJ's face.

"Whoa, wrong question," he said. "Sorry. I'm like one of those fucking clueless civilians who says, 'Oh, you're a Marine. Have you ever killed anyone?' What are you supposed to say to that? 'No, I'm a fucking lousy shot, every one of my bullets probably missed?'"

"Mine don't miss," Echo said.

DJ grabbed her hand, resisting her effort to flinch away. She could have broken his grip, but she didn't. The burning heat was gone, leaving only ordinary warmth. "Listen, I don't know what's going on here or who you're working for, but you know this is wrong, don't you? I'm a US Marine. I haven't committed any crimes. I have a family that loves me. I have a buddy in deep, deep trouble who needs my help. Not to mention that I'm supposed to be in Afghanistan. I have a life and I need to get back to it."

"It isn't up to me." Echo wished she'd interrupted him earlier. She didn't want to know about his family. It made her feel guilty for keeping him from it, sorry that he'd never see them again, resentful that he *had* a family, and angry at him for making her feel guilty and sorry and resentful.

All those feelings. What was wrong with her? Charlie was the one who was forever *feeling* things. That was fine for Charlie, but for Echo, emotions were a liability. A weakness. Possibly a lethal one. And if they didn't kill you, they still hurt like hell.

Echo imagined the feelings as scurrying bugs, and stomped on them. *Squish. Gone.*

"Drive me to where I can walk to a town, and let me go. No one will ever have to know." DJ spoke so persuasively that Echo wanted to agree.

"I can't."

"Just say you never found me. People die in Death Valley every year. Half the time they never find the bodies."

Echo jerked her hand from his grasp. "I can't."

"Why not?"

"None of your business."

His black eyebrows rose. "It couldn't be more my business, if it's the reason you're kidnapping me and stopping me from saving my buddy and breaking my mother's heart and—"

"Hey! *I* didn't kidnap you."

"That's right. And—" He was interrupted by a coughing fit. Echo watched, uncomfortable, as it went on and on, his muscular chest heaving in painful-looking spasms. When it finally ended, he wiped his watering eyes, took a sip from the bottle, and went on as if nothing had happened, "And you don't have to. If you won't drive me to town, give me some water and point me to it."

"You're crazy. It's fifty miles from here. You'd never—" Echo broke off, realizing that he'd tricked her into revealing exactly how far he was from help. "You think you're so smart."

He shook his head. As the animation faded from his face, she could see how exhausted and sick he still was. "No. Just desperate. Come on, Echo. Please. This isn't just for me."

"*I can't.*"

With equal intensity, DJ demanded, "*Why not?*"

"Because they'll hurt my sister!" Echo shouted.

"Oh." DJ looked at her with sympathy, which was more than she'd have felt for someone who'd kidnapped her and punched her in the mouth. "So that's it. Is she a hostage?"

Echo pressed the heels of her hands into her forehead. She never talked about this, and didn't intend to start now. But without intention, she found herself replying, "Sort of. It's complicated. But if I let you go, they'd take it out on Charlie."

"So, let me make sure I've got this straight. You've got nothing against me and you're not actually on board with kidnapping innocent people, but there's absolutely no way you'll help me if it means risking your sister."

"That's right." She resisted the urge to apologize. Facts were facts. Sorry didn't change reality.

"I get it. I have a sister too." There was that sympathetic look again, making Echo feel guilty. Again. Then DJ's eyebrows rose. "Wait, Echo and Charlie? Are Alpha, Bravo, and Delta back at the lab?"

"Althea, Brava, and Della," Echo said. In for a penny, in for a pound. She flung her next words at DJ, hoping to make *him* feel guilty for a change. "They died. Charlie and I are the only ones left."

DJ did look guilty. But Echo didn't find it satisfying. Instead, she felt as uncomfortable as she had when she'd watched him coughing on the floor.

"I'm sorry, Echo," DJ said. "Really, I am."

Then he threw the remaining water in her face, snatched the stunner from its holster on the wall, jammed it into her ribs, and pressed the button.

Nothing happened. His look of surprise and indignation was

almost funny. Then he dropped the stunner and dove for the back door.

Echo grabbed him, dragged him to the passenger seat, shoved him into it, and handcuffed his left wrist to the armrest. He fought, but with little strength. Once she cuffed him, he slumped in the seat, breathing hard.

She started up the Humvee and pulled out, furious with him for tricking her and with herself for being fooled. How could she have told him about Charlie? How could she have told her about her other sisters? That was what happened when you let *feelings* sucker you into telling people things about yourself— whatever you revealed was used against you.

"I *am* sorry." DJ sounded sincere.

Echo ignored him.

"I'm serious," he said. "I love my family too. I get it."

"No, you don't."

"Okay, maybe I don't get everything. But I know what it's like to have people you'd do anything to protect. I know what it's like to do things that go against everything you believe in, because you were trying to save someone's life." His voice was wearing out, but he cleared his throat and went on, "I know—"

"Be quiet," Echo said. "Doesn't it hurt to talk?"

"What does it sound like?"

"Then don't."

"You take a turn," he suggested. "Tell me about Charlie. She's older, right? How many years?"

"You don't care about her. You were just trying to distract me."

"I was trying to figure out if you'd cut me loose. Once I knew you wouldn't, I had to go for it. You guys pulled me off a battlefield. As far as I'm concerned, I'm a prisoner of war. It's my duty to resist by all means available and make every effort to escape. It's in our code of conduct. How come the stun gun didn't work? Out of juice?"

He'd switched topics so unexpectedly that she answered without thinking. "They're keyed to authorized personnel. You needed a microchip implanted in your hand."

"Oh."

He leaned his head against the window, watching the desert go by.

Echo waited for him to start talking again, but he was silent. It seemed like his energy had finally run low.

As they passed a huge rock formation, DJ said suddenly, "I feel sick. Pull over."

He did look sick and he was in no shape to run or fight, but Echo had already underestimated him twice. She wouldn't do it again.

She stopped the Humvee and unlocked the doors. "I'm not uncuffing you. Lean out if you have to throw up."

DJ opened the door and leaned out. Then he jerked his left arm, snapping the handcuff chain. Echo was so startled that he was already bolting across the sand by the time she vaulted across the seat and after him. He was headed for the rock formation, which would be full of hiding spaces.

She didn't know what surprised her more, his strength or that she'd *again* missed his intention after he'd flat-out told it to her. How did he think he'd survive, even if he escaped? And how was he managing to run? He shouldn't even be able to stand up.

Echo put on a burst of speed, determined to catch him before he got into the formation. Ahead of her, DJ slowed, then staggered. Fifty yards from the rocks, he dropped like he'd been shot.

Wondering if it was yet another trick, Echo approached cautiously. As she came closer, he struggled in the sand, trying to get up. Then, apparently exhausted, he laid his head back down. Blood trickled over the shiny cuff and broken chain around his left wrist.

"That was stupid," she said.

"I've heard that before," he muttered.

He sounded so defeated that she wished she hadn't rubbed it in. "Are you going to fight me once I'm close enough?"

DJ shook his head wearily. "I'm done. I couldn't fight a pup."

"What did you mean to do?" She was certain he'd had some plan.

"Get in there." He moved his head, indicating the rock formation. "Ambush you and knock you out, get your keys. Put you in the back and tie you up. Drive off."

Echo hadn't expected the last part. Uneasily, she asked, "What were you planning to do with me?"

"Drop you off at the nearest town, of course. I couldn't ditch you in *Death Valley*." His straightforward explanation had the unmistakable ring of truth.

"Oh." She'd imagined all sorts of things he might have intended in the few seconds before he'd explained, from kidnapping to rape to taking her to a more convenient location to dispose of her body, but his actual reason hadn't occurred to her. Now that she knew his intent had been to *save* her life, she felt doubly guilty.

Echo picked him up. He didn't resist as she carried him back to the Humvee, laid him down in the passenger seat, and locked the doors. She half-expected him to make another break for it as she fetched the first aid kit from the back. But he stayed where she'd left him.

DJ barely flinched when she took off the cuff and poured antiseptic over the torn flesh of his wrist. But he was silent as she bandaged it, which she was starting to realize meant he was either plotting something or was too sick to talk. Or both.

"Can I lie down?" DJ asked. His voice was raspy and weak.

Echo wasn't letting him out of her sight for the ride to the base. He'd undoubtedly jump out the back. But she tilted the seat until he could lie nearly flat.

"Thanks." He curled up on his side, shivering. Beneath the brutal sunburn, his face had taken on a grayish tinge.

"Are you cold?"

He nodded.

Echo took his pulse. It had sped up again, and his skin felt clammy. She turned down the air conditioning, got a blanket from the back, and put it over him.

"You don't have to do this," DJ said, startling her. She'd thought he was done talking.

"Yes, I do. You're going into shock."

"I mean, you don't have to take me back. They're holding your sister. They're holding my buddy too. We should partner up. Drive me home, we'll get allies and weapons, and we'll come back and rescue them both. You saw what I could do with nothing but a dart gun. Now imagine me with an M-16."

With that prompt, Echo couldn't help imagining DJ and an M-16, and herself at his side. They probably could tear the place down. She'd grab Charlie and carry her away. They'd find the base DJ's buddy was held at, and get him too. And then DJ and his friend would go back to Afghanistan, and she and Charlie would go into hiding.

And a week or a month or two months later, Charlie would lie ashen in a hospital bed, like DJ lay in the passenger seat now. But unlike him, she'd never get up again.

"You were imagining it, right?" DJ asked. "Now try again, but give it a happy ending."

"There isn't one."

"Come on," he coaxed. "Run away with me, Echo. We're only about five hours from my parents' home. I don't invite every girl to come meet my family, so you should feel special."

"You're unbelievable. I bet none of the girls you invite ever show up." Echo flipped on the radio. "Wildfire Base, this is Echo. Mission accomplished. Prisoner is alive and conscious, but in need of medical attention for heat stroke, shock, and a laceration to his wrist."

She clicked off the radio and added to DJ, "And a terminal inability to know when to quit." Turning the radio back on, she continued, "I've administered first aid. ETA is forty-five minutes. Echo out."

"Still not too late," DJ suggested. "If you turned around now, you'd have a good long lead before they even realized anything was wrong."

She started driving, determinedly watching the sands rather than him. If she didn't reply at all, he'd eventually give up.

"If you tell me exactly how and where they're holding your sister, I could come up with a plan to rescue her. Or, actually, this might be better— we rescue my buddy first, then *he* comes up with a plan. He's more of a strategist than I am."

DJ paused to catch his breath. "You know I'm a born wolf, right? My family knows every born wolf in the Philippines, and a whole lot of the wolves in the US. And you know how wolves are— do you know how wolves are? They're clannish. Loyal. If a wolf they trust asks them for a favor, they'll move heaven and earth to do it. Just let me get in touch with my family. I'll get together a strike force of badass wolves and take this place down. Without your sister getting hurt. I'm sure…"

The pause stretched out until Echo looked over. He'd passed out in mid-sentence.

While he'd been going on and on, making demands she couldn't fulfill and offering happy endings he couldn't deliver, she'd wished he'd shut up. But it was eerie to see him so silent and still, his bright eyes closed, his expressive features slack.

Echo floored it back to the base. She was met in the underground parking lot by a handful of nervous medics, a crowd of wary security guards, and Mr. Dowling.

Mr. Dowling stepped up as she got out of the Humvee. "Good job, Echo. I knew I could count on you."

"Of course," she replied absently, watching the medics load DJ on to a gurney.

As they strapped him in, DJ woke up and started to struggle, shouting hoarsely, "Roy! Suppressive fire, ten o'clock! Weiss, get down! Get down!"

A medic circled him with a syringe, but couldn't find a still target. Blood began to soak through the bandage around DJ's wrist as he threw himself against the straps.

"DJ!" Echo grabbed his hand. He was burning up again. "Stop fighting!"

He whipped his head around, angry and confused. "Get Suarez! We need the radio."

"You're not in combat. You have a fever. You're delirious."

"No— Really? Are you sure?" DJ started to relax. Then he spotted the medic trying to creep up on him, and began thrashing around again, yelling, "I'm a US Marine! Drop your weapon!"

"Back off!" Echo snapped at the medic, who obeyed. Then she turned back to DJ. "You're sick. Let the medics help you."

"But Roy— He's out of ammo—"

She squeezed his hand harder, so he'd be sure to feel it. "You're hurting yourself. Lie still."

To her surprise, he did. She nodded at the medic, who edged forward and jabbed the syringe into the bulging muscle of his shoulder.

DJ didn't seem to notice. Urgently, he said, "My buddy needs help."

"He's already in the hospital," Echo assured him.

He calmed as the sedative began to take effect. "Oh. Good. Make sure someone stays with him, will you? He doesn't like to be alone."

Echo didn't want to make any lying promises, so she tried to distract him. "What about you? Should someone stay with you?"

The question seemed to surprise him. "Me? Oh, you don't need to do that. But… If you're off-duty anyway… It'd be nice."

Echo hadn't meant it as an offer. But since he'd taken it as one, she supposed it wouldn't be too much of a hardship to visit him. If he started harassing her to let him go again, she could just walk out. "All right. I'll come by later."

He didn't seem reassured, but eyed her with growing incredulity. Finally, he said, "This is a *dance club*. No Christmas carols!"

As Echo laughed, his eyes closed and his hand relaxed in her grip.

She watched as the medics took him away. Both times he'd been delirious, he'd worried and worried about his friend. And now he'd revealed how much he cared about his buddy in front of Mr. Dowling. Echo's stomach clenched unpleasantly at the knowledge of how that would play out. But, to her confusion, her handler was eyeing her as if he'd just learned something important about *her*.

"What?" Echo demanded.

Mr. Dowling gave her a bland shrug. "Nothing. Let me take your mission report now. Then you can visit Torres in the hospital, if you like."

"Thanks." Occasionally, just occasionally, Mr. Dowling managed to not be a *complete* asshole. Echo decided that she ought to encourage those moments, so she added, "Really. I appreciate it. Maybe he'll be awake by the time we're done. There's no point sitting with him if he doesn't know I'm there."

Mr. Dowling smiled.

FIVE

DJ

Marine Wolf

DJ fought his way through an onslaught of fever dreams.

His pack had turned on him and was tearing him apart. He was trapped in a web of sticky strands, desperately trying to reach a sword that lay just out of reach, with a spider the size of his Harley approaching him. Marco was dead, Alec lay dying with a bullet in his head, Roy was down on the sand with blood pouring out of his mouth, and DJ was trapped in a burning Humvee with his body on fire.

When he woke at last, reality wasn't much of an improvement. He was in a small hospital room, right back where he'd started, with the addition of a needle in his arm, tubes snaking out from under the sheet, a wire running from his chest to a humming machine monitoring his heartbeat, straps around his chest and wrists and ankles, and Echo guarding him.

He'd given everything he had in his effort to escape, he'd nearly killed himself trying, and he'd accomplished absolutely nothing.

His head throbbed, his back ached, and the sheet that covered him felt like red-hot metal molded to his skin. Forgetting the straps, he tried to turn over in the hope of finding a less painful position. He barely moved, but even that slight friction was excruciating. He couldn't suppress a groan.

Echo looked down at him from her seat beside his bed. "About time you woke up. I was just about to leave."

"Don't let me keep you," DJ muttered.

"*Now* I may as well stay." Her eyes narrowed as she frowned. "You said you wanted me to."

"Wanted you to what?" DJ asked, confused.

"Oh. You don't remember. You must not have really wanted it. That'll teach me to make promises to delirious people."

Echo stood up.

"Hang on." It was ridiculous to think of any encounter with an enemy as getting off on the wrong foot— what would the right foot be?— but DJ couldn't help feeling like he'd done so with Echo. Repeatedly. "The last thing I remember, we were driving in the Humvee. I felt like hell."

"You looked like hell." Echo sat back down and examined him critically. "You still do."

"Then I got delirious, huh? I wish I remembered it. I've always wondered what that would feel like. It's never happened before, unless you count the time I overdosed on No-Doz. That was last year and my platoon is probably still laughing about it. Did I say anything funny?"

"You thought I'd requested a Christmas carol at a dance club."

DJ smiled, feeling a little better. "Anything else?"

"This isn't funny, but you were worried about your buddy. You said he doesn't like to be alone and asked to have someone stay with him—" Echo broke off. "What's the matter?"

"Nothing." DJ tried to keep his face blank while his mind was screaming, *How could you let that slip? They could use that against him. What the fuck is wrong with you?*

"Nothing." Echo clearly didn't believe him.

"I'm in pain," DJ said hastily. "When you change shifts, tell the doctors to up my morphine."

"They don't give you morphine for a sunburn, you baby."

DJ moved as much as he could, wincing as the restraints rubbed against his chest and the mattress rubbed against his back and the sheet rubbed against everything. "They should if it's this bad. Tell them to up whatever they're giving me. It hurts like a son of a bitch."

"All right." She paused. "What do you mean, 'change shifts?'"

"You know, when you go and the next guard takes over."

Her upswept eyebrows rose even higher. "I'm not guarding you."

"You're not? Wait, are you a medic? I thought you were in black ops." As soon as he said it, he remembered the context in which he'd learned it. "Shit, sorry. You don't like to talk about that."

"I don't care. I'm not some delicate flower." A flash of the mischief DJ had seen so briefly in the Humvee returned as she added, "Unlike you, you little rosebud. You were right the first time. I'm an assassin. Your guards are outside."

Maybe it was the lingering effects of the heat stroke, but DJ was completely lost. "If you're not my guard and you're not a medic, then what are you doing here?"

Echo spoke as if she was confessing to some embarrassing crime, like spying on people while they undressed. "You said you wanted me to stay with you. My handler didn't mind. So I did."

DJ stared at Echo, seeing her anew with this new information. She looked as impossibly flawless as ever, in form-fitting black jeans that showed off her long legs and a green tank top that clung to her slim waist and small (but, of course, perfect) breasts. Her ivory skin was unmarked by weary smudges under her eyes, though she had bruises around her wrists and upper arms that he was pretty sure he'd left in their struggle. Her eyes, blue without a trace of red, reminded him of arctic ice, of ocean depths, of a swimming pool on a summer day.

He had a flash of longing to have her lay her hands down on his body, and cool his burning skin.

But her posture lacked the catlike grace he'd seen before, and she'd risen as stiffly as if she'd slept in that uncomfortable-looking chair. Surely she wouldn't have...

"How long have you been here?" DJ asked.

Looking away, she muttered, "All night."

"Doing what?"

"Just staying with you." Defensively, she said, "You said you wanted me to."

DJ found this nearly impossible to process. "I did? And you did?"

She rolled her eyes as if he was an idiot. Just as he was starting to think that he'd somehow misunderstood the entire conversation, she said, "Yes."

DJ was struck dumb, which didn't happen often. He was the enemy. He'd fought her, stomped on her ankle, gotten her shot with a tranquilizer dart, thrown water in her face, tried to stun her, and informed her that he'd intended to tie her up, dump her in the back of a Humvee, and then ditch her. In return, she'd sat by his side all night, just because he'd asked her to while he was in some pathetic feverish state that he was now glad he didn't remember.

"I left the medical stuff to the doctors, of course," Echo said. "Once they took off, all I did was cool you off whenever you started moaning about being on fire." She jerked her head at a side table with a basin and some wash cloths.

Even more defensively, she added, "They said I should. Since I was here anyway. It wasn't something that just spontaneously occurred to me."

DJ was torn between being embarrassed and wishing she'd do it again. Maybe she would if he asked her nicely. Then he decided that she couldn't possibly be telling the truth, but was playing good cop to Dr. Semple's bad cop. But surely if that was the game, she'd be more friendly.

However he turned it over in his mind, he kept coming back to the same conclusion: he'd deliriously begged her to stay with him, and she had. All night.

His pack would have done that for him, of course, and so would his fire team. He supposed a serious girlfriend would too, though given the rarity of him being that sick and the rarity of him having a serious girlfriend, the two had never overlapped. But this strange, fierce woman, who had only ever sounded warm when she'd spoken of her hostage sister? He didn't understand it. But it touched him.

"Thanks," DJ finally managed. "I mean, thanks a lot. I really appreciate it."

"You're welcome," she said, sounding distinctly doubtful.

"But why? We're enemies. You weren't under orders. And it couldn't have been any fun."

Her blue gaze met his, so clear and deep that he felt like he was falling into it. "Temporary insanity. Don't get used to it."

"That'd be pretty stupid of me, considering that it's *temporary*." He contemplated her eyes. Tide pools. Wishing wells. Lagoons. "Okay, I have another guess about you. You're some kind of water-shifter. That's why I haven't seen you change yet. It must be miserable to be a were-otter in Death Valley. Did they at least give you a tank to swim around in?"

She made another "you idiot" face at him, but her lips twitched as if she was trying to suppress a smile. "Yes. It has kelp and everything."

"And abalone?"

"Of course."

"Sea anemones?"

"Anemones, starfish, little transparent shrimp. The works."

"Would you let me have a swim in it?"

She smiled, for real this time. "I don't know. Your fur might clog up the circulation vents."

"No, it won't. It's waterproof. You forgot: I'm a *Marine* wolf."

"No wonder you did so badly in the desert."

DJ nodded solemnly. "I'm adapted for an aquatic environment."

"Like a Navy SEAL."

"Exactly. They only let you into the SEALs if you're an actual—"

"— seal-shifter," they said together.

To his surprise, DJ was enjoying himself, his pain and discomfort and worry fading into background noise. Hardly anyone would play along with him like this. Roy, sometimes, if you caught him in the right mood. Some of Five's actor and writer friends, when he went to her parties. Just his luck, he'd finally found a woman who'd take a thread of absurdity and run with it, and she was a mysterious, cranky assassin forced to work for the bad guys.

He tried to turn over again, only to be stopped again. "Goddammit. Can you unbuckle the straps? They're driving me crazy."

"So you can bolt again? Forget it."

"I won't," DJ assured her. "I *can't*."

"That's what I thought before."

"So if I do try, you'll stop me like you did the last time. I won't even make it to the door."

Echo seemed to find that more persuasive. "I'm not taking the manacles off your ankles."

"Manacles?"

She lifted the sheet. Sure enough, his ankles were chained to the bed. "Well, you broke a pair of handcuffs."

"I couldn't break those," DJ said glumly. They were steel links, half an inch thick.

He could, however, turn into a wolf and slip the cuffs. But he hadn't been lying when he'd said he wouldn't make it to the door. Besides, now that he knew where he was, he wouldn't try to escape until he could take some water with him. Or a Humvee. He had to locate the vehicle bay.

To his immense relief, she unbuckled the straps around his chest, then the ones at his wrists. They hurt as she peeled them off, but he couldn't wait to move again. The instant she took off the last one, he quickly sat up.

He could barely hold himself up. The room swung around him, and the pain in his head went from throbbing to splitting. DJ hastily lay down again, but the damage had been done. The room wouldn't stop spinning, and his skin burned worse than ever. He closed his eyes, willing the pain to subside. It didn't.

"DJ?" Echo said, a little uncertainly. "Are you awake?"

"Yeah. I feel terrible, though. And I'm on fire again. Would you mind cooling me off?"

A wet cloth came down on his forehead, then slid over his cheeks and throat, touching lightly but leaving exquisite relief behind. She must have been getting it ready even before he'd asked.

"Thanks," he sighed. "That helps a lot."

"It's only what any platypus would do for another," replied Echo.

Temporary insanity, DJ thought. He hoped it wouldn't wear off any time soon.

She kept rubbing the cloth over his body, dousing the flames. For once, DJ didn't feel the urge to speak or move. He lay as quietly as if they were both wolves, and she was grooming him to make him feel better.

One of the hardest things about living with one-bodies was the lack of touch. In the world outside the pack, men could shake hands, slap each other on the back, or maybe, under extreme circumstances, lay a hand on a shoulder. They could touch out of necessity, and they could fight, of course. But that was it. Touching women was even more limited, unless he was dating them. Most touch came across as sexual or aggressive, not as communication or play or camaraderie or any one of the million other ways that wolves used it to relate to each other.

It was a price he had to pay for being a Marine. But it grated on him, especially whenever anyone in his platoon was wounded or sick. They felt like pack, but he couldn't comfort them in the way of wolves.

When he'd spent a month in a military hospital in Germany, his pack had flown in to visit him. At first he was too weak to shift, so they didn't either. Instead, they got as close to him as they could without disturbing the wires and tubes, and took turns holding his hand, rubbing his back, and stroking his hair. When he got stronger, one would guard the door while he and the others became wolves, so he could be groomed from head to tail. Grandma Steel always made sure to arrive in a decrepit, shedding fur coat, to explain any hairs that might be left on the bed.

DJ didn't know how he'd have made it through without his pack and their touch, nor why one-bodies were so skittish about such a natural thing. But while a wolf might lick a stranger as a greeting, only pack and close friends would groom a wounded wolf for hours. What Echo was doing meant something. But DJ had no idea what, especially since he still didn't even know what she was.

The washcloth was getting uncomfortably warm. Echo lifted it from his chest. DJ heard her dip it in water, then wring it out. When she laid it back down, it was cool again.

He opened his eyes, and saw that she was resting her other hand on the pillow. The impulse was impossible to resist; he turned his head, laying his cheek down on her hand. The warmth of it burned and stung, but he didn't move and neither did she.

"I think you're not a platypus after all," DJ said dreamily. "You're something with a pack. You said you're not a wolf. A lion? A dolphin? An orca? That's it, right? You're a killer whale."

"A whale," said Echo. "That's flattering."

"A *killer* whale. Sleek and deadly. That has to be it."

"You were closest when you guessed I was a tree. I'm a saguaro shifter. Tall and prickly."

DJ laughed. Then, comforted by her touch, he drifted into sleep.

The first thing DJ noticed when he woke again was how much better he felt. The second thing he noticed was that the straps were back. And the third thing he noticed was that Echo was gone and Dr. Semple was standing over him, having apparently just shaken him awake.

A man stood beside the doctor. Though he was a stocky black man in a suit, while Dr. Semple was a skinny white woman in a doctor's coat, there was some sort of non-physical resemblance between the two. DJ frowned, trying to figure out what it was.

"Good morning, Torres," the new guy said. "I'm Mr. Dowling. I'm going to be your handler."

DJ knew, he *knew*, that he should play it cool, gather information, and act like all the fight had been beaten out of him. But what came out of his mouth was, "What the fuck is a handler?"

"You can think of me as your new commanding officer," Mr. Dowling said smoothly. "You take your orders from me, and you give your reports to me."

"You're going to have to unchain me before you can order me to do anything but lie down some more," DJ pointed out.

Mr. Dowling didn't so much as blink. "Before I do that, I want you to understand why you shouldn't run away again."

"Nearly dying in Death Valley once was enough for me." DJ wished Mr. Dowling would finish threatening him and let him get up already. He was ready to jump out of his skin, plus there was something vaguely embarrassing about having to talk from a bed to someone looming over him.

"Yes, but you'll be leaving this base eventually. I want to make sure you come back."

DJ didn't like the sound of that. Nor did he like how Dr. Semple was standing there silently, watching him with unnerving anticipation. DJ's frustrated restlessness melded with an even more unpleasant anxiety.

Dr. Semple set up a laptop on the side table where the basin of water had been. As she turned it so DJ couldn't see the screen and began typing, DJ wished Echo was still there, touching him and making him feel almost like his pack was with him. Sure, she too was keeping him captive, but at least it wasn't by her own free choice.

And that sums up exactly how fucked this whole situation is, he thought.

"We made a deal," said Dr. Semple, making DJ jump. Or try to, anyway; all he could do was twitch against the restraints. At least the sunburn had healed enough that it didn't hurt. Much.

DJ remembered the deal, but now he wasn't so sure he wanted to stick with it. But he couldn't not know, either. "Let's see the video."

"This is Farrell when he first came out of surgery." Dr. Semple turned the laptop so DJ could see the screen.

It was surveillance video, but high-quality. Roy lay unconscious, hooked up to a bunch of noisy machines. What DJ could see of his face beneath the tubes and electrodes was as white as his pillow. Even so, he looked better than he had in the helo.

"Got anything more recent?" DJ asked, trying not to betray his nerves. If they put any electrodes on him, his heart rate would probably overload the machine.

Dr. Semple turned the laptop away and typed. As he did, Mr. Dowling addressed DJ. "You ran before Dr. Semple could explain the consequences of doing so. As you may have figured out, Farrell isn't here. But what happens to him depends entirely on your actions. Due to your escape attempt, his sedation and painkillers were withdrawn."

Dr. Semple turned around the laptop. DJ had just enough time to see a freeze-frame of Roy, still unconscious and under bright lights but hooked up to fewer machines, before the doctor hit "play."

Roy was the most stoic person DJ had ever met. DJ had seen him go for days without eating or sleeping, take a bullet to the thigh, nearly die of shrapnel wounds, and endure the agony of becoming a werewolf, all without uttering a word of complaint. The most reaction DJ had ever seen from him was when he'd just woken up from a nightmare and wasn't fully conscious yet. But as soon as he was completely awake, he'd say nothing until he'd recovered enough to claim that he was fine.

On the laptop screen, Roy shifted in apparent discomfort, groaned, then opened his eyes. Then he made a sound that DJ had never heard from him before, a cry of startled agony that made a stab of pain go through DJ's own heart.

"You sick fucks!" DJ shouted.

Rage blurred his vision and sent heat rushing to his face. He became a wolf and threw himself against his restraints, so set on ripping out his captors' throats that he could almost taste the blood in his mouth. But he had no leverage, and the straps held him tight. However he snarled and snapped at them, he couldn't break free.

Finally he subsided, panting, and became a man again.

The fucking video was still playing. Roy had his forearm flung over his face, the IV needle ripped out and blood running down from where it had been.

"It hurts," Roy gasped. "Everything hurts. DJ—"

"That's enough!" DJ yelled, loudly enough to drown him out. If he had to helplessly listen to Roy's pain— pain that DJ was responsible for— for one second longer, it would kill him. "You made your point! I won't run away again! Now turn off that fucking video and give him his fucking morphine!"

Mercifully, Mr. Dowling reached over and closed the laptop. "Please inform Farrell's doctors that they can give him his medications now."

Dr. Semple stepped out of the room.

DJ lay shaking with fury and pent-up adrenaline, an acrid taste in his mouth and bitter guilt in his heart.

"Are you ready to listen now?" Mr. Dowling asked.

His expression was as mildly curious as if he was waiting for DJ to give him a non-urgent report, not as if he'd just been participating in torturing a wounded man. Dr. Semple had looked like that too, when she'd lied to DJ that Roy was dead.

That was when DJ figured out the nature of the resemblance between Mr. Dowling and Dr. Semple. It was an aura of asshole.

Dr. Semple came back into the room. "Farrell is resting comfortably. Whether he stays that way is up to you, Torres."

DJ gritted his teeth, refusing to give them the satisfaction of getting a rise out of him. "Just tell me what you want from me."

Mr. Dowling smiled pleasantly at him. "We want to recruit you."

"Too late. I'm the property of the US Marine Corps."

The smile grew wider. "Excellent. In that case, we'll skip the paperwork. Congratulations, you're our new black ops operative."

DJ had seen that coming, but he couldn't resist arguing. "You mean assassin, right? I'm a Marine, not a ninja. I'm an automatic rifleman— a machine gunner. Have you ever heard a SAW? It's not exactly stealthy. You want a guy who'll creep up and kill people and creep away unseen, you go kidnap yourself a scout sniper."

DJ hoped they'd try. With any luck, the sniper would snipe them.

Mr. Dowling inquired, "Do you know any who can turn into wolves?"

"*Wolves* aren't stealthy," DJ retorted, frustrated. "What's going to be more conspicuous practically anywhere, any person ever, or a fucking wolf? Unless you want to put a hit on a lumberjack."

"How to make the best use of you is our problem, not yours," replied Mr. Dowling. "Think of it as a transfer to a different branch of service. We're part of the Department of Defense. Like the NSA, but more secret."

Like the NSA, but more evil. DJ wondered if it was true. It wouldn't entirely surprise him.

"If I take off your restraints, do I have your word of honor that you won't attack us or run?" Mr. Dowling inquired. "Backed up by the fact that even if you managed to kill us, someone else would pick up the phone and give the orders for your friend to die in pain."

Secret evil branches of the US government ought to count as foreign powers, as far as DJ was concerned. As he'd told Echo, he considered himself a prisoner of war. Captured Marines weren't allowed to promise not to escape. And Roy would undoubtedly rather be tortured than have DJ violate the code of conduct for his sake.

Roy wouldn't have made repeated, useless attempts to escape, but would have patiently waited for the perfect opportunity. Roy would have given them his name, rank, and serial number, and then shut up for all eternity. Roy would never have admitted to Echo that he was in pain, let alone asked her for help, let alone laid his head down on her hand.

DJ wasn't Roy. He couldn't be bound by what Roy would do or what Roy would want. He had to do this his way.

"Your other option is to go to the lab and help with my

experiments," said Dr. Semple.

"Awesome. I've always wanted to be a lab rat," DJ said sarcastically. "I choose black ops, of course! Take off the straps. I give you my word of honor that I won't kill you or run."

Mr. Dowling undid the straps, then unlocked the manacles. DJ sat up quickly before he remembered why that might not be a good idea. But this time nothing happened. His body ached and his skin was tender, but he felt confident that he had the strength to rip out these assholes' throats.

And then someone else would give the order, and Roy would die. DJ had to protect him.

"You shouldn't hurt Roy. I mean, not just because it's fucking sadistic and you'll burn in hell for it, you fucking—" DJ caught himself and hurried on before they could interrupt. "He's too valuable to screw with. You want a werewolf Marine? He's a werewolf Marine. Bring him here. Let him bond with me. Then you'll have both of us."

"We already have a pack of made wolves," Mr. Dowling said. "They have... problems."

DJ could imagine exactly what sort of problems they might have. Every horror story Grandma Steel had told him flashed into his mind.

"Forget your fucked-up made wolves," DJ argued. "Roy's more than that. He's a much better Marine than me. Seriously, look up our records. Roy has medals. I've got nothing but reprimands. I barely even made it through boot camp!"

"We've examined your records," Mr. Dowling replied calmly. "And under the pretext of trying to locate you and Farrell, we also had our operative interview the other members of your fire team, your lieutenant, and the doctor at your base."

DJ tried to keep a straight face on the off chance that Mr. Dowling was bluffing, but his heart sank.

Sure enough, Dr. Semple added, "We learned that Farrell was suffering from severe post-traumatic stress disorder. His record does suggest that he was a better Marine than you. *Once.* But he's useless to us now. He'll never fight again."

Her words were a double blow to DJ. They knew about Roy, and they didn't value him. And though DJ knew that they'd say anything to manipulate him, hearing that dispassionate evaluation from a doctor was crushing.

"He could get better," DJ said, hating the doubt that he heard in his own voice.

"Highly unlikely," Dr. Semple said dismissively.

"Farrell *used to be* valuable," Mr. Dowling said, rubbing it in. "And that's not even considering whatever problems might have come with his transformation. Right now he's not even well enough for us to determine what those might be."

"Maybe he doesn't have any," DJ suggested. "Hey! Maybe becoming a werewolf cured his PTSD. You never know. It's healing his shrapnel wounds, isn't it?"

DJ was first excited, then unnerved to see this idea visibly catch Dr. Semple's interest.

"What an intriguing thought," Dr. Semple said, her eyes glinting creepily. "We've tested werewolf healing on a number of diseases and injuries."

DJ felt sick imagining how she'd probably done that. Being forced to be an assassin would be a day at the beach compared to being infected with things to see if he healed.

Ignoring DJ's horror, the doctor continued, "But it never occurred to me try it on psychological disorders. A cure for PTSD has been the holy grail of military medicine since World War One."

DJ was relieved when Mr. Dowling interrupted the doctor. "As far as PTSD is concerned, the holy grail isn't curing it, it's predicting who'll get it so they can be weeded out in advance."

"And identifying who's immune." Dr. Semple turned to DJ, so eager that she was practically licking her lips. "I only asked about combat stress in our initial interview to distract you. But now I'm curious. You have quite a paper trail. Demerits, recommendations that you be discharged, recommendations that you be considered for a medal, and a fascinating set of medical records. But you've never been treated for combat stress. Is it true that you've never had any serious trouble with it?"

DJ's mind leaped ahead to the likely outcome of this line of questioning. The only way to test whether someone was immune to something was to try to give it to them. "I lost my shit in the medevac helo, remember?"

Dr. Semple raised a patronizing eyebrow. "An obvious fake to distract the corpsmen from Farrell's transformation."

"Got me there," DJ admitted. "But everyone gets combat stress sometimes. Including me. I already told you that."

"The difference between combat stress and PTSD is that PTSD doesn't go away. Is it true that your combat stress has never lasted for more than a few hours? And that you've never had any symptoms other than subjective feelings of 'things moving too fast?'"

"I'm having a flashback right now. To Afghanistan. And you know what? It's a lot nicer than here. I think I'll stay there."

Neither Dr. Semple nor Mr. Dowling looked amused.

Quickly, DJ said, "Now you see why I have all those demerits. Me and my big mouth. Look, I was lying the first time. No one wants to admit that they have PTSD. They think it makes them seem weak. Like they can't be trusted. I didn't want people to think that everyone who said I couldn't be a Marine was right— that I couldn't hack it. That I wasn't strong enough."

"Exactly what symptoms do you have?" Dr. Semple asked.

DJ couldn't tell whether or not the doctor was buying it. But he could certainly provide some plausible symptoms, based on what he'd seen in other Marines. It would be too noticeable if he borrowed Roy's, since they'd already researched him, so he went with Alvarado's.

"I'm tense all the time," DJ began. "Anyone comes up behind me, I'll whip round like I think they're a hit man. Anyone touches me when I'm sleeping, I'll attack them before I realize what's going on. If I hear a loud noise, I'll hit the deck, and when I get up, I'm sweating and my hands are shaking. And I drink too much."

"In Afghanistan?" said Mr. Dowling, his eyebrows raised.

"You can get alcohol there if you really want it. Foreign contractors can bring it in, or your friends can mail it to you in mouthwash bottles. And drinking is the only way I can stop remembering." DJ shut up, figuring he'd said enough. Besides, that last bit was getting into territory *he* didn't like to remember. He'd never been personal friends with Alvarado, but DJ had always thought he was a good guy.

Dr. Semple appeared to at least be considering what DJ had told her. "Stop remembering what?"

DJ showed them his scar. "This. I mean, how I got it."

"Tell me about that," said the doctor.

"I don't want to talk about it," DJ said promptly. If there was one thing everyone with PTSD had in common, it was that they didn't want to talk about it.

"I already know what happened," Dr. Semple said. "I want to know how it felt to you. Did you think you were going to die?"

Mr. Dowling, evidently bored by the entire discussion, went to the laptop and started typing. Probably checking his email.

"I don't remember," DJ said.

"Do you dream about it?" Dr. Semple asked.

"Sometimes."

"How do you feel when—"

A gunshot shattered the still air of the room. DJ ducked and grabbed for his M-16. As his fingers closed on emptiness, he spotted Mr. Dowling looking up from his laptop and realized how he'd been tricked.

"Incoming!" DJ shouted, several seconds too late.

Mr. Dowling actually rolled his eyes. "Good thing we're not recruiting you as an actor. Dr. Semple shook you awake when we came in, and you didn't so much as flinch. *I'd* have probably reacted more, under the circumstances."

"I did go for my rifle just now," DJ pointed out, though he didn't know why he was even bothering. He'd obviously failed the test. He should have said he had flashbacks. No one could prove that he didn't.

"You're a Marine," said Dr. Semple. "That's a trained reflex any soldier would have. You didn't hit the floor, your hands are steady, and you're not sweating. Hold still."

DJ forced himself to obey as the doctor took his pulse.

"Interesting," remarked Dr. Semple. "If you did have PTSD, your heart rate would have been elevated. In fact, it should be regardless, because you were startled. But it's *below* the baseline we got from you when you arrived."

"What's that mean?" The last thing DJ wanted was to be

interesting to Dr. Semple.

The doctor smiled. "I don't like to speculate without further data. But preliminarily, it means you're even more special than I thought."

DJ ran through all the words he knew that expressed fucked-upness— snafu (Situation Normal, All Fucked Up), fubar (Fucked Up Beyond All Recognition), and so forth— before deciding that none of them expressed the utter fuckedness he was searching for. He'd need to invent a new one. Fucking Asshole Sadistic Scientist Thinks I'm Special. Whatever that spelled out.

It was funny— funny-weird, not funny-hilarious— how words came so easily to him in his mind, when they were so fucking impossible on the page. If he'd only known that some day he'd be trapped in a lab with a doctor who wanted to traumatize him to see if he was immune to PTSD, he'd have been a lot more tolerant of all those excruciating sessions of educational therapy he'd gone through as a kid. At least Dr. Semple wasn't going to torture him with cut-out letters.

"And that isn't the only one of your neurological anomalies," Dr. Semple mused.

Of course. If she'd gone digging through his medical records, she'd learned all about the funny— funny-weird— way he was wired.

Condescendingly, the doctor went on, "That means 'brain differences.' Like learning disabilities. Why haven't you ever been diagnosed with ADHD? That stands for attention deficit hyperactivity dis—"

"I know what it stands for," DJ said, then wished he'd kept his mouth shut and pretended he wasn't that familiar with it. Since he'd once again given himself away and it hardly mattered now, he added, "I've never been diagnosed because I've never been tested. Test me yourself, if you care. If I do have it, it doesn't bother me any."

"It doesn't bother *you*," Mr. Dowling remarked snippily.

Dr. Semple ignored him. "But if your medical records are correct, your dyslexia is unusually severe. Perhaps there's some clue in that. Have you ever worked with cut-out letters?"

At that, the situation became so spectacularly fucked that it tipped over into funny-hilarious. DJ laughed. And kept on laughing, until his eyes watered and his captors stared at him as if he'd lost his mind. Maybe he had.

Finally, he managed to pull himself together. "All right, you've got me. Let's make a deal."

There went the "you are totally insane" stares again. But DJ was used to that.

"You are in no position—" Mr. Dowling began.

"Actually, I think I am." DJ went on, faster and louder, before they could interrupt. "Mr. Dowling, I'm a born wolf Marine with the power of super strength. I could do a lot of damage on your behalf. Dr. Semple, you might never find a lab rat as *special* as me. I'm worth a lot to you both, assuming Dr. Semple doesn't break me by accident."

"She won't," Mr. Dowling said, giving the doctor a warning look.

"So here's *my* deal," DJ went on. "I'll do whatever you say. Within reason. I won't murder innocent people who're just in your way. But if you want me to go after bad guys we're not legally allowed to kill, I'll do that. If you want me to cooperate with your creepy experiments, I'll do that too. Your part of the deal is that I want Roy here with me."

"Unacceptable," said Mr. Dowling. "You'll grab him and run. Farrell stays where he is."

"Then I want to talk to him."

"Also unacceptable. I can't risk coded messages."

"Fine." DJ was disappointed, but unsurprised. "Now here's the part I won't budge on. You don't hurt him. Ever. I want to see video of him every day, and I want to see him being treated well and getting better."

"We can't guarantee that he'll get better," Dr. Semple pointed out. "You of all people should know that."

DJ tried not to visibly flinch. Marco must have told their operative *everything* on the theory that even the most seemingly irrelevant details might somehow help rescue Roy and DJ. "I want to see you taking good care of him, all right?"

He wondered if he should say anything about pack bonding. If they let Roy bond with someone, it would undoubtedly be someone evil who would fuck with him. If Roy didn't bond with anyone, then DJ would have two months maximum to get to him before the loneliness drove him crazy.

DJ thought Roy would vote for the latter. But if DJ requested it, these assholes might go ahead with the bond-of-evil just to spite him. And without talking to Roy, DJ wouldn't be able to tell whether he'd bonded or not. He decided to let that part alone.

DJ recalled the icy calm of combat as he stared first into Dr. Semple's eyes, then into Mr. Dowling's. Neither broke his gaze, but he saw discomfort creep into each of their faces. "Hurt him again, and I'll kill as many of you as I can before you take me down. I know, then I'll be dead and you won't have any reason left to keep him alive. But that's the deal. Take it or leave it."

"Deal," said Mr. Dowling.

"Fine," said Dr. Semple.

"And I want my family to know I'm alive," DJ added. "They're wolves. They can keep a secret."

"We'll consider letting you send a message," Mr. Dowling said. "No live communication, though."

"I want them to reply in video or audio, so I know they got the message."

As Mr. Dowling started to agree, Dr. Semple said, "Do any of your family have useful powers? Where do they live?"

Though DJ knew the doctor was just screwing with him— if she wanted to go after his pack, she could easily find them without his help— anger and fear flared through him. "You stay away from them! My sister's famous. She disappears, it'll be all over the news. My brother's a corporate lawyer with a heart condition. He's not James Bond— he's not even allowed to play racquetball. My grandmother's seventy, my oldest niece is six, my parents—"

"Enough, Torres. We're not interested in your family. So long as you cooperate." Mr. Dowling pointed to a door. "Take a shower. Get dressed. We'll get some food for you. And then—"

"And coffee. Unlimited coffee. That has to be part of the deal." *Should I push my luck?* DJ figured he had nothing to lose. "And an iPod."

"Excuse me?" Mr. Dowling said icily.

"You've completely fucked up my life," DJ pointed out. "The least you can do is give me an iPod. With speakers. And internet access—"

"No internet." Mr. Dowling and Dr. Semple spoke in perfect

unison.

Without missing a beat, DJ continued, "Then I want it to come loaded with music. I'll tell you what songs— actually, albums would be simpler. I'll tell you what albums I want. I can sort through them later."

"*And then*," Mr. Dowling went on, with an edge in his voice, "We'll introduce you to your partner."

SIX

Echo

Roommates

Charlie stretched luxuriously out on the sofa, *Flames of Desire (Billionaire Firefighters # 3)* discarded at her side. "…and then Kevin said his cast itched, and he didn't know how he could take a bath without it getting wet. So I said I'd help him…"

Normally Echo enjoyed hearing about Charlie's escapades with her boyfriend-of-the-month. Last month it had been Juan the lab tech. But as Charlie recounted all the details, Echo's mind kept drifting away from Kevin the security guard, to what might be happening to DJ. When she'd returned to check on him, the guards had told her that Dr. Semple and Mr. Dowling were in there with him. The head of medical research and the head of covert ops: whatever was going on in there couldn't be pleasant. She hoped that at least his sunburn was better.

"But I didn't take care of him *all night* like you did with DJ," Charlie said, poking Echo in the ribs. "That's so romantic! Was he grateful? Did he—"

Echo's attention returned to Charlie so quickly that she felt like it had been yanked with a bungee cord. "There was nothing romantic about it. I accidentally promised him I would, that's all."

"What's he look like?" Charlie asked. "Is he devastatingly

handsome? He is, right?"

"Ask Kevin," Echo said, grinning.

"Kevin never saw him. He got knocked out when DJ kicked the door in."

"The first time I saw him, I was too busy fighting him to see if he was devastating or not. The next time I saw him, I'd punched him in the mouth and he had second degree sunburns. His face was all red and swollen. He definitely wasn't devastating then."

"Do you think he will be when he heals?"

"No," Echo said firmly. "Stop trying to set me up with him. It's a terrible idea. He's a born wolf who's been cut off from his pack. He—"

He probably won't live very long hung in the air between them, unspoken.

Charlie laid a gentle hand on Echo's shoulder. "Everybody dies. Kevin will, some day. I—"

Echo couldn't stand hearing her sister talk like that. "He's not my type, all right? But maybe he'd be yours. He's dark and handsome."

"I thought you were too busy fighting to notice."

Caught out, Echo protested, "I never said he wasn't handsome. I just wasn't sure about the devastating part."

"Forget the devastating. Is he tall?"

"Well… He's not short."

"Average height," Charlie said dismissively. "Is he a dominating alpha male?"

"He might be an alpha *wolf*. He didn't seem dominating, but you never know. He could be into bondage and spanking and giving orders, the whole nine yards. Besides, he's a werewolf. That's sexy, right? Why don't you ever read any werewolf romances?"

Charlie made a face. "Too much like real life."

The knock at the door made Echo jump. "Who is it?"

To her dismay, Mr. Dowling opened the door. Normally the apartment she shared with Charlie was a refuge. It was going to start feeling exactly like everywhere else if her handlers kept invading it.

"What do you want?" Echo asked ungraciously.

Mr. Dowling smiled as if she'd welcomed him in. "I want you to come with me."

Echo followed him through the unmarked corridors. She thought they'd go into the office, but he kept on walking. They passed medical research, then the hospital.

"Where are we going?" Echo asked.

"Residential quarters."

That told her nothing. Apartments were scattered all over the base. "Whose residence?"

He stopped at a door and waved her toward the retina scanner.

"It's keyed to me?" she asked.

"Yes. Open it."

"Why?"

As she widened her eyes for the scanner and the door began to slide open, a blast of music hit her, a swaggering rap song in... Hindi? Echo didn't speak it, but she was familiar with the sound. Charlie loved Bollywood movies.

Mr. Dowling spoke loudly, to be heard over the music. "Because it's your new apartment."

"What?" She swung on him before she got a look inside.

From inside the apartment, an equally startled voice said, "What? Seriously? *She's* my partner?"

Echo didn't have to turn around to see who was speaking. She recognized that scratchy voice.

"He's my *partner?*" Echo exclaimed.

Mr. Dowling gestured her inside. DJ was leaning against the living room wall, adjusting the sound on an iPod with a tiny speaker system attached. Their eyes met, and he turned it off.

He looked much better than he had the day before. The blisters and swelling and redness had subsided, but a pink line still cut across his mouth. The sight again made her feel guilty, which made no sense. It was a trivial injury, inflicted on a werewolf. It would be healed into invisibility by the next morning.

Then she remembered the other bomb Mr. Dowling had dropped. "What do you mean, my new apartment? I have an apartment!"

The door slid shut as Mr. Dowling took a seat on the sofa. "You two will be roommates while we train Torres. We want you to learn to work as a team. It's a method that should be familiar to you, Torres."

"You mean the way guys who don't get along in boot camp get assigned as battle buddies? You know, that doesn't always work out so great." DJ shot a furtive glance at Echo, then earnestly informed Mr. Dowling, "Anyway, she and I get along fine. Mission accomplished. We don't need to room together."

"If you both behave, it won't need to be permanent," Mr. Dowling said blandly, as if he was addressing a pair of recalcitrant teenagers. "You're lucky it's just the two of you, and you have a nice apartment instead of bunks in a barrack."

"That's true," DJ remarked, then shut up when Echo glared at him.

Echo's temper rose rather than cooling. "I've always lived with my sisters— my sister. Charlie needs me. What if she has a medical crisis and I'm not there?"

"She'll press her alert button, the same as she would if you were on a mission or she was alone for any other reason," said Mr. Dowling.

DJ had been staring at Echo ever since she'd mentioned her sister. But to Echo's relief, he didn't comment. Instead, he tugged at the sofa until a shred of cloth came away in his fingers. He examined it, dropped it, started to tear off another shred, and then jerked his hand away and began to pace around the living room.

Over his shoulder, he said, "I want to see more video. I want to know that Roy's recovered from you torturing him."

Echo's stomach lurched. She hoped Mr. Dowling would deny the accusation or say that DJ was exaggerating, but he only said, "I'll consider it. Echo, you can visit Charlie, of course, but you sleep here at night."

Her eyebrows flew up. DJ's jaw dropped.

Mr. Dowling rolled his eyes. "There's two beds. I'm your handler, not your matchmaker."

Echo didn't know what was most embarrassing, that she'd thought Mr. Dowling was ordering them to sleep together, that Mr. Dowling knew what she'd thought, or that DJ had obviously thought the same thing.

"In that case, could we get a two-bedroom?" DJ asked.

Mr. Dowling was clearly impervious to embarrassment, because he spoke without a hitch. "No. The point is to force you to interact. I don't want you hiding alone in your rooms."

"If we promised not to…?" DJ suggested.

Mr. Dowling ignored him. "Echo, show him around the base. We'll collect him for training after lunch. Torres, you know what happens if you don't honor our agreement."

DJ stopped pacing and looked straight at Mr. Dowling. With no expression whatsoever, he said, "So do you."

The temperature seemed to drop thirty degrees.

"The door will unlock from the inside now." Mr. Dowling retreated, the door sliding shut behind him.

There was a brief silence. Then the ice melted from DJ's face, and he once again looked like the sweet innocent guy whom Echo had been so sure couldn't hurt her. But though it had only been for a second, she'd seen the real man beneath the cheerful mask. He was a ruthless killer, just like her. She wasn't sure if that made her feel better or worse about being stuck with him as a partner.

Better, she supposed. At least she didn't have to worry that he couldn't pull his own weight. If Echo was forced to have a partner, she could do a whole lot worse.

"I'm sorry I got you booted out of your apartment," DJ said. "About being partners—"

Echo put a finger to her lips. DJ fell silent while she scanned the living room. She spotted the heat-glow of two bugs in the walls, got a knife from the kitchen, pried them out, and smashed them underfoot. DJ followed her as she went from room to room, scanning for bugs and destroying the ones she found.

The apartment was similar to the one she shared with Charlie, except that the bedroom was very small, with a pair of single beds about two feet apart and no room to push them further away from each other. The gym was larger, with a hot tub and an empty area that was presumably for free-sparring. There was a bug in the bedroom and another in the bathroom, plus two in the gym. Echo destroyed them all.

After she crushed the last one against the floor of the gym, she said, "We can talk now."

"Aren't they going to notice that you smashed their bugs?" DJ asked.

"Of course. But I don't like being spied on, and they know that. I guess they felt like they had to try. But I never let them bug our— my apartment." Now that she could speak freely, there was something she'd been wondering about. "What was that song you were playing when I came in?"

"'Kali Denali.'" DJ grinned. "I'll turn the speakers to 11."

The bass line made the walls shake, and the few lines in English were pure gangsta rap. Echo wished she hadn't been so quick to smash the bugs— she liked the idea of blasting her eavesdroppers with it. Then she remembered that DJ had been playing it when the bugs had still been in the walls, and her grin matched his.

"Was that Hindi?" she asked, when the song ended.

"You're close. It's Punjabi."

"Do you speak it?"

"Not a word. But I'll play you something in a language I do speak." DJ turned on another song. Echo couldn't even guess what language it was in, but she liked the catchy tune of the sung part and the expressive voice of the rapper. Without understanding a single word, she was certain that it was a love story that ended sadly.

"Did you like it?" DJ asked after the last notes faded.

"Yeah, I did. What language was it in?"

"Tagalog, from the Philippines. It's 'Magda,' by Gloc-9."

"What's it about?"

"The way our lives can change, and how we look back and can't even figure out how it happened. The narrator is this guy Ernesto, who was childhood friends with this girl, Magda. They lost touch with each other, and he went looking for her. Finally he found her in the big city, where she was stripping in clubs. I think she might be a prostitute too, but I'm not totally sure about that part."

Apologetically, he added, "I'm fluent, more or less, but my vocabulary's not that great when it comes to words my parents wouldn't say in front of a kid."

Echo laughed. As DJ started playing another song by the same guy, tapping out the beat on the wall, she peered over his shoulder at the song list.

She put her finger under the word 'ng.' "How do you say that?"

DJ stopped tapping. He hit the song she'd indicated, interrupting the one that was playing and starting a new one.

After the first few notes played, he said, "'Alalay Ng Hari.'"

"I meant..." She still hadn't caught the pronunciation; the word had blended together with the others as he'd said it. She found a different song with it and again indicated it. "This word. By itself."

DJ peered at it for longer than it could possibly take for anyone to read a two-letter word, then said it again, distinctly: "Nang."

Echo was still trying to figure out what had struck her as so odd about what he'd done when he turned off the music.

"I'm dyslexic," he said matter-of-factly. "I have to sound out every single letter, every single time, and it's hard to figure out which letters are which. I can't automatically recognize words, even short ones. By the time I get to the end of a sentence, I can't remember the beginning. I can write, but my spelling and handwriting are terrible, and it's just as hard for me to read what I've written myself as it is for me to read anything else. It's not that bad for most people with dyslexia, but I guess I'm just special. Dr. Semple sure thinks so."

Echo wasn't a book fiend like Charlie, but she couldn't imagine not being able to read so much as a single sentence. "How do you DJ if you can't read song titles?"

"Icons. Numbers— don't ask me why I can read numbers but not words, maybe Dr. Semple will figure it out. If I'd gotten this iPod more recently, I'd have the song lists memorized. My laptop at home has voice software, like blind people use."

Echo looked at his iPod again. The Gloc-9 list had 114 songs on it. "You memorize lists of a hundred songs each?"

"No, that's just because I haven't had time to sort everything. If I was performing, it'd be broken down into smaller chunks. It's easier to memorize five lists of twenty songs than one list of a hundred."

Echo was used to memorizing important information. She could hardly take her dossiers with her on missions. But the thought of having to memorize *everything* was staggering. Flight itineraries. Entire city layouts, if you couldn't read street signs...

"Sorry I tried to pull the wool over your eyes," DJ went on. "I don't actually mind if you know. It's just that a lot of people have given me a hard time over it, so faking it got to be a habit."

"What sort of hard time?"

"Calling me stupid." He shrugged, but his look of unconcern wasn't especially convincing.

Anger flared hot and red within her. "Anyone who'd think you're stupid is a fucking moron."

"Thanks. I think so too, actually." His fingers, which had been tracing their way over the walls, hit one of the holes where she'd extracted a bug. "Hey, how did you know where the bugs were?"

"They're hotter than the walls."

"You can see heat, huh?" DJ's bright smile flashed. "That narrows it down. Not many animals can do that. Snakes can. And some bugs can, I think. I mean the insect type. Please tell me you're not a bedbug-shifter."

Echo knew she couldn't play the game much longer, but she couldn't resist letting it go for one more round. "We're not sharing a bed, so what do you care? Are you prejudiced against an entire species?"

"'Fraid so," DJ admitted, hanging his head. "It's terrible, I know. But I'd sleep better if you could reassure me that you're something I'd be more comfortable sharing a bedroom with. Like a pit viper."

Echo opened her mouth to tease him with the possibility, then closed it. She might as well tell him. If she didn't, Mr. Dowling would. And though she didn't know why, she wanted it to be her.

She sat down at the bench press. "I'm not a shifter."

DJ leaned against the bar, catching her serious mood. "You're not? What are you, then?"

"I was genetically engineered to achieve the untapped maximum potential of the human body."

"That sounds like a press release," DJ said, looking both intrigued and amused. "Are you quoting someone?"

"Dr. Semple," she admitted. "It's true, though. More or less. I'm stronger. I'm faster. More agile. I can endure extremes of heat and cold and pain. I can see into the infrared. I can consciously control a lot of physical functions that normal humans can't, like my heart rate. And I heal fast. Not as fast as a shifter, but almost."

"Wow." DJ looked impressed. "You really are perfect. Except for not being able to turn into a tree. That's a real disadvantage, you know."

Echo wanted to smile, but she couldn't. Not after *you really are perfect.* "I was created here. We're clones. Me and Charlie and…"

When she couldn't finish, DJ asked, "And Althea and Brava and Della?"

Echo nodded. Her eyes and the inside of her nose prickled, threatening tears. It wasn't so much the reminder of her sisters and their fate, as that DJ had remembered their names. She didn't know why that moved her so much, but it did.

After a brief silence, DJ said, "I know this has got to fall into the category of 'I don't want to talk about it,' so I'm not asking for details or anything, but I'm really hoping to survive this whole thing. If there's some specific way they got killed on the job that I might be able to avoid if I knew about it advance, can you tell me what it is?"

While DJ spoke, Echo managed to pull herself together. To her relief, her voice was cool and steady as she spoke. "They weren't killed on the job. Genetic engineering is tricky. My sisters all had major health problems, and that's why they died."

And if Mr. Dowling wanted DJ to know the details, he could tell DJ himself.

"I'm sorry." DJ abandoned the bench press bar, which he'd been spinning around with one hand, and sat down beside her. "So you all grew up in the lab, huh?"

"On the base," Echo corrected. "It's more than just a lab. There was a set of clone boys, too. Alan, Brian, David, and Ethan."

"Four boys, but five girls?"

"No… There must have been five boys originally. There should be a C. But I don't remember him." Echo frowned, wishing she could at least recall his name, but nothing came to mind. "He must have died as an infant. The boys had worse problems than my sisters. I didn't know them too well because they spent most of their time in the hospital. The last one died when we were about ten."

Even before Althea, she thought, but didn't say. DJ looked so sympathetic already that it was making her uncomfortable.

"My brother Nutmeg— Dominic— " DJ broke off. "Do you know

about scent names?"

Relieved by the change of topic, Echo said, "Sure. The made wolves here have them."

"Can you smell people's scents?"

"I can, but I have to be close to them. I can't do it from across the room. And I have to focus on it. I don't do it automatically."

DJ looked startled, then pleased. "Can you scent me?"

Echo closed her eyes, concentrated on her scent receptors, and took a deep breath. She smelled salt and hot ash, burning wood and a richness like oil or butter. His scent was wild yet homey, hard-edged yet sensual. It made her think of a fire burning brightly under a starry sky.

"Well?" DJ asked hopefully. "What do I smell like to you?"

Echo opened her eyes, and saw that she'd leaned in close without realizing it. She practically had her nose in his hair. She jerked back. "Like someone built a campfire on a salt flat and they're frying eggs. What's your scent name, Sunny Side Up?"

DJ looked so disappointed that Echo smacked him across the shoulder with the back of her hand to jar him out of it.

"I'm teasing," she informed him. "You don't smell like eggs. Let me try again. Salt Fire … Bonfire?"

DJ laughed. "That's nice. Much more dignified than my real scent name. It's Lechon: suckling pig. So you see, you weren't that far off. Has anyone ever told you what you smell like?"

All the sisters could scent people, so Echo knew. But she said, "Sugar and spice and everything nice."

"It's nice, all right. But it's not sugar and spice. Your scent name would be New Leaves or Cut Grass. Or maybe..."

"I don't want a scent name," Echo said hastily, since DJ looked all too pleased at the prospect of naming her. "I'm not a wolf, so I don't have to get stuck with something like Air Freshener or Nutmeg."

He snapped his fingers. "Nutmeg! I meant to tell you about him. He's my older brother, and he was born with a heart defect. He didn't get out of the hospital until he was four months old. He can't play sports or do anything too strenuous, and every now and then, he lands back in the hospital. Last time was two years ago. I'd like to think he's fine now, but he's probably just overdue."

DJ looked away from her, idly lifting and lowering the bench press bar in one hand like a normal person might exercise their wrists with a ten-pound barbell. He didn't seem to expect a response. But she was certain that he'd told her the absolute truth.

Maybe that was why he was so oddly easy to talk to. They had more in common than physical strength and that someone they cared for was held hostage to ensure their cooperation. He too had grown up worrying about a sibling.

"The genetic engineering went wrong for all my sisters," Echo said. "Charlie too. They were supposed to have immune systems that could fight off anything, and they ended up with immune systems that attacked their own bodies. They were supposed to be able to consciously control their heart rate, and they ended up with hearts that stopped beating if they weren't consciously making them beat."

"That sounds terrifying. How does Charlie manage?"

"She has a pacemaker. And she wakes up if she stops breathing while she's asleep. Most of the time, she does breathe automatically. But sometimes her heart or lungs or stomach or something switches over to only working if she makes it work, and then she has to stay on life support until it goes back to automatic again. It's usually only for a couple of days. But she couldn't survive outside of the base. The doctors here have had her entire life to learn how to keep her going. No normal hospital could manage it."

"Oh." DJ set down the bar and rested his forehead on his hands, as if the exercise had worn him out. "No wonder you didn't go for 'Let's run off together and rescue your sister.' I thought she was locked up somewhere, like Roy."

"No. She could run if she wanted, but she'd be throwing her life away."

"I'm sorry," DJ said again. His dark gaze met her squarely. "What a fucked-up situation we're in, huh? Your sister can't leave the lab, and you can't leave without her. I don't know where my buddy is, and I can't leave without him."

"At least he *could* survive outside, if you did find him." Echo didn't wish anything bad on DJ or his buddy, but her own bitterness was like ash in her mouth.

"Yeah..." DJ sounded doubtful. He got up from the bench and began to pace. "They nabbed us when our helicopter was shot down. He got half the metal in the helo buried in his chest. He couldn't speak. He was coughing up blood. It was..."

He trailed off, for once seeming at a loss for words, and shook his head. "I had to save him. But I don't know if I did, really."

"Did something go wrong when he changed?"

"I don't know." DJ paced faster, agitated, tapping his fingers along the wall, the weights, anything within reach. "I didn't notice anything. But it could be too early to tell."

He stopped suddenly, facing her. His words came in jagged bursts. "I don't know what I've done to him. I don't know what they're doing to him. They showed me a video of him. He'd just come out of surgery. They took away his pain meds to get me to agree to work for them. So I did."

The bitter taste in her mouth got stronger. "They did that to Charlie once. I told them I'd kill them all if they ever did it again, and to hell with the consequences."

DJ's lips quirked in a sardonic smile. "We've got a lot in common. I told them the same thing."

He dropped down beside her, leaning in as if he was going to whisper in her ear. His breath slid over her cheek like a summer breeze. But he didn't speak.

On impulse, she focused until she could catch his scent of salt and flame. It made her head spin as if she was lying outside, watching the stars until she felt as if she was falling into the sky. She tried to pull her focus away from it, but she couldn't. The only way she could stop breathing in his scent was to turn off her sense of smell entirely. Frustrated and unnerved, she did so.

The room abruptly seemed cold and sterile, shorn of the scents of metal and chlorine and all the other barely-noticeable odors that she'd experienced without registering them.

Echo felt adrift. Automatically, she focused on her other senses, trying to ground herself. This steady rush of air through the vents. The tap-tap-tap of DJ's feet drumming against the floor. The darkness of his eyes, one shade lighter than black. The ripped muscles of his arms that didn't even begin to show his actual strength. He wasn't touching her, but she could feel the heat of his skin. She could *see* the heat of his skin when she looked into the infra-red, glowing like a burning coal.

She pulled away until she couldn't feel his breath or the closeness of his body beside her. "They can't hear us. You saw me get rid of their bugs. If you have something to say, just say it."

He gave her a wry smile. "Well, see, that's the problem. I can ask, but I don't know if I can trust your answer. For all I know, those bugs were dummies and the real ones are still there."

"*I* don't know that you haven't been planted here to fuck with me," Echo retorted. "If you're right, the real bugs are probably there to spy on *me*."

"I'm not a spy," DJ said earnestly. "I swear it."

Echo gave a dismissive wave of her hand. "You don't need to be a spy to lure me into talking as if I think no one's listening. You could do that without meaning to. But if you care, I think you're exactly what you say you are. You were about half an hour away from dying when I found you in the canyon."

His eyes widened in surprise. "I was? I knew I was sick, but I didn't realize it was that bad."

"I'm not a doctor. But it was 117 degrees out, you were burning up, your heart was going a mile a minute, and—"

You were calling for your mother.

Echo couldn't say it. Not, she realized, because it would embarrass him. Now that she'd gotten more of a sense of him, she didn't think it would. He adored his family and didn't care who knew it. But remembering him lying on the sand, a grown man momentarily a boy again, made emotion well up in her like blood from a wound.

Compassion and protectiveness. The desire to comfort him and make him feel better. Jealousy that he had a mother and she loved him. He'd sounded so utterly trusting that if he called to her, she would come. Resentment and anger and bitterness. Why had he gotten a mother and a family and the ability to trust, when Echo never had and never could?

Echo tried to think of something else. Anything else. Preferably something that had nothing to do with feelings, families, or DJ. Butterscotch brownies. Dominating billionaires. DJ's brother with the ridiculous scent name and the heart defect, whom he obviously loved so much.

Goddammit.

DJ waited expectantly. When she didn't continue, he said with total sincerity, "I absolutely believe that you saved my life. Thank you. I owe you one. Actually, I owe you two. If it wasn't for you, I would have had a miserable time when I woke up here. I felt awful, and wolves don't like to be alone when they're sick. Wolves don't like to be alone in general, to be honest."

Echo felt more awkward than if he'd called her a liar. "It's fine. You don't have to be grateful."

He shifted on the seat, and she couldn't tell if he too felt awkward or if it was just his general fidgetiness. "Let me start over. I know you don't want a partner and you don't want me for a roommate, so I'll try not to annoy you too much, but I just wanted to tell you that I'm glad I'm not locked up alone. Or with some asshole."

Echo couldn't resist the straight line. "Maybe I'm an asshole-shifter."

DJ laughed, and Echo felt the tension between them break. "Nope, I don't buy it. But I hope Mr. Dowling and Dr. Semple are, because that would mean sometimes you can catch them in their non-asshole form."

"I wish. They're always like that."

"Maybe they shifted once and got stuck that way," DJ suggested. "My grandma warned me that could happen."

"Maybe they shifted once and decided they liked being an asshole better than they liked being human," Echo put in.

DJ snapped his fingers, still smiling. "Okay. I've made up my mind. Let's both lay our cards on the table."

"What do you mean?"

The smile vanished, and the intensity of his gaze pinned her in place as if she'd been hit by a stunner. "I mean that I'll tell you exactly what my intentions are, and you can tell me what yours are, and then we go from there. All right?"

Echo opened her mouth to refuse, but DJ was already talking. "I intend to cooperate exactly as long as it takes for me to find out where Roy is and figure out how to break him out without getting him hurt.

The instant I have that, I'm gone. If you figure out a way for Charlie to survive outside, we should all go together. Otherwise, let's make it look like you tried to stop me and failed. I won't kill you to escape. When we're on a mission, I'll back you up like you're a sister Marine. But I'm not staying here forever."

Echo jumped up from the bench, her paralysis broken. "You're crazy. I can't believe you told me all that. How do you know I won't run straight to Mr. Dowling and report everything you just said?"

DJ shrugged. "I'm sure he's figured out that I'm planning to make a break for it eventually."

"Yes, but— But—" Echo's fists clenched. She couldn't even explain to herself why she felt so outraged. Probably because he was being so *stupid*. Stupid and reckless: traits that got people killed.

"You sound like you *trust* me," she burst out, putting her finger on the problem. "I'm the enemy!"

"Yeah. I did notice that. But I trust you anyway." His smile was ironic but sincere. "I mean, I trust that whatever you tell me about your intentions will be true. You might tell me I can go fuck myself and if I try to escape, you'll feel honor-bound to kill me."

"I won't feel honor-bound, you idiot. I don't believe in honor. I might kill you if that's what it takes to save Charlie. But that's the only reason." Echo's jaw snapped shut as she registered what she'd just said.

"I'm good with that," DJ said cheerfully. "So, assuming Charlie can be protected, will you let me escape?"

Echo felt boxed into a corner. "I didn't say that."

"I know. But will you?"

As she thought about it, DJ picked up a 40-lb barbell and tossed it from hand to hand as if it weighed nothing. He didn't seem to be doing it to make any particular point, but only to have something to occupy his hands.

Another wave of bitterness broke over her. All that strength, contained in a man completely willing to put at her disposal, and it was useless to her. She'd been trapped before he'd come, and she'd still be trapped after he was gone. Why should she help him when he couldn't help her? What right did he have to be so infuriatingly confident that she'd risk herself and even her sister for his sake, when they barely knew each other?

I broke him and I couldn't fix him, Echo remembered him saying, his voice weighted with guilt. *I'm such a fuck-up.*

She bet he wouldn't look so self-assured if she were to quote that back at him. But she recalled the bleakness in his gaze, and she didn't want to see it again. Let him keep his guilty secrets. Ferreting them out would do nothing but get her even more entangled with him than she already was.

If she agreed to let him go when the time came, then he and his teasing and his fidgeting and his distracting scent and his funny scratchy voice and his body heat and his blithe self-confidence and his ability to stir up feelings she didn't want to feel would all be out of her life.

"Deal," Echo said.

DJ beamed at her. "Thanks, Echo. I knew I could count on you."

Before she could explain that she was only agreeing to get rid of him, he'd set down the barbell and grabbed her hand. His grip was strong and warm, his palm dry. Her sense of smell had returned when she hadn't been paying attention; she caught a whiff of fire and oil, smoke and salt, before she hastily shut it off again and disengaged her hand.

"Do you have any idea where the other bases are?" DJ asked.

"No. I think you'd have to get into the computer system to figure that out."

"Or I could get my fangs into Mr. Dowling's throat."

Echo liked that idea, but she couldn't let DJ get himself killed for nothing. "He'd say anything to get off the hook. He's probably got fake records in the system for exactly that sort of situation."

DJ got up and started pacing again. "Yeah, you're probably right. And I can't have someone else finding him dead and sending a message to kill Roy. Well, I'll keep thinking about it. Now you ask me for something."

"I don't want anything from you," Echo replied.

The expression flashed so quickly across his face that she wasn't sure she'd correctly identified it. It had looked like sadness, but that made no sense. She'd turned down the opportunity to put him under an obligation. He should be relieved.

She dismissed it from her mind. DJ was obviously like Charlie, constantly *feeling* random things. It was impossible to keep track of all those fleeting, pointless emotions.

"If you ever do, just let me know." He held her gaze, unblinking and still. She again had the unsettling sense of being pinned in place. "Whatever it is, I'll help you. I swear it on my honor. You may not believe in honor, but I do."

SEVEN

DJ

Meet and Greet

"Honor." Echo repeated it like it was a dirty word. "I said I'll let you go when the time comes, and I will. You don't need to swear any vows to me."

DJ could tell that she'd meant it. Once again, he'd proved that sheer persistence could create miracles. He ought to be overjoyed. But he felt a strange sense of let-down. He could get out but Echo couldn't, and that made his triumph seem stale and flat.

When he'd sensed her resistance wearing down, he'd been certain that she'd not only let him escape, but would go with him. The thought had lifted his spirits. It wasn't that he'd imagined she'd *stay* with him. He just liked the idea of her running free under some wide-open sky almost as blue as her eyes. It made sense that she wasn't a shifter, once she'd explained it to him. There was nothing in the world, no cat or shark or flying thing, that could move more gracefully than her own human form.

"Come on," she said, standing up. "Let's get some lunch."

DJ jumped up. "That sounds great. I'm starved."

As they headed for the door, she said, "Once we leave, don't say anything you don't want Mr. Dowling to hear; the entire place is bugged.

The cafeteria included."

"Does it have coffee?"

To his surprise, she smiled at him. It didn't make her look any softer, but she looked less like she might try to kill him at any second, and more like she was standing ready to kill anyone who might attack him. Maybe he was only projecting what he wanted to see. But he couldn't help being comforted by even the possibility that someone in this hellhole had his back.

"It's got a coffee *bar*," Echo promised, heading down a featureless corridor. "Espresso machine, flavored syrups, the works. You like the fancy girly drinks with fifteen non-fat ingredients, right?"

"No way. I drink my coffee like a man. Like a man with a serious caffeine addiction. Espresso, when I can get it. How about you? Drip black, right?"

Echo shook her head. "Caffeine doesn't affect me, so I only drink coffee for the flavor."

"Don't tell me you like the fancy girly drinks."

Amazingly, she was still smiling. "I like the fancy girly drinks. Iced frappuccino, Vienna coffee…"

"What's that?"

"Two shots of espresso, then fill the mug with whipped cream."

"You have a sweet tooth." DJ's own teeth ached as he imagined sucking down a cup of whipped cream. "You should meet my sister Five."

"There's five of you, too?"

"Just three. It's her scent name," he explained. "Chanel Number 5. She also goes by Danielle. Anyway, she's obsessed with desserts. Especially pastries. Once she mailed a box of macarons to Afghanistan. They arrived in about the condition you'd expect."

"A box of crumbs?"

"A box of stale, multicolored dust."

"I bet you poured it into your mouth." Echo opened an unmarked door and led DJ into yet another anonymous passageway.

"I didn't, but some of the guys did. You would have, right?"

"If I didn't have anything better, I'd probably do that with sugar packets."

"My buddy Alec used to eat sugar like that. But I couldn't tease him about it, because I used to chew instant coffee crystals. There *wasn't* anything better, and Marines are adaptable. You'd make a good Marine." Though he knew better, he couldn't help adding, "If you ever get out of here, you should think about enlisting."

Echo ignored that. She also ignored the pair of security guards she passed by. DJ nodded a greeting at them. They didn't nod back. Belatedly, it occurred to him that they might have been some of the same ones he'd shot with tranquilizer darts.

She turned left at an unmarked T-intersection of corridors. None of the doors were marked, either. DJ memorized the layout as they walked. He'd had lots of practice doing that, since written signs weren't much good to him. But he usually had more visual cues to assist him, like different colors of paint or graphic symbols.

A maze of twisty passages, all alike, DJ thought. *If I wander around long enough, I'll probably be eaten by a grue.*

She stopped at a door and opened her eyes wide. The scanner flashed, and the door slid open.

DJ started to step forward, then stuck in the doorway. Echo grabbed his arm and hauled him inside. He heard the door slide shut behind him, but his attention was on the woman who sat curled up in an armchair. Echo had told him that Charlie was her clone, but it was one thing to know it and another to see it.

His first thought was, *They're exactly alike.*

The cloud-white hair, the flawless skin, the ice-blue eyes, the elegant features, and the slim figure: the women were more identical than twins. It was as if Echo was in two places at once. DJ was dying to become a wolf and find out if their scents were identical, too, but he managed to restrain himself.

His second thought was, *They're not alike at all.*

While Echo's hair was snipped carelessly short and rumpled as if she'd just come in from a workout, Charlie's hair was long and loose, falling down to her lap like a shawl. While Echo had the spare yet strong build of a gymnast, Charlie was simply thin. And while Echo was in her apparently inevitable jeans-and-a-tank-top (currently rust-red jeans and a black top), Charlie wore a gauzy dress swirled blue and white, like a summer sky.

To complete the impression of *not alike at all,* Charlie proceeded to do something that Echo wouldn't have done in a million years: she checked him out like she was on the prowl at a dance club and had no intention of going home alone. Then she glanced away with a shrug, just like the dance club women did when they decided he wasn't to their taste.

He was unsurprised that he didn't pass muster. In that, the sisters were exactly alike. Whatever they were into, it wasn't him. If he was less thick-skinned, he might have been stung by the look of horror Echo had shot at her handler when he'd accidentally made it sound like he was trying to set them up.

Not that it mattered. DJ had more important things to care about than whether his genetically engineered assassin roommate wanted to jump his bones. He didn't have time to do any bone-jumping anyway. Not to mention how complicated that would get, given that he meant to escape and she couldn't leave.

It was just as well she wasn't into him. He wasn't into her, either, which made it all even more utterly and completely irrelevant. She wasn't at all the physical type he preferred. Or the personality type, really. Though she was his talking type, if there was such a thing. And maybe his musical type. What were the odds that a woman who didn't even recognize Tagalog would like Gloc-9?

"DJ, Charlie," Echo said loudly.

He jumped, realizing that she'd repeated herself. He'd gotten so caught up in his own thoughts that her first words hadn't quite registered.

"Pleased to meet you." DJ hastily shook Charlie's offered hand. Her bones felt brittle, her skin thin as an old woman's. He kept his grip loose to make sure he didn't hurt her.

Echo spoke to her sister as if DJ wasn't even there. "Mr. Dowling laid it out for you, huh?"

"Yeah." Charlie glared up at a small hole in the ceiling, where something had been dug out with a knife. "Fucking asshole! I hope he gets hemorrhoids. And leprosy."

Echo glanced around the apartment. "I don't see any new bugs.

Sorry. If you want him to know what diseases you hope he'll get, you'll have to tell him in person."

"I hope he gets Ebola too," Charlie muttered.

"Dengue fever is a good one," DJ suggested. "They have it in Afghanistan. It causes excruciating joint pain."

For the first time, Charlie looked at him approvingly. "I'll add it to the list."

"Let's get lunch," Echo said.

Charlie set the book she'd been holding down on the table. The cover showed a woman with lots of cleavage plastering herself to a man riding a motorcycle along a mountain road. He wore leather pants, an unzipped leather jacket, no shirt, and no helmet. She wore a crop top, a miniskirt, and no helmet. DJ imagined the title: *Our Worst Road Rash Ever.* Or maybe *Future Organ Donors in Love.*

Charlie grabbed a cane that leaned against the chair and hauled herself up, and they walked out. She told him what everything was as they passed through more anonymous corridors and unmarked doors: housing, pass and ID office, bathroom, gym, pool, disbursing and finance, human resources, and more housing. It was weirdly similar to Camp Pendleton, though much smaller. And, of course, evil.

"So people work here?" DJ asked at last. "They're not all prisoners?"

Echo made a hand gesture like she was threatening to stab him. Then he realized that it referred to her using a knife to extract a bug from the wall. Probably.

"No, most of them are just employees." Charlie spoke as if he'd asked a perfectly reasonable question. "It's like any top-secret agency. They have to sign documents swearing that they'll never tell anyone anything, not even who they work for. The pay is good. And they know that if they did spill the beans, well…" She looked meaningfully at Echo.

Echo pretended not to hear the entire exchange. DJ wondered if she ever had been sent after some disgruntled or greedy or disillusioned employee. He couldn't imagine her voluntarily killing a whistle-blower, but if she was told that she had to do it or they'd take it out on Charlie…

"Mission Cafeteria accomplished!" Charlie announced, and threw open the door.

It was like a Marine commissary, only smaller. And with superior food. Not to mention the coffee bar.

"Hi, Jamie," Charlie said to the barista. "How's it going?"

"Not bad." He fixed her a mug of pink lemonade without her having to ask.

DJ put in his own order, unable to resist adding, "How do you get to be a secret agent *barista*?"

Echo kicked DJ's ankle, but Jamie only smiled. "I answered an ad, and I'm not an agent. I just work here."

"And if you tell anyone where you work...?"

This time DJ got an elbow in the ribs.

"She'll kill me," Jamie said, jerking his head at Echo. "So I say I'm a barista at a company that makes parts for air conditioners. The pay is good, the benefits are great, and every now and then I get to see someone turn into a wolf. It's the coolest job I've ever had. By far."

DJ took his espresso and started sucking it down as he waited in line for his food. As always, the caffeine hit made him more relaxed, not more jittery. Maybe that was related to the way that being startled by the recorded gunshot had made his heart beat slower rather than faster. He never felt as calm as he did when he was in combat, not even when he was a wolf or half-asleep. Just another way he wasn't wired quite like everybody else.

As he stacked three steaks on his plate, he decided not to mention his peculiar relationship with caffeine to Dr. Semple. Let her lose her chance at a Nobel because he withheld vital information. DJ didn't intend to deliberately fuck with her experiments, in case she caught him and took it out on Roy, but he wasn't going to volunteer anything, either.

No one spoke to Echo other than to ask her what dressing she wanted on her salad, but Charlie seemed to be buddies with everyone. When they went into the cafeteria, Echo started to head for an empty table in the corner, but Charlie pointed to an occupied one, where two men and three women sat eating.

DJ had already noticed it. A black wolf crouched at the feet of the older man, eating raw meat from a bowl on the floor.

"DJ, you should meet the pack," Charlie said.

He let her lead him over, uneasily aware of Echo's silent presence beside him... and of the black wolf. A tame wolf— an animal? No werewolf would eat off the floor like a dog, except maybe as a joke. But no one was laughing.

The black wolf jerked up his head, blood dripping from his muzzle. DJ felt a touch on the pack sense.

He was so startled that he nearly dropped his tray. For a split second of joy, followed by a split second of fear, he thought a member of his family was at the base. Then he reached out, and found a presence he didn't recognize.

It was eerie. Bonded packs could only communicate with each other. Unbonded werewolves could reach out to anyone, but their touch was uncertain and weak. This presence was strong and wild, wordless and feral. It was what DJ would imagine a true wolf— an animal— would feel like, except that true wolves couldn't talk to werewolves. Nobody knew if true wolves had some version of the pack sense with each other, though DJ had always figured they probably did.

The wolf pushed harder at the pack sense, in a distinctly aggressive gesture. DJ's mental shields went up so fast that the wolf's head jerked up, his lips curling away from his gleaming fangs. DJ braced himself, ready to shift or fight, but the wolf's head lowered and his tail went between his legs.

An animal with the pack sense— another genetic engineering experiment?

DJ looked into the yellow eyes of the wolf, and felt a creeping disquiet that was halfway to fear.

Echo clapped him on the shoulder. This time he did jump. She grabbed his tray before anything could spill. "You're too quiet. It's making me nervous. Say something."

"You're weird," DJ said promptly. "Normally people tell me to *stop* talking." He addressed the table. "Hi, I'm DJ Torres. My scent name is Lechon, my power is strength, and I'm a kidnapped US Marine."

Echo's elbow smacked into the exact place on his ribs she'd hit last time.

"Ow. Pick a different target next time, that one's getting sore."

"That's the idea," Echo said.

"Echo!" Charlie snapped. "Stop hitting him."

DJ opened his mouth to say that he didn't really mind. Marines roughhoused like that all the time. So did wolves, nipping at and tussling with each other. It made him feel at home.

"It's not fair," Charlie went on before he could say so. "He can't hit back."

"Sure he can," Echo said, shrugging.

DJ's elbow instantly found its mark on her ribs. Charlie stared at them, her mouth half-open with what looked like genuine alarm.

"It's *fine,* Charlie." Echo spoke with an edge in her voice. "He's not hurting me. Don't be such a mother hen."

"That wasn't what I—" Charlie broke off, shaking her head. Then she turned to the table. Since DJ and Echo had failed at introductions, Charlie took over, "DJ is Echo's new partner. He's a born wolf. DJ, this is the pack."

DJ stuck out his hand to the closest person, a blonde woman in a business suit and, oddly, white gloves.

She leaped backward, knocking her chair over. "Don't touch me!"

At the same time, Echo grabbed DJ's shoulder and yanked him away. "Don't touch her!"

DJ looked from one woman to the other, Echo hovering over him protectively— that was nice, she *did* have his back— and the gloved woman with her eyes wide with horror.

Made wolf. Gloves. Right.

"Your power's fucked, huh?" DJ asked. "What is it, a death touch?"

The blonde woman righted her chair, took a deep breath, and answered calmly. "In a way. Anyone who touches my skin has a severe allergic reaction. Like a peanut allergy. It could kill you. We all carry EpiPens, in case someone brushes up against me accidentally."

"That's too bad. I guess you spend lots of time as a wolf." As soon as he said it, he hoped he hadn't put his foot in his mouth, in case she was one of the rare people whose powers carried over to their wolf form.

To his relief, she nodded. "Yeah. But don't feel too bad for me. I was dying anyway. I got the flu and accidentally overdosed on Tylenol. It destroyed my liver. I ended up in the hospital with three days to live. Two days in, Mr. Dowling and Emmett showed up. Oh, and I'm Amber

Killeen, formerly with Homeland Security. Pleased to meet you." In lieu of a handshake, she bobbed her head.

When she didn't go on, DJ prompted her. "And your scent name is…?"

"Oh," she said, seeming surprised. "It's Sangria."

The white man with graying hair stood up. "I'm Emmett Anderson. My scent name is Oak, and my power is to attract prey animals."

DJ shook his hand. "That would've been great for your pack in the old days. You'd never have to worry about feeding the pups."

Emmett yanked his hand back like DJ had told him his power sucked and he was a fucking loser, then sat down with no further explanation.

What did I say? DJ tried to telepathically beam at Echo, but she was busy giving Emmett a lethal glare.

Weird. And Amber hadn't even known to tell him her scent name. Maybe the entire pack was made and had never had anyone to teach them wolf traditions beyond the existence of scent names.

DJ wondered if Roy remembered his own scent name.

The Indian woman bounced up. "Pushpanjali Malakar, former FBI. I go by Push. My scent name is Campfire, and my punch can shatter concrete."

"That's badass," DJ said admiringly.

"I know!" Push grinned at him.

The woman with the black eye patch and scarred face didn't stand; she had braces on both legs and a pair of crutches leaning on her chair. But she held out a strong-boned hand. "I'm Guadalupe Cordero. Mechanic. I'm a *veteran*—"

"Marine," DJ said with her. He'd guessed from her bearing and her regulation knot of braids that she had some kind of military background, and he'd known which one as soon as she hadn't said "former." "Military police?"

She nodded. "I got blown up by an IED while I was on vehicle patrol. They had to shoot me full of stimulants just to get me conscious enough to understand what I was being offered. The healing didn't work 100%, but I probably wouldn't have made it at all, otherwise."

Echo poked DJ, right in her favorite spot on his ribcage. "How'd you know what her job was?"

"Women can't be infantry, so that's where female Marines go if they want to see combat."

"Or in helicopters," Guadalupe said. "But I wanted to be on the ground. As for my power, it's easier to show than tell."

She pointed to the ripe plum on Amber's plate. "See that?"

"Sure." DJ eagerly waited for it to explode or spontaneously combust or even disappear.

Guadalupe stared hard at it, but nothing happened. Then she opened her hand to reveal a small lump of yellow stuff oozing liquid on to her palm.

At first DJ couldn't figure out what it was. Then he realized. "Is that...?"

"Yup." Guadalupe dropped the lump to her plate, picked up the plum, and sliced it in half with a paring knife. Juice poured out from the hole that had opened up near the pit.

DJ caught himself pressing his fist to his chest like he'd been hit by shrapnel and was trying to hold back the blood. He removed his hand and let it fall to his side, fingers open. He was an automatic rifleman. Guadalupe's power was no different from what he did with an M-16. It just *seemed* more gruesome.

"What's your range with that?" DJ asked, trying to sound matter-of-fact.

"I have pinpoint accuracy within fifty meters, and I can hit a general area at ninety," Guadalupe replied calmly.

A general area, DJ thought, unable to help wondering if she meant that she couldn't target a specific person or that she couldn't target a specific body part. *Right into her hand.*

Guadalupe returned the plum to Amber. DJ was unsurprised to see Amber turn it over with the hole side down, then drop a napkin over it.

The last person at the table, a tall black man with a shaved head, seemed unperturbed. He extended a lanky arm and gave DJ a pleasant smile and a firm handshake. "I'm Ty Roberts. I guess it doesn't matter now if I say I was CIA. My story's a lot like Guadalupe's, except I was wounded by a terrorist car bomb. My power is clairvoyance— I can see things going on miles away and behind closed doors. But it gives me such bad migraines that I can't use it for long. And this'll sound weird, but my scent name's Sidewalk."

"Actually, that's one of the less weird things I've heard recently." DJ turned to address the whole table. "Shall we shift?" When everyone looked blank, he added, "To catch each other's scents, so our scent names make sense?"

Emmett looked startled, then guilty. To the others, he said, "It's a wolf tradition. Let's do it."

The others got up and shifted, leaving DJ standing alone. Though he was the one who'd made the suggestion, it was hard to get used to the idea of shifting in public, under the eyes of one-bodies. He tried to focus on the pack, but the black wolf kept drawing his attention.

DJ wished he'd inquired about the strange wolf, rather than waiting for someone to explain. He could ask Echo or Charlie now, but it felt wrong to talk to a one-body about a wolf— even an animal, if he was an animal— right in front of the wolf.

He made sure his mental shields were raised to full strength, then shifted.

Green.

Lechon hadn't shifted to scent Echo, but her scent was the one that captured his attention. He inhaled deeply, taking it in to experience it with all his senses. Soft emerald moss lining a forest floor. Shining dewdrops on fresh-cut grass. Tiny new leaves unfurling at dawn.

Now that he knew what to focus on, he could tell that it was a human scent. But the usual markers— sweat and musk and flesh— were a little different, a little more... Lechon sniffed again... A little more delicate, maybe.

Charlie's scent was also delicate, but it wasn't the same as Echo's. If Echo's was green, Charlie's was orange-brown. Thick layers of fallen leaves on damp earth.

Lechon pulled himself away from the sisters to scent the pack. They were sniffing at him too, though the strange black wolf hung back.

Since Lechon couldn't touch Sangria as a human, he made sure to butt his head against her side and give her a nice long nuzzle in greeting.

Her tawny wolf smelled tangy, bittersweet. Dry red wine and nearly-ripe raspberries, with a touch of citrus.

The scent of Campfire's sleek gray wolf reminded DJ of how people described his own: burning wood, charcoal, and ash. And something fresh, like country air.

Oak's heavyset brown wolf smelled of old wood, Sidewalk's smallish gray wolf of sun-warmed concrete. Lechon touched noses with Mechanic's black-tipped gray wolf, and inhaled her scent of hot metal, old leather, and engine oil.

Then he found himself face to face with the black wolf. Lechon took a sniff, catching the sulfur-and-smoke odor of a struck match. The black wolf stiffened, and Lechon felt another powerful shove at the pack sense.

Lechon bristled. How dare that wolf try to exert dominance during a peaceful pack introduction! He lowered his shields, meaning to give the wolf a shaming slap of disapproval.

Raw emotion roared through the pack sense. Grief tore at him, ripping his heart open with the knowledge that a precious thing was gone forever. There was a hole inside him that could never again be filled. He'd lost everything that made his life matter, and he'd never get it back.

Then, following the grief, a tide of rage, hot as blood. If he couldn't have what he wanted, what he needed, he'd kill the people who'd taken it from him. He'd kill everyone who had what he'd lost. He'd—

Someone grabbed him, sending him tumbling backward. He whipped around, teeth bared, ready to rip out his attacker's throat.

Cut grass. New leaves.

Echo.

Lechon forced his shields back up. The punishing emotional onslaught vanished, leaving him disoriented. He shifted. DJ knelt behind an overturned table, with Echo's arms clasped tight around his chest.

All hell had broken loose. People were yelling. Wolves were snarling. Chairs and tables were flying. Some people had fled the cafeteria already, others were bolting, and still yet others were trapped in corners or hiding under tables. Lights flashed. Sirens screamed.

Calm washed over DJ like cooling water. He was the still point around which everything else moved. Unhurried and unafraid, he examined the scene.

Ty had returned to his human form and was throwing chairs and tables, his pleasant face contorted in irrational rage. Push was punching the walls, screaming a shrill, wordless battle cry. Each blow smashed a hole in the concrete and sent cracks radiating outward like a spider web. The black wolf was tearing around the cafeteria, howling and snapping at anyone within reach.

Emmett and Amber were pursuing the black wolf, Emmett in human form and Amber as a wolf. Guadalupe was on the floor, stealthily wriggling her way toward Push. Two security guards were firing tranquilizer guns. A dart bounced off the table shielding DJ and Echo.

"What the fuck is going on?" DJ asked.

"Ty and Push and Match went berserk," Echo said tersely.

A stray dart hit Emmett. He stopped short, plucked it out, then collapsed.

"Great. There goes any chance of the alpha shutting this down. Fucking moron." Echo grabbed DJ's shoulder, her blue eyes intent on the scene. "You take Match— the black wolf. It won't matter if he bites you, right?"

"He's a—" DJ started to ask, then caught himself. Obviously he was a werewolf. "No."

One of the flying tables hit a guard. She went down and stayed down, her dart gun skittering across the floor.

"Try not to hurt him," Echo said.

She plunged into the fray, making a beeline for the fallen guard's tranquilizer gun. Darts were still flying.

"Cease fire!" DJ yelled at the top of his lungs, wishing Echo had given him more notice that she was going out. "Cease fire!"

He grabbed a fallen chair to use as a shield and bolted out. To his relief, the second guard had indeed ceased shooting, so DJ didn't have to worry about friendly fire.

Push knelt and slammed her fist into the floor. A shockwave sent a crack shooting outward to the guard who was still standing. He staggered, off-balance, as the floor shattered beneath his feet. The black wolf leaped at him and took him down.

DJ tackled Match, yanking him off before his fangs could close over the guard's throat. The wolf snarled and struggled in his arms, but DJ was easily able to control him.

If he'd wanted to kill the wolf, DJ could have broken his neck. But he wasn't sure how to incapacitate a wolf without harming him, other than hanging on to him. DJ hung on and looked up to see how Echo was doing.

She'd gotten the tranquilizer gun and was firing at Ty, who was still hurling chairs. Push was down with a dart in her arm. DJ couldn't do anything while he was occupied with an armful of raging, snapping wolf.

DJ turned to the security guard. "Tranquilize the wolf I'm holding!"

The guard sat up, then stared down at his right wrist. "He bit me."

Oh, shit, DJ thought.

The guard was a young man with black hair in a buzz cut. He could have been a Marine. The bite wound was minor. It was even odds whether he'd be dead by the end of the day.

"Pick up your gun and fire!" DJ ordered. "Now!"

The guard snatched up his gun. A dart hit Match's side. A few moments later, he went limp in DJ's arms.

DJ put the wolf down and looked up. Ty was sprawled on the floor. Echo seemed unhurt. She took a quick glance at DJ, then ran out the door. Amber became a woman and went to join Guadalupe.

The peace and clarity of combat faded, leaving nothing behind but a bone-deep weariness.

DJ sat down beside the guard and took the gun out of his hands. "What's your name?"

"Justin. Justin Graham."

"I'm DJ Torres. Thanks for shooting the wolf. That was a big help."

Justin lifted his bleeding wrist, turning it back and forth as if he hoped that getting the right angle would make the wound disappear. "I was too off-balance to get the shot. I should've clubbed him with the gun. I don't know why I didn't think of it."

"He was on top of you before you got a chance."

"I should've dropped the gun and gotten him in a headlock, like you did."

"Forget what you maybe should have done. Seriously. I'm shaking it out of your head, okay?" DJ caught him by the shoulders and gave him a gentle shake. "Do you know what's going to happen?"

"We all know. You become a wolf, or you die. Fifty-fifty chance if you're not already dying. They tell us in case we want to volunteer."

DJ had to unclench his jaw to speak again. Shoving down his fury, he said, "You have to feel inside yourself, find the part of you that's the wolf, and be the wolf. Once you become a wolf the first time, the change is complete. After that, it's easy to switch between bodies. But doing it for the first time will be the hardest thing you ever do. You'll have to give it your all."

Justin took a deep breath. "I can do that."

"My best friend was wounded in Afghanistan," DJ said. "I bit him to save his life, and then I talked him through the change. He made it. You will too."

Justin looked up, over DJ's shoulder. Echo had come up so quietly that DJ hadn't heard her.

"I saw Match bite you, and I called it in to the hospital," she said to Justin. "The medics are on their way."

"Where's Charlie?" DJ asked. "She's okay, right?"

Echo nodded. "I carried her out before I tackled you."

"Um…" DJ wasn't entirely sure he wanted to know, but he had to ask. "What was I doing? I didn't hurt anyone, did I?"

Unexpectedly, Justin was the one to reply. "You just sat there and howled. Don't worry about it."

"Oh. Good." DJ still couldn't figure out how he'd even perceived the fucked up made wolves' pack sense, let alone been overwhelmed by it. Maybe it was the power of mass craziness.

A team of medics ran up and had Justin lie down on a gurney. He caught at DJ's arm. "Can you come with me?"

DJ remembered Roy sprawled on the sand. Roy clutching DJ's hand, his expression as urgent as if he had something he desperately needed to say. Blood spilling out of his mouth every time he tried to talk.

I can't do this again, DJ thought. *I can't.*

Justin had put on the mask you wore when you were scared to death and determined not to show it. He reminded DJ more than ever of a Marine. A new one, a recruit in boot camp or a fucking new guy on the first day of his first deployment.

If the fucking new guy was lucky, someone more experienced would take him under his wing, like Roy had done for DJ. DJ's fucking new guy days were six years gone. He could take on Justin, and teach him what he needed to survive.

"Of course I'll stay with you," DJ said. "I'm a Marine. We never leave anyone behind."

"I'm just a security guard," Justin said, but his desperate grip relaxed.

"You and I fought together," DJ said. "Close enough."

DJ and Echo walked beside the gurney as the medics rolled it out. Justin told DJ he could sense the wolf inside him, which DJ took as a good sign.

Mr. Dowling intercepted them in the corridor. "Echo, come with me. I want your report." He glanced at DJ. "Or if you prefer, you could stay with him and report later."

Echo froze, then said, "I can stay if you want."

DJ wasn't sure if she was speaking to Justin or him. Justin made a 'take off' gesture, and Echo's shoulders sagged with relief. Then she turned to DJ, her eyebrows rising in inquiry.

Much as DJ wanted to say, "Please don't leave me alone with this," he too waved her on. Justin was the one whose life was in danger, and he didn't want her. Not to mention that Echo clearly didn't want to stay. But as DJ watched her walking away with Mr. Dowling, he felt abandoned. Left behind.

In the hospital, DJ was pushed aside as a medical team, overseen by Dr. Semple, stuck Justin full of needles and attached him to a bunch of machines. Justin was tense but calm as he answered the medics' questions about how he felt. But he kept his gaze fixed on DJ like Justin was drowning in the ocean and DJ was the rescue helo.

DJ had heard how excruciating it was to have your body pulled apart and rebuilt, fiber by fiber from the inside out. But Roy was the only person he'd ever watched go through the change, and though DJ had seen his muscles seizing up, Roy had been hurt so badly already that he had barely seemed to notice.

First Justin simply reported that he was getting muscle cramps. Then his body locked into a spasm so intense that his back lifted off the bed, arching like a bridge.

DJ pushed his way to Justin's side and caught his desperately grasping hand. "Find your wolf, Justin! The pain will stop as soon as you change."

Justin's hand clenched over his. "I can feel it, I just can't *do* it."

"Yes, you can!"

DJ searched his memory for what had helped Roy. It had all happened so fast. One minute he'd been coaching him like he was coaching Justin, and the next minute Roy was passing out. Dying. Frantic, not knowing what else to do, DJ had hit him in the face. And then a gigantic white wolf lay panting on the sand, his fur soaked through with blood.

"You've had one success, Torres," said Dr. Semple.

DJ jumped. The woman was hovering over them like a vulture.

"Do whatever you did for Farrell," she went on. "This is all being recorded. If you succeed, whatever you do will become our new protocol."

Justin's muscles relaxed. With a shuddering sigh, he lay still and exhausted, his eyes half-closed.

"You're doing fine, Justin," DJ said. "Just rest for a minute. I'll be right back."

DJ beckoned Dr. Semple out of earshot. "You've got six wolves here. What do you think I know that you don't?"

"Most of our subjects were already dying. Our success rate has been very low. Of the subjects who survived, Cordero was only partially healed, Roberts' power has serious drawbacks, and Killeen can't control hers. And then there's O'Donnell."

"Who the fuck is O'Donnell?"

She looked at him like he was an idiot. "The black wolf. Special Agent Richard O'Donnell. He was never able to change back to human form. Over a period of several weeks, he lost his memories and his ability to comprehend most human speech. Now he's nothing more than an unusually intelligent wolf who doesn't remember that he was ever human."

"Jesus Christ." DJ felt sick.

"Anderson is a born wolf," Dr. Semple went on, as coolly as if she hadn't just topped Grandma Steel's horror story about the made wolf who'd burned himself to death. "Malakar was our only complete success. On the one hand, she was a healthy volunteer. On the other hand, she was the only one of four healthy volunteers to survive. So you know as much as we do, Torres."

"This is the most fucked-up thing I've ever *heard of*."

"I seriously doubt that, even if you slept through your high school history classes." The doctor pursed her thin lips. "As I said, most of them were dying. They were grateful for the opportunity."

DJ forced himself not to punch her. "Can you give Justin something for the pain?"

"No. Mild painkillers don't help, and stronger ones seem to interfere with the subject's ability to change. None of the subjects who were administered morphine or nerve blocks survived."

Justin screamed, then managed to choke it off. "DJ!"

DJ bolted back and grabbed his hand. "I'm here. Just hold on. I won't leave you again."

When he looked up, Dr. Semple was giving him a ghastly wink. "Work your magic."

DJ talked until his throat was raw, and kept on talking. He said everything he remembered saying to Roy, and then he said it again. On the theory that Justin would fight harder if he remembered what he was fighting for, DJ quizzed him about his family, his hobbies, his ambitions, his favorite music. He told him what it felt like to be a wolf. He asked him if he'd ever thought about joining the Marines.

He told Justin that he was strong and tough and easily could have been a Marine if he'd wanted, that he was exactly the kind of guy DJ would want watching his back, and that he was going to make a fucking badass wolf. He held Justin's hand and wiped the sweat out of his eyes. He hit Justin across the face, in case that had been what had done the trick for Roy.

It didn't do the trick for Justin.

"Sorry," DJ said. "I thought a shock might do it. That's why I didn't warn you."

"Do whatever you have to do," Justin said.

DJ went back to just talking. And Justin lay there gritting his teeth, still a man, so pale that he looked like Roy when he'd been bleeding to death.

"I'm giving it everything I've got, I swear," Justin whispered. "What am I doing wrong?"

DJ wished he knew. "Nothing. You're doing everything right. Just keep trying."

"I can do that." Justin's eyes closed, and all the machines sounded their alarms.

As the medics sprang forward, DJ slapped him as hard as he could without breaking his jaw. His cheek was slack and cool. DJ's hand left a crimson imprint in his skin. Desperate, DJ hit him again, driving his lips into his teeth.

The medics pushed him aside. DJ sat on a bed and watched, numb, as they did CPR. The blood from where DJ had hit Justin got smeared all over his ashen face.

Finally, Dr. Semple held up her hand. "Time of death: 6:49 PM."

All DJ could think was that he'd had nearly seven hours to save Justin, who competed in triathlons, didn't like most hip hop but loved Eminem and Kanye West, had a date scheduled with a lab tech named Catalina, and had decided not to join the military because his father still had nightmares from Desert Storm. DJ had probably only had fifteen minutes with Roy. In seven hours, he ought to have been able to do more.

After they took Justin's body away, Dr. Semple seemed to notice DJ. With a greedy light in her eyes, she asked him, "How do you feel?"

"Fucking fabulous." DJ's head ached. His bones ached. He felt like he'd been in combat all day. "Guess you won't be using my methods for the new protocol."

"I might. Some other factor was more likely to have been the cause of the subject's death."

White-hot rage seared away his weariness. "His name was Justin,

116

you fucking Nazi!"

He was on his feet, his fists clenched, a heartbeat away from knocking the doctor across the room. She jerked up her stunner. Behind her, two guards covered DJ with their tranquilizer guns.

"Remember what happens to Farrell if you lay hands on me," she said calmly. "Thank you for your assistance, Torres. You may go now."

DJ sank back down. "I want to see how Roy's doing. Our deal was that you show me video of him every day."

"You saw some this morning."

"That was your sicko torture video. That doesn't count. You agreed to show me footage of him being treated well, every day. I haven't seen that yet."

DJ was ready to bust up the place if she didn't agree. If he could just see that Roy was still alive, he'd know that he hadn't fucked up *everything*.

To his relief, Dr. Semple didn't argue. "I'll see what I can do."

EIGHT

Echo

Days

Echo stayed in Mr. Dowling's office as he reconstructed the entire disaster, bringing in all the witnesses and getting periodic reports from the hospital. The ones who'd been most centrally involved, like Echo and the members of the pack who weren't still tranquilized, stayed while others went in and out.

At the end of Charlie's brief account, she asked how Justin and Ning were doing.

"Who's Ning?" Echo asked.

"The other security guard," Mr. Dowling said. To Charlie, he said, "Liu has a concussion. Graham's in critical condition."

"Oh." Charlie's eyes welled up with tears.

"Are you friends with him?" Echo asked.

"No." Charlie limped out. Her hip always hurt more when she got stressed.

"Take a muscle relaxant," Echo called after her.

Charlie was followed by a parade of random employees who'd been eating lunch at the time. Every now and then Mr. Dowling asked Echo a question to clarify or corroborate something they'd said.

Whenever her mind strayed, she pictured DJ's strong brown hand in Justin's white-knuckled grip, the split second of horrified refusal that had crossed DJ's face when Justin had asked him to stay, or the even briefer flash of pleading in his eyes before he'd told her to go. And then she started imagining what was happening in the hospital.

Echo forced herself to pay strict attention to the interviews and to the reconstruction of events that Mr. Dowling had an agent draw on a whiteboard.

Finally Echo and Mr. Dowling were left alone. As much to himself as to her, he said, "So, to sum up: O'Donnell felt threatened by Torres for some kind of wolf dominance reason and got upset, Anderson failed to slap him down, it got into the pack sense, Anderson prioritized shielding the most lethal members of the pack, and Malakar and Roberts and O'Donnell went berserk. Torres was briefly affected, but was able to bring himself out of it. You and Torres successfully worked together to contain the situation, but despite your efforts, we had six minor injuries and one casualty."

"Casualty?"

"Dr. Semple just emailed me. Graham died a few minutes ago."

So that was that. A sharp pain pierced her chest, as if she'd cracked a rib. Echo checked her watch. Justin had been bitten nearly seven hours ago. DJ must have stood by him all this time.

She took several deep breaths, and the pain faded. "I don't know why you keep the pack. They're more trouble than they're worth."

Mr. Dowling addressed her as seriously as if she was a colleague rather than an asset. "You think I should terminate them?"

"No!" Echo didn't have fond feelings for the pack, but neither did she want to see them all killed. "I meant you could cut them loose."

"And have them running around with no hold on them whatsoever, knowing what they know? I don't think so." Mr. Dowling rubbed his forehead wearily. "Take off, Echo. You're done."

Echo walked through the corridors on auto-pilot, only realizing what she was doing when she found herself inside her apartment. Her old apartment. Charlie's apartment.

Charlie was curled up on the sofa, crying. Echo sat and held her until Charlie said, "Michelle emailed me some of the details."

"Who's Michelle?"

"Michelle Green. The medic. She said Justin fought right up to the end. The way she described it, the whole thing sounded so much like—"

Echo stood up. "I'll call… um…" She fished for the name. "Kevin! I'll call Kevin for you."

"I can call him." Charlie sniffled. "Where are you going?"

"To work out."

To Echo's relief, Charlie didn't question that. Echo did intend to work out, but by the time she reached her new apartment, every limb felt like dead weight. She stumbled to one of the beds, lay down on top of the blanket, and stared up at the ceiling, trying to think of nothing.

Echo wasn't sure how long she'd been there when the front door hissed open. DJ stopped in the doorway of the bedroom.

"Echo. Hey." He came closer, till he was standing over the bed. "Are you all right?"

"No." As soon as she said it, she wished she'd lied.

"Were you and Justin friends?"

She shook her head tiredly. "I didn't even know his name before today."

"Combat stress?"

"That wasn't combat."

"Then what?"

She turned her head to focus on him. He looked weighted down, his usual energy spent. Even the light in his eyes had dimmed. "I'm fine. But you look beat. Go to bed."

"Ah…" DJ sat down on the edge of her bed. He was so close that all she'd have to do to touch him was roll over. "Mind if we talk for a while first?"

The last thing Echo wanted was to hear all about how Justin had died. But after DJ seemed to have poured everything he had into trying to save him, the least Echo could do was let him talk. "Go ahead."

DJ kicked off his shoes, scooted up to the head of the bed, and leaned against the headboard. "What's your favorite movie?"

That was more like it. She was definitely up for a distraction. "*Little Women.*"

He blinked down at her. "Seriously?"

"No. That's Charlie's favorite."

"Well, what's yours?"

"What's *yours*?"

"It's—" DJ broke off, the hint of a smile hovering at his lips. "I'll guess yours if you guess mine. If you guess wrong, you have to give a hint."

"*Full Metal Jacket*," Echo said immediately. "You identify with Private Gomer Pyle."

"Stop flattering me, I'll get conceited," DJ said, but the smile became a real one. "And no. Though it did make me feel better about my time in boot camp— it sucked, but at least no one committed suicide. Give me a hint about yours."

"It's science fiction."

"*Terminator 2*. You identify with Sarah Connor." He indicated her arm muscles. "You've got the guns."

Echo was secretly pleased, but said, "I could knock her out with one hand. My hint."

"My favorite isn't a war movie."

She tried to think about other genres he might like, but her mind kept being tugged toward Justin's death, like iron drawn to a magnet. Maybe if she put her thoughts into words and released them into the air, they'd be out of her head and gone.

She sat up beside DJ. Even as far as she could get from him, she could feel his body heat across the narrow bed. "I told you my sisters died because their genetic engineering went wrong."

DJ didn't seem thrown by the change of subject. "Yeah."

"Some of them had worse problems than others. Althea died when we were kids. Della lived into her teens. Brava was twenty-two. We—" Echo couldn't bring herself to tell DJ the details. "We really thought she was going to make it."

DJ put his hand on her shoulder. "I'm sorry."

Echo stopped herself from leaning into him. She could feel every one of his fingers. Where they touched was the only warm part of her body. "She got worse and worse. It was obvious that she was dying. The made wolf pack wasn't here then, but they did have this one born wolf they'd captured—"

"Son of a bitch." DJ's hand slid off her shoulder. He pressed his knuckles into his forehead and rubbed it like he had a headache. "I know where this is going."

"Yeah." Echo was relieved that she didn't have to explain everything. "Brava figured, what did she have to lose?"

DJ flinched. "Were you with her?"

"We both were. Charlie and me. And a medical team. And Valerie, the wolf." Echo bit her lip. The 'getting it out of her head' idea wasn't working at all. Instead, the entire thing was more vivid than ever. "She screamed— Brava never screamed. Valerie kept telling her not to give up. So Brava didn't. For nine hours. And then she died."

"That was pretty much exactly how it went with Justin." DJ lowered his gaze to his hands. He was shredding the top of the thick quilt into a fringe, like an ordinary person might shred a piece of paper. "You know, that's the part of combat you usually miss. I mean, I've seen people die. Of course. But you don't normally stay with them for hours, thinking you're going to save them, and *then* see them die. Normally you see it from a distance, or it's over in seconds, or you're with them for maybe a couple minutes and then they get medevaced out. Someone else stays with them, somewhere else…"

He sat quiet and still. Not even his fingers moved. Finally, he said, "I think I'm done."

"Done with what?"

"Watching people die." He looked up at her, an ironic twist in his mouth. "Perfect timing, huh? Right when I get drafted to be a hit man. I guess I'll think of it as my last deployment. What happened to Valerie?"

"They wouldn't let her contact her pack. They said they'd kill someone in it if she did, so she didn't try. She refused to bite anyone else after Brava, so she had no one. They sent her on missions, but with a partner to monitor her. She got more and more careless, and finally one of her targets got the drop on her. And that was it."

DJ sighed. "Great. And that was when they decided to make their own wolves?"

"Not exactly. They decided to try again with a small pack of kidnapped born wolves, so they wouldn't snap like Valerie did. Emmett Anderson, his wife Julia, and Taylor, their seventeen-year-old daughter. Taylor was the one they really wanted— she could possess people. Take

Prisoner

over their bodies. Just for a couple minutes at a time, but you can do a lot in a couple minutes. They were going to train her, and keep Emmett and Julia as hostages to make her cooperate."

DJ went back to shredding the quilt. "This is going to have a depressing ending too, isn't it? What happened? Did she commit suicide?"

"No, they all tried to escape. Back then the guards had regular guns as a back-up to their tranquilizer guns. Someone shot the guard Taylor was possessing. It turned out that if you kill the person she possesses, it kills her too. Julia got hit with six tranquilizer darts and overdosed. Two months later, Emmett caved and agreed to bite whoever they gave him, so he could have a pack again."

DJ's fist slammed into the headboard, jarring Echo and making her jump. "This is *fucked.* Someone needs to take this entire fucking place down."

"I wish," Echo sighed.

He whipped around to face her. "You know, there's good hospitals out there. Maybe better than what they have here. My family's got money. They could get Charlie the absolute best medical care that—"

"*No.*" Echo heard the ice in her own voice. "DJ, don't even ask. Charlie's happy here. She's got books and movies, she's got friends, she's got guys to date, and she's got a medical team that'll drop everything to take care of her. She could have years left to live. If she leaves, she'll have months. If that."

"What if just you left?" DJ spoke as quietly as if he thought the place was still bugged. His breath blew a strand of hair against her cheek.

Echo too spoke softly. "Then she'll have days."

DJ slumped back against the headboard. "Okay. Forget it. Sorry. That's the last time I'll ask. I didn't mean to pester you about that again, I swear."

Echo felt as exhausted as he looked. "Well, I didn't mean to depress you *more.* So I'm sorry too. I was hoping if I told you, I'd feel better. Fucking feelings."

"Fucking feelings," DJ agreed.

They sat in silence for a while. DJ seemed to get bored with shredding the blanket, and started peeling flakes of paint off the wall.

123

"If you're going to sit here and destroy my sleeping space, at least be entertaining," Echo said at last. "Talk to me. I mean, about something else."

"I can talk about anything," DJ said easily. "Pick a topic. Or I can just go off and you can smack me if I start boring you."

"I've been wondering about your buddy Roy." Echo barely stopped herself from saying, *The one who got you into this mess.* It was hardly Roy's fault that he'd nearly died in a helicopter crash. "How did you guys meet? Were you in boot camp together? Was it love at first sight?"

DJ chuckled. "No, and no. But in a way, that story does start at boot camp…"

NINE

DJ

DJ's Story: An Infinite Number of Monkeys

My family didn't want me to join the Marines. Not because they were pacifists or anything like that, but because I'd be so far from the pack for so long, surrounded by one-bodies on the other side of the world. Wolves are supposed to live with wolves, and packs are supposed to stick together. Also they thought I was impulsive and reckless and I'd get myself killed.

Once they realized that "it's dangerous" and "you'll be far, far away from your tiny, cozy, familiar world" were exactly what appealed to me about it, they started telling me I'd never make it through boot camp and even trying would be bad for me. They said washing out would make me feel humiliated and crushed and like I was a failure, and instead I should go for something I knew I could succeed at. We fought and fought over it for literally years.

Later they admitted that they were sure I *would* succeed, and that was why they didn't want me to try. But at the time, I didn't pick up on that and I just thought they had no confidence in me.

It's funny how the pack sense works. I always knew what they were feeling. They loved me and they were scared to death for me and they wanted me to stay with the pack. But the pack sense doesn't give you the subtleties— it tells you the what, but not the why.

I finally gave up on convincing them, and I just went and enlisted. So there I was, twenty years old and in boot camp for the first time.

Yes. There was more than one time.

You're probably thinking, "But DJ, your power is super strength, you should've breezed through boot camp."

Or maybe you're thinking, "DJ and his big fucking mouth, I'm not at all surprised he had problems at boot camp, he must have talked back to the drill instructor."

It wasn't either of those, actually. Remember, I wanted to be there. I was planning to do exactly as I was told and keep my mouth shut except to say, "Yes, sir!"

Mostly, I did. I had some trouble keeping still and not fidgeting and not letting my eyes wander. I *can* do that. It's just that it takes all my concentration, so there isn't any left for other stuff. Like hearing that I just got an order. So I had some problems with that.

But on the flip side, even when I'm holding back and only using my natural strength, I'm pretty strong. I had no trouble with the physical side of things. Some guys were bigger than me but some were smaller, so I didn't stick out that way. There were a couple other Pinoy— you know, Filipino— guys there, so I wasn't the only one. At first I thought I'd fit right in.

I was maybe a little too eager. Any time the drill instructor, Sergeant Hahn, asked for a volunteer, I volunteered. I got stuck with a shit-ton of shit jobs, and one day he said, "Torres, you remind me of a terrier I used to have, a little Scottie dog. All I had to do was blink in his direction, and he'd rocket to the door and sit there wagging his tail, waiting to go for a walk. I think I'll call you Scottie."

And for the rest of boot camp— my first go at boot camp— everyone called me Scottie. I pretended it annoyed me, but actually it made me feel like I belonged.

The problem with boot camp is that it isn't just physical. The class work was all right. I fell asleep in class a couple times, but I wasn't the only one. The problem was the written tests.

I did know that was coming, so I'd studied in advance with read-aloud software. But it didn't matter if I knew the answers when I couldn't read the questions.

The Marines will let you in if you're dyslexic, but they won't give you any special accommodations. The idea is that you won't have any on the job, so if you can hack it without them, you're fine, and if you can't, they don't want you.

I got through the first tests by reading a few words in each question and taking my best guess about what it was. Sometimes I squeaked through. I'm pretty good at guessing, and some questions had diagrams— like, a drawing of an M-16 with arrows pointing to all the parts. That was easy. I'd misspell the names, but at least the instructors could tell that I knew what they were. Sometimes I failed, and they made me repeat the test. But since it was the same test, I remembered the parts I'd read before, so I could squeak through the second time.

By the time I was near the end of boot camp, I'd gotten over-confident. Combat is what Marines are for— they say, "Every Marine is a rifleman." They don't say, "Every Marine is a reader." I figured they could see how good I was at everything combat-related, and they'd want me for that and let the written work slide.

Then I hit the final written exam. Right before we took it, Sergeant Hahn told me I wasn't getting a second chance to repeat that one. I had one shot, pass or fail.

"Just like you might only get one shot at an enemy," he said.

I panicked, and reading gets even harder for me when I tense up. I floundered my way through that fucking exam, but at the end I knew I'd failed it. No second chances. I felt like I'd missed my one shot and the enemy had nailed me in the fucking heart.

Sure enough, I got called into Sergeant Hahn's office. He handed me a pen and a piece of paper with a sentence written across the top and said, "Last chance, Torres. You have three minutes to write down the answer to this question."

That was when I knew I was done— he wasn't even calling me Scottie. I wasn't one of them any more. In three minutes, I was going to be a civilian again. My pack had been absolutely right. I'd failed, and it was going to crush me.

He took out a stopwatch, clicked it, and said, "Go."

My brain just froze. I stared and stared at the words, and I couldn't concentrate enough to read any of them. Finally, I managed to go letter-by-letter and figure out that one of them said *rifleman.*

Just then, Sergeant Hahn said, "Either you don't know the answer or you're very confident, Torres. You've got one minute left."

There was no way I could read the rest of the sentence in one minute, let alone write the answer. But I figured it had to be asking me to write out the Rifleman's Creed, which is this thing we have to memorize about the importance of taking care of our weapons. So I started scribbling it as fast as I could. *This is my rifle. There are many like it, but this one is mine. My rifle is my best friend.*

That was as far as I'd gotten when the stopwatch clicked. I handed over the paper. Sergeant Hahn eyeballed it like I'd written, *Fuck you and the horse you rode in on.*

"Are you having a joke with me, Torres?" he asked.

I said, "No, sir."

He looked back down at the paper and said, "Then can you tell me why *every single word* is misspelled? Why *is* is misspelled, which I didn't even realize was possible until this moment? And why rifle is misspelled *two different ways?*"

I said, "I'm dyslexic, sir. I disclosed it upon enlistment, sir."

He gave me that drill instructor stare, and said, "I'm aware of that, Torres. You are not the first person with dyslexia to go through boot camp. But among that select crowd, you are something truly unique. Now take your time, read the question, and repeat it back to me when you're done."

I have no idea how long it took me to read it, because by then ninety percent of my brain was taken up with "I've completely fucked this up, it's all over, what do I do now, why was I born this way, it's not fair," and so forth. But finally I did. And then I felt like the world's biggest tool.

I repeated the question back to Sergeant Hahn. "Sir, it says, 'Is every Marine a rifleman, yes or no?'"

That fucking sadist said, "Well?"

I said, "Uh, yes, sir. Yes, every Marine is a rifleman. Sir."

"How much do you want to be a Marine?" he asked.

I said, "It's the *only* thing I want, sir."

Sergeant Hahn leaned back in his chair, put his hands behind his head, and said, "There's a theory that if you give an infinite number of monkeys an infinite number of typewriters and an infinite amount of time, eventually the monkeys will write *Hamlet.* If you repeated boot camp an infinite number of times, do you think you could eventually pass the written exam?'

At that point I felt like it was more likely that I'd write *Hamlet,* but I said, "Yes, sir. I did pass the ASVAB, sir."

That's the test you have to take to even get into boot camp. I got the minimum qualifying score, but I did pass.

"How did you manage that?" he asked.

I thought, *A miracle, sir.*

I said, "I was less nervous, sir."

Next thing I knew, he'd sprung out of the chair and was yelling in my face. "If you're *too nervous* to read *in my office,* how nervous will you be in combat?!"

"I think I'll be *less* nervous, sir," I said.

As soon as I said it, I was sure he'd think I was being sarcastic. I wasn't, though. And I hadn't even flinched when he'd jumped at me.

He said, "I think you might be, too."

I took a second look at him. I still thought he was a sadistic bastard. But I was beginning to get the impression that he hadn't gone to all that trouble just for the pleasure of fucking with me.

"There's a reason we require you to be able to read," he said. "What are you going to do if you're in combat and you need to radio in your position, and you don't know where you are because you can't read the street signs?"

I thought that if I was in combat, the street signs probably wouldn't be in English and I wouldn't be able to read them even if I wasn't dyslexic, but I kept my mouth shut.

He said, "That wasn't a rhetorical question. What do you think you'd do?"

"I'd cover the Marine who's reading them for me," I said. "We're never supposed to be in combat alone, sir."

"If something's never supposed to happen, you can be certain that it will," he said. But I guess my answer was good enough, because he said, "Torres, I'll offer you a second chance to become a Marine. It's conditional on you going through boot camp until you pass the written tests, though."

I was willing to go through boot camp fifty times, if that was what it took.

"Yes, sir! I'll do it, sir!" I said. If I'd had a tail then, I'd have wagged it.

Sergeant Hahn told me, "It's also conditional on promising me that you'll disclose your problems reading to everyone you have to work with. In advance, not when you're under fire."

I was fine with repeating boot camp, but that pulled me up short. I understood why he wanted me to do that. But if I did, everyone would think I was an idiot and a pain in the ass and wonder how I'd even gotten into the Marines.

He nodded like he was reading my mind, and said, "Every unit has the guy everyone thinks got in by mistake. That's going to make you that guy. They might change their minds later. Or they might not. So you've got to ask yourself, 'Do I want to be popular? Or do I want to be a Marine?'"

I said, "I want to be a Marine, sir."

And then I repeated boot camp. Twice. I failed the written exam the second time, too. But by the third go-round, I was less stressed about it, or someone decided I was needed for the war, or a miracle occurred. I made it out of boot camp, got through combat arms training which thank God had more diagrams and less reading involved, and made it into my unit.

I faithfully explained to everyone that I couldn't read. And sure enough, everyone thought I was an idiot and a pain in the ass and wondered how I'd even gotten into the Marines. Some guys called me stupid, I punched them, I got in trouble, rinse and repeat. There's a limited time that I can keep myself to "yes, sir, no, sir," and I'd long since passed it. I got a reputation as a stupid, mouthy asshole.

I'll cop to the mouthy asshole part. It wasn't a great time for me.

This was all in the US. Then I got transferred, possibly because someone was sick of me, and deployed to Afghanistan with a bunch of guys I didn't know. But they all knew each other already. I was the fucking new guy who was replacing a Marine who'd rolled his car and smashed up his ankle so bad that he'd never be fit for combat again. That guy, needless to say, everyone had liked. So even apart from everything else, I had big shoes to fill.

I couldn't face going up to a whole new set of guys who already didn't want me and saying, "FYI, not only am I not your awesome buddy, but I can't read." I decided that unless I really was in combat and had to read a street sign or something, I wasn't saying a thing.

I got assigned to a fire team as the assistant automatic rifleman. That meant I carried extra ammunition for the automatic rifleman. That was Roy.

Roy was a couple years older than me and much more experienced. He'd fought in Iraq. He'd fought in Afghanistan. He had friends all over the Corps. He had a reputation for being a Marine's Marine, you know? The guy everyone looks up to.

Oh, and he's fucking huge. Like a Viking. An Irish Viking. Black hair, gray eyes, tallest guy in the platoon and built like a tank.

I was intimidated, so I decided to make a show of not being intimidated, which basically made me act like an asshole again. The whole first day, I could see that everything about me was irritating everyone, especially Roy, but I couldn't figure out how to stop.

I decided to at least do something useful, and reached for the SAW. That's the squad automatic weapon, the machine gun I was carrying the ammo for. Roy grabbed it and glared at me like it was a child and I was a molester.

I said, "I'm just going to clean it."

"*I* clean the SAW," he said. And that was that.

The capper was that our base was in the middle of nowhere. The electricity wasn't too reliable and we weren't allowed to have personal electronics because they needed to save the juice for important things. So since there wasn't much else to do on our off-hours, everyone read a lot.

I really wanted to get along with Roy, so I kept trying to talk to him. Usually when he was trying to read. I figured he was only reading because he had nothing better to do. Actually, Roy would way rather sit down with a book than a video game. So the more I tried to befriend him, the more I drove him up the wall.

One night he shoved a book at me and said, "Sit down, shut up, and read this."

It was a fat book I couldn't have read in an infinite number of years. And it had rabbits on the cover. I thought he was hazing me.

I said, "Who sent you this, your ten-year-old sister?"

Roy said, in that extra-patient way people talk when they're really pissed, "It's not a kids' book. The guy who wrote it served in World War II. It has some of the best battle sequences I've ever read. Just read the first chapter. I think you'll like it if you give it a chance."

I could tell he was serious. So I sat there and turned pages until I figured it was safe to say, "It's boring."

Roy just shrugged, but I could tell he was wishing I'd fall into a black hole and never emerge to bother him again.

Meanwhile, we'd been patrolling around, but I hadn't seen any combat yet. I was getting antsy, waiting for the other shoe to drop. You can't know for sure how you'll do till you actually experience it.

Then the shoe dropped. One second our platoon was patrolling in broad daylight, next second we were taking fire. We all took cover and ended up scattered around the street. I was behind a wall with my fire team and two guys from another one. Next thing I know, Marco's telling us we're going to breach the building where the enemies were.

It was like someone hit a switch on my nervous system. A sense of absolute calm washed over me. All my usual jitteriness and restlessness and obsessing over what people thought about me and whether I was good enough went right out the window. Instead of having five million thoughts bouncing around my head, I had one: *We're going to breach the building.* It was like being a wolf in a man's body: wolf instincts, human intelligence. I wasn't afraid at all. Everything was perfectly clear.

It felt fucking amazing.

"You stick by me, Torres," Roy told me. "I've got your six."

"I've got your back, too," I said.

He said, "Thanks," but I could tell he was thinking, "Sure you do, fucking new guy. Fucking new guy who hates my favorite rabbit book."

We breached the building and fought from room to room. It was my first time in combat and it fried my brain. I only remember fragments. A crow flying past a window. My shoulder banging into the wall when I ran through a doorway. Shell casings bouncing on concrete. A man's shoe in the middle of the floor.

After we secured the building, Roy started yelling for Sibrian, the hospital corpsman. I thought he'd been hit but it turned out it was for me. My helmet had gotten ripped off somehow, and there was blood all over my head and running down my face. I remember Roy trying to make me lie down and me arguing with him. Sibrian showed up and told us both to cool it. I was fine— just a few cuts from flying glass. They'd bled a lot but I didn't even need stitches.

Back at the base that night, everyone else collapsed into bed. But instead of getting exhausted, I got wired. It occurred to me that if I'd moved my head even a quarter of an inch, the glass could have hit my eyes or my throat. And once I thought that, I started thinking about all the other things that could have gone differently. I could see every way I could have died, and there were thousands of them.

My heart was slamming into my chest. My skin was too tight. Blood was pumping through my veins like water in a fire hose. I felt like I was standing on a conveyor belt, and I had to move fast or the ground would get yanked out from under my feet.

Roy grabbed me by the arm and took me outside. I paced around, talking a mile a minute, and he just walked with me. I don't think he said a single word for over an hour, while I went on and on about fractions of an inch and the rotational speed of the earth and alternate timelines where I was dead. I must have sounded like a lunatic.

Eventually I ran out of energy. It happened so suddenly that I had to sit down on the ground. Roy sat beside me.

I was shaking. It had just hit me that not only could I have died, but I'd killed someone. I don't mean that I'd fired my rifle and later I'd seen bodies. I remembered shooting a man who'd appeared around a corner with an AK-47. Sure, he was the enemy and that was what I was there to do and if I hadn't shot him, he'd have shot me. But still. I shot a man, and I watched him fall down and die.

When I'd joined the Marines, I hadn't just been going toward something, I'd been going away. I love my pack but they drive me crazy too, and there's a lot about wolf culture that's suffocating and rigid and small-town and not me.

But right then, all I could think was how much I wanted to be a wolf and feel the pack sense and have one of my pack groom me till I felt better. And there I was, about a million miles from my pack, stuck in the middle of the desert with a bunch of one-bodies who couldn't stand me. I felt more alone than I had in my entire life.

Roy put his hand on my shoulder. If we'd been wolves, he'd have shoved his whole body up against mine and licked my fur. But it meant the same thing. He was telling me I wasn't alone.

I said, "I'm really fucked up. I don't know what's wrong with me."

"Nothing's wrong with you," Roy said. "This is combat stress. They taught you about it in boot camp, didn't they? You've got kind of a weird version of it, but otherwise, this is normal. You'll be fine tomorrow." He took another look at me, then he said, "Or maybe the day after tomorrow."

I laughed, and he said, "Or maybe in an hour. Hard to say."

"Why don't you have it?" I asked.

"This wasn't my first time," he said. "Once you get more experienced, it takes more to shake you up. You'll get there. You did fine. You did better than fine."

"I did?" I asked.

"Yeah," he said. "You did great. At first I wasn't sure I could rely on you, but now I know I can. I'm glad you're on my team."

I could tell that he meant it. Then I remembered that fucking rabbit book, and I felt guilty for lying to him. And I was still pretty wired.

I said, "Farrell, there's something I should tell you. About that rabbit book…"

I told him everything— well, everything but that I was a werewolf. I told him all about boot camp and what happened after it and how I'd wanted to turn myself into a brave, honorable, disciplined Marine, and instead I'd turned myself into an obnoxious asshole.

Roy sat there and listened to the whole story. Then he said, "So, should I call you Scottie?"

He wasn't ragging on me. I'd told him it had made me feel like I belonged. But everything had gotten so fucked up after boot camp, I wanted to start from scratch.

I nearly said, "No, call me Lechon." But that was a wolf thing, and I wanted my life to be more than just pack. And also people who knew what it meant and weren't wolves would laugh their asses off.

Then I thought of saying, "No, call me Dale." But that was my civilian name.

I didn't DJ seriously then, just at parties for friends. I used to announce myself as DJ Torres, but it was a joke. No one called me that. But I liked the idea of a new name to go with the new leaf I was hoping I'd turn over.

So I said, "No, call me DJ."

He said, "Okay. Then you call me Roy. What was your drill instructor's name?"

"Sergeant Hahn," I said. "Black, my height, weighs twice what I do. At least."

"I know him," Roy said. "Not that well. But he's a smart guy. I think you should do what he said."

It never even occurred to me that I could refuse. I said, "Here we go again."

"No," Roy said. "It won't be like that. Not after I tell everyone how you saved my life."

By then I was starting to sober up. I said, "Thanks, but don't lie just to make people like me. Fuck them if that's what it takes."

Roy started laughing. He said, "Did you think I meant I'd make something up? Don't you remember?"

"Remember what?" I asked.

"One of the enemy got the drop on me. You shoved me out of the way and shot him."

Once he said it, I remembered the part I'd blanked out before: *why* I'd shot that guy. "Oh. That."

"Yeah. *That*," he said. "Think you can sleep now?"

"Uh-huh." I could barely keep my eyes open.

The last thing I remember was him hauling me to my feet. He must have practically carried me back inside and put me in bed.

I did feel more-or-less back to normal the next day. And the next time everyone got out their books, Roy grabbed me, sat me down next to him, picked up the rabbit book, and started reading out loud.

I was so embarrassed, I thought my face would burst into flames. I jumped up.

Roy looked at me over the book and said, "Sit down, DJ. If I read aloud, I get to read without you pestering me, and you get to hear a great story. Win-win. And since your hands aren't occupied, you can clean the SAW while you listen."

I got the SAW and sat back down. Roy started reading. It took months, but he read me that whole book. When he finished it, he started another one.

He was right that no one hassled me about being dyslexic. First it was because he had my back, but eventually it was because they saw I could do my job anyway. I've never had to read in a combat situation, by the way.

He was right about the combat stress, too. It didn't hit me as hard the second time. The third time, I was just tired and went to sleep along with everybody else.

Eventually the electricity situation improved. We got our iPods and so forth back, and I started playing Roy music. But I never listened to audiobooks when he was around. Every book he read while we were deployed together, he read aloud so I could read it too.

TEN

Echo

The Replacement

If Echo had known how DJ's story was going to end, she never would have asked him to tell it. She had to deploy all her bio-control to stop from crying.

"Hey." DJ tilted his head back, looking her over. Pinpoints of reflected light shone in his dark eyes as he brushed her cheek with a fingertip. His touch was so light and warm that she briefly thought a tear had overflowed after all. "What did I say?"

She relaxed her throat and breathed until her voice could come out steady. "My sisters and I used to read to each other."

"Do you still?"

"No. Charlie and I don't have the same tastes. It used to not matter because Brava and I could tease Charlie about her raven-haired heroes, and she and Della could tease me about how I always picked books where something exploded every few pages, and so forth."

"Now that I know, my next story will have more explosions," DJ said cheerfully. "You can make a mini-bomb out of the heating element in the packaged meals we got. I used to have lots of fun with those."

Echo smiled, letting him distract her. "How did you like the rabbit book? What *was* the rabbit book?"

"It was *Watership Down*, and I liked it a lot. But my favorite parts weren't the battle scenes, they were the ones that described what it was like to be a rabbit. I honestly wonder if the guy who wrote it was a rabbit shifter. It felt so real. Not that I know what it's like to be a rabbit."

"Were there any other shifters in your unit?" Echo asked.

"Not that I ever figured out. For a while I was convinced Roy was secretly a wolf. I tried dropping phrases wolves would know into conversations, but he never picked up on any of it. In a lot of ways he was a better wolf than me, except he couldn't shift."

"What makes a good wolf?" Echo asked.

"Courage. Loyalty. Selflessness. Instinct. Respect for tradition, respect for your elders, respect for your alpha. And above all, pack. Your pack is your life. You live for your pack and you die for your pack. That's Roy. Except he had a platoon instead."

"Do you know how's he doing?"

The energy seemed to drain out of DJ. "Not so great. Dr. Semple showed me some video. It had gone through some encryption process. The light was weird. Flickering. But otherwise, it was clear. A nurse was changing his bandages."

"How did he look?"

"His wounds were healing. But he'd lost a lot of weight. He lay there and stared at the ceiling. The nurse talked to him, but he barely even responded. When she was finished, she left him alone. The look in his eyes— I wanted to reach through the screen and put my hand on his shoulder. He's lost everything he cares about, he's all alone, and he doesn't even know I'm trying to find him."

He sounded desolate. Echo looked at him sharply. Fucking feelings, but she had to ask. "How are *you* doing?"

"I'm not doing so great, either," he confessed. "Justin's dead and Roy's in bad shape and I'm still stuck here. I don't know why I'm not bouncing off the walls from combat stress."

"You didn't kill anyone," Echo suggested.

"I didn't save anyone, either."

"Sure you did. People were trapped in the cafeteria. What do you think Match would have done to them if you hadn't grabbed him?"

His mood seemed to lift a fraction. "Thanks, Echo. That makes me feel better. You must have saved people, too."

DJ put his hand on her shoulder and squeezed, pressing on her tense muscles until they loosened under his fingers. "I'm sorry about Brava. And Althea and Della. I've lost people too, people who were like family. Listen, I have to get some rest— I'm dead on my feet— but if you need me, I'll be right here. If I'm asleep, you can shake me. It doesn't startle me. And I don't mind."

Echo couldn't imagine herself shaking him or anyone awake to say, "I need you." But before she could say so, he'd let go of her shoulder, stumbled to his bed, and dropped on it like he'd been stunned.

He seemed to fall asleep immediately, lying on his stomach with his back exposed, his hands open and relaxed. His face was turned to the side, his lips barely parted, his eyelashes long and black. He was still wearing the white T-shirt he'd fought in, with smooth brown skin showing through the rips where Match had nearly clawed it off his body. There were a few spots of dried blood at his side; his burn scar must have torn open again. Echo could hear his breathing, rhythmic and deep. Peaceful.

It unnerved her to think how easily he could be taken by surprise. He'd even been reckless enough to reveal that he slept so deeply that he wouldn't wake unless he was shaken.

Maybe he was so exhausted that he'd neglected his usual precautions. Or maybe he and Roy had watched over each other for so long that DJ had forgotten that Roy wasn't there to guard him any more. If that was it, Echo hated to leave him unprotected. Maybe she should keep watch for him, like she had when he'd had heat stroke.

She shook her head fiercely, driving out those ridiculous thoughts. His safety was his responsibility, not hers.

Echo turned off the lights, then belatedly looked into the infrared to check for new bugs in the walls. She found none. DJ glowed with warmth a few feet away, his bare skin crimson and his body beneath his clothes a darker red, like blood from a vein.

She lay on her back and controlled her breathing into a pre-sleep rhythm. DJ could let his guard down all he liked, but if anyone tried to break in, Echo would be ready for them. She'd wake in a flash and be on them before they even saw her coming. No one would get past her to where DJ slept so soundly.

The next morning, the first sight to meet Echo's eyes was DJ, asleep atop the covers and curled on his side with his arms held tight to his chest. Huddled, as if he was cold.

She got up, rummaged in a closet, and draped a quilt over him. He shifted in his sleep, pulling it around himself. Echo couldn't help smiling. He looked so cozy. If she lay down beside him, he'd probably reach for her the same way, tugging her close to his body.

She'd touched him enough, and seen enough of him shirtless, to imagine what that would feel like. His muscles would be firm against her body, his skin smooth and warm. If she laid her head against his shoulder, his clipped hair would be soft against her cheek. His restless hands could squeeze the tension out of her back and shoulders, as he had so briefly done the night before.

The scar on his side was new and fragile enough that it might still be painful to a careless touch. She'd have to ask him about it before she put her arms around him, so she'd be sure not to hurt him by accident. That was a bad place to be burned, and its sheer size made it a critical injury. Even with his werewolf healing, he must have come very close to death. It had to be a bad memory.

In that case, she wouldn't ask about it, but would simply avoid touching it. She'd rest her arm above it, and reach around to caress the elegant curve of his shoulder blade, the perfect skin of his back...

She pulled herself up short, cutting off the fantasy. It alarmed her that she'd had it at all. It wasn't so much the sexual aspect as the tenderness. Sex was nothing. It was a physical need, like hunger, though thankfully one that didn't need to be satisfied so often. When she wanted sex, she drove into Las Vegas, went to a bar or casino, selected an attractive man, gave him a false name, had sex in a hotel room, and left as soon as it was done.

The sex itself might be rough or gentle, depending on her mood. But the man was only the delivery mechanism. He didn't matter to her, and she took care to chat just enough beforehand to make sure that he wouldn't try to make himself matter. Having sexual feelings for someone she saw as a person— a man who had told her stories, fought against her and at her side, slept within hand's reach of her, joked with her, confided in her, trusted her— was new and disturbing.

Echo took a quick, cold shower, threw on some clothes, and nearly ran to her— to Charlie's— apartment.

To her relief, Charlie was there, in a fuzzy pink bathrobe and brushing out her hair.

"What do you think of DJ?" Echo demanded.

Charlie's eyebrows flew upward. "*You've* had an interesting night."

"Not like that," Echo said, heat rising to her face. "He told me some war stories."

"War stories, huh?" Charlie snickered.

"Not like that," Echo repeated, annoyed. "Don't be a pain. I want to know what you think of him."

"You've seen much more of him than I have. You tell me."

"I want your take on him. You understand people better than I do."

Charlie's lips pressed together as if she planned to go to her death without speaking. Finally, she said, "I have an opinion, but you're not going to like it."

"It's fine if you hate him," Echo assured her. "I don't care."

Her sister gave a bitter laugh. "It's working already. You didn't say, 'it's fine if you like him.'"

"Charlie, what is with you? It's fine either way."

"He seemed nice," Charlie said grudgingly. "Funny. I'm glad I'm not rooming with him, because all that energy of his would wear me out. But I liked him. And Michelle said he knocked himself out trying to save Justin, so…" She sighed. "I think he's a good guy."

Echo waited for more, but that appeared to be all her sister had to say. "Is that it? What was the big deal, then? Why shouldn't I like it if you think he's nice?"

Charlie put her hand over Echo's. "Why do you think they're throwing you two together?"

"They think I'm careless and reckless, and I need someone to keep me in line."

Charlie's veil of platinum hair rippled as she shook her head. "That's not it. I mean, that's true, but that's not why they're pushing him on you. You really don't see it?"

"No," Echo snapped. "Just tell me. You're making me feel stupid."

Charlie looked abashed. "Sorry. I didn't mean to. Echo, they gave you a nice guy because they want you to like him. They gave you a trustworthy partner because they want you to trust him. They gave you a playful guy because they know you've missed that since Brava died. And it's working. Before all hell broke loose in the cafeteria, I saw the two of you smacking each other in the ribs and grinning like you were on the best date ever."

"They're trying to set us up?" Echo asked, bewildered. "Why?"

"Not like that. Or not necessarily like that." Charlie's hand closed over Echo's. "They want you to get attached to someone other than me. Because otherwise, there'll be no power on Earth that can keep you here after I die."

"Don't talk like that!"

An angry pink line drew itself across Charlie's cheekbones. "Why shouldn't I? Denial doesn't make you live longer. I'm dying, and he's my replacement."

Echo wrenched her hand free and jumped up. Her heart was pounding, and she didn't bother to control it. "Fuck him! Who cares about him? No one can ever replace you. And you're not dying!"

Charlie snatched up her cane and stood, her gaze like blue flame. "What are you going to do when I die, Echo? I know you've thought about it."

"I haven't!"

"You have!" Charlie yelled. "You're going to do as much damage as you can before they kill you, Echo! Right?"

Echo forced her heart rate back to normal levels. "So what if I am?"

"So I don't want you to commit suicide on my behalf! You know what, Mr. Dowling had the right idea. You *should* get attached to someone else, if you can't get it together to live for yourself!" Charlie was trembling with anger, her breathing shallow, her face bright red.

"Your heart," Echo hurriedly reminded her. "Your breathing!"

Charlie sank back down in the chair. The color faded from her face as she controlled her nervous system.

Echo waited till she was sure her sister was out of danger before she spoke. "Thanks for being honest."

Charlie sighed. "I'm already regretting it."

Echo stroked Charlie's fine hair. "You're probably right. I mean about what Mr. Dowling's trying to do. But it won't work. DJ won't be around long enough for me to get attached. Once he finds out where they're holding his buddy, he's making a break for it. I promised I'd let him."

Charlie twisted her head around to stare at Echo, her mouth open wide enough for something to fly in. She was probably worried that Echo was being reckless again.

"We'll make it look like I tried to stop him," Echo assured her.

Charlie's mouth fell even wider open. She never did trust Echo to be cautious.

"I don't care about DJ," Echo said firmly. "I've never cared about anyone but my sisters. You're my last sister, and I'll never care about anyone but you. Believe me, I won't do anything that could rebound on you. And if you want me to keep living, you'll just have to keep on living, too."

Charlie kept on staring, then suddenly laughed. "I'll do my best."

Echo was only somewhat reassured. And she had no intention of falling in with her handlers' plan, like a perfectly conditioned lab rat. Fury simmered beneath her skin when she thought of how close she'd come to doing so, if Charlie hadn't tipped her off. She'd not only had that sexual fantasy about DJ, she'd actually liked him!

She still liked him, much as she now didn't want to. She was certain that he had no idea of her handlers' plot to attach them to each other. Like her, he was a pawn on the board. A rat in a maze.

But now that Echo knew what was going on, she didn't have to follow the path laid out for them. She could see all the possible end points, and she didn't like any of them.

The best-case scenario involving DJ was that she'd be stuck with him for a while, and then he'd leave and she'd never see him again. But it was just as likely that he'd be killed trying to escape. The more attached she was to him in either outcome, the more painful the inevitable end would be. In the worst-case scenario, Echo got so attached that she missed DJ making some ruthless plan to save Roy at any cost, and Charlie got killed in the crossfire.

Echo needed to be cool and detached. DJ ate away at her cool detachment like flames licking at dry wood. The only solution was to avoid him as much as possible.

To Echo's relief, DJ didn't spend much time in the apartment. He was gone most of the time getting intensively trained in assassinating and so forth, and when he wasn't doing that, he was at the lab, getting tested and examined by Dr. Semple.

They were still stuck sleeping in the same room, but there was an easy fix for that. She took to going to bed early, so he always returned to a darkened bedroom where she lay pretending to be asleep, and was gone before he woke.

It was impossible to avoid him entirely, and in the brief times when they ran into each other in the apartment or the corridors or the cafeteria, he gave her an earful, talking as if he intended to cram an entire day's worth of reports into five minutes.

The first week, it was mostly worry about his family and worry about Roy. Then the powers that be let him send a message to his family and get a message back, so the second week consisted of worry about Roy, asking her personal questions that she evaded, quizzing her for info he could use to make his escape, and playing music and trying to discuss it with her.

Echo wanted to discourage the "What sort of music do you like, Echo?" and "Wanna hear classical cellists playing Metallica, Echo?" and "Listen to this, Echo, it's a rock band covering the Korean National Anthem," so she made non-committal noises in response. But some of DJ's music was so annoying that she was forced to either leave or ask him to turn it off. And some of it she couldn't help enjoying, though since she was trying to not to interact, she couldn't say so.

After two weeks of successful avoidance, he came in while she was feigning sleep. But instead of going to his own bed, he turned on the lights and said, "I know you're not asleep. Stop pretending."

Echo sat up, perplexed. "I was breathing exactly as if I was. I even set my heart rate to mimic sleep. How did you know?"

DJ smiled briefly, leaning in the doorway and tapping on it with the fingers of his left hand. "I didn't. Now I do."

She scowled, irritated at him and irritated at herself for falling for his trick. "What do you want?"

"I want you to stop avoiding me." DJ sat on his bed, earnestly facing her. "I get why you're doing it, but we're going to have to interact anyway once they're done training me, and they're pretty close to done."

Echo froze, horrified at the thought that he knew exactly what she was afraid of feeling about him. "Why do you think I'm doing it?"

"You're afraid that if the powers that be think we go together like peanut butter and chocolate, you'll be stuck rooming with me forever. You're hoping that if they see that throwing us together isn't doing anything to make us get along better, they'll let you move back in with Charlie. Right?"

"That's right," Echo said, immensely relieved. "Sorry. It's nothing personal. I've lived with Charlie my entire life."

DJ sighed. "I know. But I don't think your plan is working. And it's driving me crazy. Anyway, the apartment's not bugged. Right?"

Echo glanced around the room again, even though she'd done so when she'd come in earlier that night. "No, it's not."

"Then what about acting like we hate each other in public, and acting however we like in private?"

Echo wanted to object, but she couldn't think of a good reason other than her actual one. "Well— why's it driving you crazy?"

DJ's gaze was straightforward, but his voice held the faintest tinge of hurt. "Because it feels like you really do hate me."

Guilt made Echo's stomach clench. "I don't."

"I know that. But it doesn't feel like it."

Feelings! With no further recourse, Echo said, "Fine. From now on, we just hate each other in public."

DJ's smile turned on like a light. "Great! Want to listen to some music?"

Resigned, Echo said, "Sure." It was better than talking, anyway.

He threw himself on his bed and flipped through his iPod, cheerily telling her that he'd once gotten hooked on a Norwegian death metal band and only belatedly learned that the members were white supremacists.

"Oops," DJ said, laughing. "It was embarrassing, I'd been enjoying the neo-Nazis for weeks before someone tipped me off. At least I hadn't played them in clubs. By the way, if you ever want to hear some incredible stories, look up Norwegian black metal. Murder, suicide, arson, cannibalism, lawsuits over a guy getting hurt when the band flung a decapitated sheep head into the audience, you name it. Anyway, the song I'm going to play is by the group I got into as a substitute. They have a similar sound, but they're not evil."

He paused. "I may have phrased that wrong. They're Satanists. But they're not Nazis."

While Echo was still trying to figure out if the entire story was an elaborate leg-pull, DJ started the song. The shrieking, head-banging, headache-inducing sound made Echo wish she'd kept a bug around. If anyone deserved Norwegian Satanists, it was Mr. Dowling.

She tried to tune it out, but that only made her focus drift to DJ, who had sprawled out on his bed with his hands behind his head, the picture of contentment. What did he have to be so happy about?

Echo leaned over and stopped the song. "Sorry. I hate it."

"I could play something more peppy," he offered, already rifling through his song lists. "How about some J-pop?"

Echo didn't want peppy, she wanted to know why *he* was so peppy. "Is Dr. Semple still hauling you into the lab for experiments?"

"Uh-huh."

"What's she doing?"

"She thinks the funny way I'm wired might make me immune to PTSD." DJ rolled his eyes like it was the stupidest thing he'd ever heard, then shrugged like maybe there was something to it. "Well— It would be nice if she was right. Then it'd be good for something, instead of just being an endless fucking hassle and annoying everyone around me."

"What do you mean, the funny way you're wired? You mean being dyslexic? What difference would that make?"

"It's not just dyslexia." DJ tapped his temple. "It's lots of stuff. I could give you a whole list. But here's the interesting part. Dr. Semple says her tests show that I have trouble learning from experience—"

Echo started laughing. She couldn't help it.

DJ leaned over and thumped her in the ribs. "Shut up. She means on a neurological level."

"Even your *nerves* don't learn from experience," Echo gasped, still laughing. "I believe it."

"Very funny." DJ thumped her again, considerately selecting a different spot. "Anyway, she says that people learn by seeing similarities between different situations. If you touch a flame once, you learn that all fires burn. It doesn't matter whether it's a candle or a campfire, all the flickering orange things hurt if you stick your hand in them. With PTSD, you learn too much. You get blown up by an IED in the desert, and you learn that everything around you at the time is dangerous, down to the song you were humming when the blast went off. So whenever you see sand or hear that song, you feel like you're about to get blown up again and you have a panic attack."

"And she thinks you won't do that?" Echo asked, intrigued.

DJ nodded. "Apparently I have trouble seeing similarities. The same cut-out letter looks completely different to me if she pins it to a different board. So I don't see sand and get reminded of being burned, because the sand anywhere but where the IED actually blew up seems completely different to me. Anyway, that's her theory."

Since DJ seemed undisturbed by the subject, Echo asked the obvious question. "*Were* you burned by an IED?"

"Yeah, that's what the scar's from. Put me in the hospital for a month."

"And it doesn't bother you to remember it?"

"Ah." DJ glanced around. "There's definitely no bugs in here, right?"

Echo double-checked. "No."

"Stuff that's only associated with what happened doesn't bother me. She can show me video of Afghanistan and burn victims and IEDs till the cows come home, and I'm never going to give a shit. I even still like the song I was humming when I was hit. It was Dessa's 'Crew,' I'll play it for you some time. But…" DJ fell silent, his lips trembling and his teeth clenched.

Grief, Echo thought. She'd seen that expression on her sisters' faces, the mirrors of her own, so many times before. *And guilt.* Maybe DJ felt guilty for having lived when someone he cared about had died. Echo knew all about that one, too.

Finally, he said, "When I let myself think about what actually happened, yeah, it bothers me. Just because I don't have PTSD doesn't mean I don't hurt."

That hurt was so raw in his voice and eyes that Echo wished she hadn't asked. He wasn't even trying to conceal it, like it had never occurred to him that his pain could be used against him.

As if he'd read her mind, he said, "Obviously, that's the part I don't want Dr. Semple to know."

He shook himself, like a wolf shaking water out of his fur. It seemed to successfully shake out the feelings, because he continued with seemingly genuine enthusiasm, "But I do think her theories are interesting. When I was in educational therapy, I was too frustrated to care why I was the way I was. But now it's cool to learn what makes me tick. And like I said, it'd be nice to think I'm getting something worthwhile out of the rat's nest up here." DJ again tapped his temple.

"But what are you actually doing in the lab?"

He began rapidly thumbing through his iPod. Norwegian death metal blasted from the mini-speakers, making Echo jump.

"Sorry. Sorry." DJ hastily turned it off. His fingers drummed jerkily against the headboard. "Sorry."

"What's with you?" Echo demanded. "What are you so nervous about?"

"Nothing. Must've drunk too much coffee."

"Coffee doesn't make you jittery. It makes you relaxed."

DJ stopped tapping and peered at her, looking oddly pleased. "You noticed that?"

"We've been stuck together for two weeks. Of course I noticed."

"Most people don't. Not even when we're stuck together for an entire deployment."

"Most people aren't very observant." Echo realized that DJ had deftly shifted the topic. He could evade all he liked, but she'd yet to catch him lying in response to a direct question. "DJ. Answer the question. What exactly is Dr. Semple doing to you?"

"It's not as bad as I expected," DJ assured her. "I was afraid she was going to try to *give* me PTSD. But it hasn't been like that. She hooks me up to machines that measure my heart rate and brain activity and so forth. And then she has me play games and try to read and watch news footage of combat and so forth."

"What else is she doing?" Echo asked suspiciously.

"Having me shift. Measuring my strength and endurance."

"What else?"

"Pain threshold," DJ said, after a moment's pause.

"She's testing your pain threshold, and it's not as bad as you expected? What's she using?"

"Ice water." DJ shrugged, as if to underline "not so bad," then looked away and muttered, "Electric shock."

Echo's belly knotted. "You should complain to Mr. Dowling. Tell him she's endangering your mission fitness."

"I will if she goes too far," DJ promised. "Honestly, I can take it."

"And she'll find out exactly how much you can take," Echo said grimly.

DJ scooted to the edge of his bed, propping his chin in his hands, his face creased with concern. "Did she do that to you?"

"A long time ago. Years."

"Did you complain to Mr. Dowling?"

"No. See, she wasn't doing those tests on Charlie, and I didn't want to give her the excuse of not having enough data on me."

DJ laughed, but it had a bitter edge. "Great minds think alike. I had exactly the same thought about Roy."

"How's he doing?" Echo asked.

"Not so good." DJ let out a ragged breath. "His wounds are healing. But he doesn't sleep unless they sedate him. I can see that he has to force himself to eat. There's books in the room but I've never seen him reading. Mostly he lies in bed and stares at the ceiling. It's like the life's gone out of him. I can't stand seeing him like that. He's my best friend— my brother. I have to get him out of there."

Echo remembered how Emmett had fallen apart after Julia and Taylor died, even more than could be accounted for by grief. And being without a pack was supposed to be much worse for made wolves. "They haven't let him bond?"

"No. They think he might not know that he's a werewolf, and they want to see if that makes a difference."

"*Could* he not know?"

"Maybe. He was really out of it when I bit him. More of his blood was on me than in him." DJ reached out across the gap between the beds and caught her wrist. His gaze was pleading, his fingers warm and tight. "How do I find him, Echo? I've been talking to everyone I meet here— discreetly, you know—"

Her expression must have given her away, because DJ said, "What?"

"You're terrible at discreet. Everybody knows what you want. But even if anyone was willing to put their own neck on the line to help you, none of them know where the other bases are, either."

"Oh." He looked even more discouraged. "Well, obviously, I've gotten nowhere with that. And the video's useless. The encryption makes it flickery and dim, and even when it's clearest, there's nothing in it I can identify. I don't know how to rescue Roy. But I have to."

So much love and determination blazed within him that Echo could almost see it as a light beneath his skin, like she could see his body heat in the infrared. He'd save his friend or burn himself out trying. His scent rose up rich and hot around her. Ash and oil, charcoal and smoke. He was a fire that would burn *her* up if she let him. She needed to get his hand off her, immediately, before she went up in flames.

Echo spoke slowly, distracted by his touch and her losing battle to pull her hand away. "I think you'll have a better chance once they start sending you on missions. You'll report directly to Mr. Dowling, in his office, and if anyone knows where Roy is, he does. And maybe you can do some research once you're outside the base."

"Okay. That makes sense." He squeezed her wrist harder. "Thanks, Echo. You've done so much for me. I wish you'd let me do something for you. Isn't there anything you want from me?"

What she wanted in that exact moment, so intensely that it seemed incredible that he couldn't see the image in her mind, was to take him in her arms and hold him tight. She wanted to feel his whole body against hers, not just the fingers of one hand around her wrist. She wanted him to open his mouth to hers and show her what it felt like to kiss a man she actually cared about.

Equally, she wanted him safe and gone from here. She wanted him to rescue Roy, mostly so DJ could stop agonizing over him, but partly for Roy's own sake, now that Echo knew more about him. DJ had said he was done with watching people die, so maybe he wouldn't return to the war. But even if he did end up back in Afghanistan, at least he'd be living the life he'd chosen for himself. And he'd be out of Dr. Semple's clutches. Echo knew from personal experience that either DJ hadn't told her everything about that, or there was plenty coming up that he hadn't yet encountered.

She wanted to take away his pain. She'd keep it as her own, if that was what it took. Echo didn't have so much happiness to begin with that it would matter if she lost some. But even imprisoned and tortured and frantic with worry, DJ brimmed with warmth and enthusiasm and caring and even joy. When he was experimented on like a lab rat, he took it as an opportunity to discover what made him tick. His ability to find happiness in the absolute worst of circumstances was a gift too rare and precious to be destroyed.

Clearly, Echo wanted a lot of things, not only from DJ but for him. A lot of completely impossible things. All else aside, he'd never shown the slightest bit of romantic interest in her.

And that was just as well.

Fine, she told herself. *Squashing and denying and avoiding your feelings was a miserable failure. The feelings exist. But that doesn't mean you have to act on them.*

"I want you to never play Norwegian death metal in my presence again," she said.

"Done!" DJ released her wrist.

She immediately missed his touch. She missed *him,* which made no sense at all. He was right there with her, very literally within arm's reach, lying down and propping his chin on his hands. If she stretched out her hand, she'd touch his soft hair.

"Hey," he said softly. "I wanted to tell you, Echo— I appreciate everything you've done for me."

"What are you talking about? I haven't done anything but punch you in the mouth and help my fucking handlers fuck up your life."

"You've done a lot more than that." DJ's smile was wry and sweet and absolutely, impossibly sincere. "You saved my life in the desert. You took care of me when I was sick. You pulled me out of the crazy pack's crazy pack sense. Every time I've asked you for the sort of favor that would make most people tell me to fuck off, if it's at all possible, you've said yes and you've followed through. We ought to be enemies, but you've got my back. If it wasn't for you, I'd have lost my mind in here."

Echo couldn't say that any part of what he said was untrue, but when he phrased it like that, it seemed hard to believe. While she was still lying there with no idea of how to respond, he reached across the space between them and laid his hand on her shoulder.

"Good night, Echo," he said. "I've got your back, too."

ELEVEN

DJ

Pack Sense

DJ awoke on his feet, grabbing for a weapon that wasn't there. The lights were on, and a siren blared. Echo leaned against the wall with apparent casualness, which probably meant she was poised to kill. She was still in her sleepwear of a black tank top and black pajama pants, and looked like a rumpled blonde ninja.

"You have reflexes after all," Echo remarked. "Good to know."

"What's going on?" DJ asked.

A voice boomed over an intercom that DJ hadn't known was there. "Do not leave your rooms. Do not leave the base. We are on full lockdown. Shelter in place until further notice."

The siren stopped. DJ looked at Echo for an explanation.

"Your guess is as good as mine," she said. "But I bet—"

The front door hissed open.

"—we're about to find out," she concluded as Mr. Dowling barged into their bedroom, a duffel bag slung over his shoulder.

"The pack's gone berserk," he said.

"What, again?" DJ asked. "Though I guess it's not surprising. Considering that the alpha is a kidnapped, grieving civilian—"

Mr. Dowling interrupted him. "Quiet, Torres. I'm sending you and Echo to deal with them, so pay attention. Anderson is in the hospital with a concussion. Based on the scene where we found him, he was struck by falling debris when Malakar smashed a wall. He's unconscious, so we can't ask and he can't end this. Torres, you said you were able to tap into their pack sense. Could *you* shut them down?"

DJ hadn't expected that. "I'm not their alpha."

Mr. Dowling spoke with calculated offhandedness. "Could you become their alpha? The alpha of a born wolf pack is the senior wolf or the senior mated pair. That suggests that all born wolves are capable of being an alpha."

It didn't surprise DJ that Mr. Dowling had asked, it only surprised him that it had taken that long. But DJ supposed Mr. Dowling didn't want him leading the pack in an uprising. The situation must be dire if offering DJ that level of power seemed like a better alternative.

"Their own alpha would have to either die or deliberately break the bond," DJ began, wondering how much of this Mr. Dowling already knew. "And even then, each pack member would have to choose to bond with me and I'd have to choose to accept them. If they're completely off their heads, they're probably not capable of choosing or bonding."

DJ forced himself to stop there, hoping that was enough to discourage Mr. Dowling. If they were dead-set on making him take over as alpha, they'd try their usual leverage. And then DJ would find out exactly how much of a wolf he was. He'd been brought up to believe that the pack bond was sacred and could only be entered into by birth or free choice. Forcing or coercing a bond was like committing rape. DJ didn't know if he could bring himself to take on a bond he didn't want, with wolves who didn't have a free choice either, even to save Roy.

Mr. Dowling brushed at his pant legs, as if he was washing his hands of the idea. "What about just getting into their pack sense like you did before, and seeing if you can bring them back to their senses?"

DJ did his best to hide his relief. "I don't even understand how I got in that one time. Anyway, it knocked me off my feet. If I try, I'll probably run amuck too."

"Or sit on the floor and howl," Echo put in. "Where are they?"

"Ah." Mr. Dowling frowned. "This is where it gets tricky. The entire pack, minus Anderson, exited the base on foot. We're not sure of the others' location, but Tyrone Roberts is on top of a mesa with a sniper rifle, firing at anyone who attempts to enter or leave the base via the main entrance."

"Goodie," DJ remarked. "What sort of sniper rifle?"

Mr. Dowling gave him an approving glance. "We think it's an M-2010."

"Twelve hundred meter range," DJ said. "That beats an M-16. I want a SAW."

The approval vanished. "I'm not giving you a machine gun. I want them alive and unharmed. You can have tranquilizer rifles."

"What's their range?" DJ asked.

"One hundred thirty meters," Echo replied. "But they're only accurate at about seventy."

"Fuck that," DJ said. "I'm not going up against an M-2010 with a dart gun. I'm particularly not going up against Guadalupe without a long-range weapon. She can rip my brain out of my skull at ninety meters."

"Only a piece of it," Echo put in. "And it's not like you're using it for anything."

DJ started to elbow her in the ribs, then recalled that they were supposed to hate each other. It was too late to take back the gesture, so all he could do was change a playful thump into a hard one. He figured Echo would rather take a hit than risk rooming with him forever.

Echo slammed the heel of her hand into his chest, nearly knocking the wind out of him. Hoping that she was just an enthusiastic actor, he grabbed her shoulders and shoved. She grabbed back, and they crashed into the wall together.

"Fuck you!" DJ shouted. "You don't talk like that to me!"

"You don't lay hands on me!" Echo yelled back.

Mr. Dowling yanked them apart. "Break it up! What the hell is wrong with you two?"

DJ bit his tongue on the impulse to say, "She started it." Instead, he said, "I don't like smart alecs."

"And I don't like roommates," Echo said sulkily. "But he can have his SAW. I don't need one, though."

"Get it together," Mr. Dowling snapped, standing over them like a pissed-off drill instructor. "You're partners. It doesn't matter if you don't like each other. Your lives depend on each other. And neither of you gets a SAW. The armory here doesn't have any." He looked at DJ. "They're not *stealthy*."

Touché, DJ thought.

But no way was he going out with inadequate weaponry. He had to protect himself, and he had to protect Echo.

"Then I want my own sniper rifle as a back-up," DJ said. "I won't shoot to kill unless I have to. But if I do have to, who's more valuable to you, a genetically engineered assassin and a born wolf Marine, or the made wolves who go nuts every other week and are currently trying to kill you all?"

"I don't like him, but he has a point," Echo said to Mr. Dowling. "If you're going to stick me with a partner, the least you can do is try not to get him killed on his very first mission."

"Fine," Mr. Dowling said. "But if you use lethal force as anything but a last resort, you're not the ones who'll suffer for it."

Echo's lips pressed together into a white line.

DJ's inner wolf leaped up, snarling. Fists clenched, a heartbeat from shifting, he said, "If you hurt Roy, I'll fucking rip your throat out."

Unperturbed, Mr. Dowling replied, "If I die, he dies. Now get dressed. I'll be waiting outside."

He tossed the duffel bag on to DJ's bed and left the apartment.

DJ forced his fury aside as he turned to Echo. "I didn't hurt you, did I? I was doing the 'hate in public' thing."

Echo unzipped the duffel bag. "I know, and you didn't. We should spar some time, though."

Brightening, DJ said, "Yeah, it was fun, wasn't it?"

She tossed an armful of desert camouflage and body armor at DJ. "This looks like yours."

DJ retreated to the bathroom, where he stripped off his pajama pants and put on the camo and armor. He wasn't in that state of perfect calm that came with combat, but in the pre-combat stage of readiness and anticipation. He trusted his teammate. He wasn't afraid. It was like he'd never left Afghanistan.

When he came out, Echo was waiting in camo but no armor.

"Didn't they give you armor?" DJ asked, horrified. "Is that some fucked-up game they're playing with you? I'm not wearing mine if you don't have any."

"No, they did." Echo opened the duffel bag, showing it to him. "But it weighs me down. I fight better without it, honestly."

"Ty has an M-2010," DJ reminded her. "You're not going to get close enough to fight him without it."

"I was thinking you could distract him while I sneak up behind him," Echo said. "You don't do much sneaking, do you?"

"People generally hear me coming," DJ admitted. "I'm not crazy about splitting up, though. Especially since we don't even know where everyone else is."

"We can survey the area and try to figure that out," Echo said. "Ideally, we take Guadalupe out first, from a distance. She's the most lethal. On the positive side, she's not very mobile."

"Small blessings."

Mr. Dowling banged on the door. "Are you two dressed? What are you doing in there?"

"Strategizing," Echo called, then plastered a glare over her face when Mr. Dowling came in. DJ made sure to get one on too.

"Put on your body armor," Mr. Dowling ordered.

Echo complied, though DJ was sure she'd strip it off as soon as they were out of sight. He wished he knew whether she'd made a cool assessment of pros and cons, or was simply reckless.

Mr. Dowling escorted them to armory, where they collected their rifles and dart guns. DJ noted its location and did a hasty inventory. He also memorized the way to the secret exit Mr. Dowling led them to. Echo had been right: his chances had improved now that he'd started going on missions. Once he figured out where Roy was, he could easily grab what he needed and get the hell out of there.

Leaving Echo behind.

Mr. Dowling opened a concealed door via hidden retina scanner. As they got the rest of their equipment together, he briefed them on the powers and capabilities of the made wolves.

DJ stole a glance at Echo. She was covered from head to toe, boots to bulky body armor to gloves to helmet. He could see nothing of her athletic figure and barely any of her elegant features. As she'd said, the armor did weigh her down and rob her movements of her usual grace. Except for the crystal clarity of her eyes, more blue than the most perfect summer sky, she looked like any sister Marine.

Never leave anyone behind.

He'd have to leave Roy, or he'd have to leave Echo. They'd both saved him, but he couldn't save them both.

Roy was imprisoned and terribly wounded, deep down to the heart and soul, completely apart from the shrapnel. He needed DJ.

Echo was hurting too, but she could make her own choices. She *had* made her choices, and DJ couldn't argue with them. Of course she'd sacrifice herself for her sister. That was what family meant. She liked DJ, and he was glad of that. But she didn't need him.

DJ had to go. Echo couldn't go. Once he left, he could never come back. However DJ circled round his dilemma, he always came back to the same place. And he always hit with nearly physical force, like crashing into a brick wall.

He supposed it could be worse. Imagine if she was his mate! Then he'd be like a wolf in one of the old tragic stories, separated from his true love by cruel fate.

DJ was lucky he hadn't fallen in love with her. Probably lots of men would have, if they'd been in his shoes. Probably DJ would have too, if he hadn't realized early on that it would be doomed and would break his heart. Even apart from the "trapped in a secret evil lab" aspect, she only saw him as a friend. And there was nothing more annoying than being stuck in close proximity with someone you weren't into who was stuck on you.

It wasn't just that Echo was beautiful, though she was. More than beautiful: she was absolutely stunning. DJ had never used to be a fan of that type of beauty, all long legs and angular bone structure and shades of pale. It made him think of supermodels nibbling lettuce in between shooting ads for high heels. He couldn't imagine having a relationship with that kind of woman. They'd have nothing to talk about. He couldn't even conceive of having sex with that imaginary supermodel. He'd probably break her nail.

But Echo had only seemed icy and unreal for the first two seconds he'd laid eyes on her. After that, he'd seen what was beneath the beauty: warmth and playfulness and caring, bitterness and anger and grief, love and courage and a dogged tenacity to match DJ's own.

And she liked Gloc-9.

And she bantered.

And he was going to leave and never see her again.

Bam. Brick wall.

"Are you listening, Torres?" Mr. Dowling barked.

Reflexively, DJ said, "Yes, sir!"

Both Mr. Dowling and Echo stared at him.

"What did I just say?" Mr. Dowling inquired.

"You were briefing us on the mission," DJ replied.

"*Specifically*, what did I just say?"

DJ had been completely checked out, but Mr. Dowling was holding an EpiPen and had a box of them in his other hand. "You were explaining how to use the EpiPens, in case we get tagged by Amber. Take off the safety cap, jam the orange end into your thigh until it clicks, hold for five seconds, then wait a minute or so and see if symptoms improve. If they don't, use another one. Then rush to a hospital."

Echo laughed. Mr. Dowling looked torn between annoyance and grudging approval.

"What?" DJ asked. He'd been so sure that was it.

"I asked if you were familiar with EpiPens," Mr. Dowling said. "Obviously, the answer is yes."

"My whole unit was trained in first aid," DJ explained.

He tucked half the EpiPens into an easy-reach pouch and handed the rest to Echo. As she put hers away, he noticed that one of the straps on her pack was loose. It was an awkward area to reach, so he tightened it for her.

As he straightened up, he caught Mr. Dowling's eye and remembered that he was supposed to hate her. "God, you're careless."

"*I'm* careless?" Echo retorted. "*You're* the one who spaced out in the mission briefing."

"Good luck," Mr. Dowling said. It sounded exactly like "Good riddance."

He opened the door, letting in a rush of cool night air. DJ inhaled deeply. He hadn't realized how much he'd missed the outside until that moment.

"Come on, Torres. Don't drag your feet." Echo walked out without a backward glance.

DJ hurried after her, hastily scanning the area for threats. He saw none, though in that desert landscape of boulders and rock formations, canyons and caves, anyone could be hiding anywhere. Though based on the pack's behavior the last time they'd gone nuts, he doubted they'd be stealthy.

The moon was full and huge, golden as a pirate's coin. There was no light spill, so the sky was black as engine oil and the stars were a spray of white-hot sparks. He could even see the hazy sweep of the Milky Way. Sand and gravel crunched beneath his feet, and the dry air was untainted with chemicals.

He was outdoors on a beautiful night, he had a mission, and he had Echo beside him. It was impossible not to be happy.

DJ took off his rucksack, helmet, and weapons, which were too bulky to shift with him, and became a wolf. He lifted his nose to the night, but the air was too dry for him to scent the pack. All he could smell was dust and sand and minerals, and Echo's incongruous scent of green leaves and clear water. It was as if he was just out of sight of an oasis.

Cool fingers came down on his back. Lechon twitched in surprise, then bent his head to offer Echo a tempting angle. To his delight, she took the bait and scratched behind his ears. Obviously, he needed to be a wolf more often. He couldn't resist nuzzling the curve of her hip.

She gave him a final scratch, running her fingers through his fur as if she liked the texture, then said, "Did you scent anyone?"

Reluctantly, he shifted back. "No. In air like this, I'd have to be right on top of them."

"I didn't see anyone in the infrared," Echo reported as he put his gear back on. "But I'll climb that and see if I can get a better vantage point."

She indicated the huge rock formation nearby. They ducked behind it. Echo promptly took off her pack and started removing her armor.

"Are you sure you don't want anything between you and the M-2010?" DJ asked. "What about just the helmet?"

"Ugh, no." Echo yanked it off and shook out her hair. It glimmered in the moonlight. As DJ watched, incredulous, she stripped off her boots and her loose camouflage shirt and pants, revealing sand-colored moccasins, jeans, and— of course— a tank top.

"You should be the spokesperson for Tank Tops of America," DJ remarked. "Do you ever wear anything else?"

"They're comfortable. I can move in them. And they come in all colors." She poked him in the body armor. "You should try one sometime. Show off your shoulders."

Did Echo just flirt with me? DJ wondered. He quickly dismissed the thought. She was probably just teasing him. And if she wasn't, he didn't want to think about it now. That would be a get-you-killed-level distracting thought.

"Let's review the plan," DJ said.

"Don't you remember it?"

"I want to make sure nothing got added or subtracted while I was busy daydreaming."

A little smile hovered at Echo's lips. "What were you daydreaming about?"

DJ couldn't tell her, but he didn't want to lie to her. "Supermodels."

Echo snickered, then took out a GPS device and indicated Ty's position, then their own. "Assuming I don't see anyone from here, we cut behind this ridge to his mesa. We'll be shielded and he'll never see us coming. We split up at the fork. I signal you with the buzzer when I'm in position. You throw flash-bang grenades to catch his attention. I climb the mesa and shoot him with the dart gun. Then I survey the area, see if I can spot anyone, and radio you. Depending on what I see, we go after them separately, we go after them together, or we meet up and search."

"Check." Then, unable to resist, DJ added, "Are you *sure* you don't want to throw the flash-bangs while I climb the mesa? Since you're set on not wearing armor…"

"Hold this." Echo handed him the GPS.

Without warning, she sprang at the sheer wall of red granite beside them. Echo flew upward, stuck way above DJ's head with her fingers and toes jammed into completely invisible crannies, then climbed up with astonishing speed. He still had his mouth hanging open in awe when she reached the top.

He expected her to flatten herself and crawl over to avoid being spotted, but to his alarm, she began to stand up. Then she froze in a wary crouch, like a cougar waiting to leap on unsuspecting prey. She must have seen something. DJ frantically beckoned to her to come down. She was silhouetted against the sky, a perfect target. They weren't within range of Ty, but the other wolves easily could have guns too. Not to mention Guadalupe.

Echo climbed halfway down the wall in seconds, then dropped the rest of the way. She landed beside DJ like a gymnast, with both feet planting firmly into the ground.

"I spotted one of them at eleven o'clock," she murmured, her breath warm against his ear. "Can't tell who. But they're running as a wolf, straight for us."

"Let's—" Before DJ could say, "sneak along the ridge and flank them," Echo had taken off to do exactly that.

DJ scrambled to catch up with her. Matching her stride, he leaned in and spoke in a lowered voice. "You've got to give me some warning of what you're doing. We haven't been partners for long enough that I can just know. I need words."

She gave him a startled glance, then nodded. "Right. Sure. I'll—"

A woman's angry shriek resounded through the still night air. With a sound like a sledgehammer hitting stone, the rock shattered under Echo's feet.

DJ grabbed her arm and yanked her away before she could fall. Echo regained her balance almost instantly, her hand resting so lightly on his arm that he could barely feel its warmth.

The crack extended straight out from the ridge. Now DJ knew Push's exact location. He signaled to Echo to go in the other direction, then moved toward Push's right side.

Another scream and crash, and DJ leaped out of the way of a small crevasse. Tranquilizer gun held ready, he scrambled up the ridge and peered over the top. Push was kneeling thirty feet away, unarmed and wild-eyed. As she raised her fist to punch the wall again, DJ sighted and fired.

A dart hit her side. DJ ducked out of sight. Another punch sent rocks tumbling down. Then silence. He gave it a count of five to make sure she was down, then peeked over the ridge.

Push was out cold in a heap of broken rocks. DJ didn't see anyone else around, including Echo. He looked back down where he'd come from, but she was still out of sight. Where had she gone?

"Jump!" Echo yelled.

Burning pain stabbed through his right arm as he threw himself forward over the ridge. DJ tumbled head over heels until he fetched up in a thankfully soft heap of sand.

He'd dropped his dart gun when he'd been hit, but he spotted it near Push. He wriggled on his belly, wary of presenting an easy target, until it was within hand's reach.

He grabbed it, and was relieved that he *could* grab. He didn't see any blood, but his upper arm burned like he'd been shot— not that he'd ever been shot, but he'd heard people describe what it felt like. He had to be within ninety meters of Guadalupe.

DJ hadn't heard any more sounds, which he hoped to hell meant Echo hadn't been hit, rather than that she had and was being stoic. He edged along the base of the ridge, in case Guadalupe was lying in wait for him to pop his head over. He'd get out of the kill zone, then go reinforce Echo.

"DJ!" Echo vaulted over the top of the ridge and landed beside him. Other than a tiny cut on her cheek, she seemed unhurt. "Are you hit?"

"I think so. It was Guadalupe, right?"

Echo nodded. "I nailed her with the tranquilizer gun. Let me see."

DJ holstered the gun and tried to roll up his sleeve. The wound or whatever it was throbbed fiercely when he tried to push the cloth over it.

"I'll get that." Echo took the edge of his sleeve and tore it all the way up to his shoulder, then ripped the sleeve off entirely.

His upper arm was swollen and bruised, as if someone had hit him with a baseball bat. DJ gingerly touched it, then winced. "I think she tore out a chunk of muscle."

"Ouch. Can you use your arm?"

DJ checked his range of motion. "Yeah. I'm good to go."

Echo nodded briskly, then picked up the radio and gave a brief report. She clicked it off, then turned to DJ. "I don't think you should bear weight on it, though. I'm still taking out Ty."

"You got no argument there. Besides, I've seen you climb now. Are you sure you're not a gecko shifter?"

"I'm sure." A beat later, Echo added, "But maybe I'm a tree frog."

She splayed out her fingers, frog-like, then turned to climb back over the ridge.

DJ tapped her shoulder. "Hey. Thanks for saving my life."

She seemed taken aback. "Oh, I don't think she would've killed you. It looks like she was going for your gun-hand."

"I was already moving when I was hit. I think she was aiming for center of mass."

"Ugh."

"My point exactly," DJ said. "So thanks for saving me from an incapacitating injury that would have needed surgery, at the very least, and easily could have killed me. And definitely would have been incredibly creepy and gross."

Echo smiled. "You're welcome."

They collected Echo's pack, then once again set off toward the mesa where Ty was lurking.

DJ rotated his right shoulder every few minutes, making sure he was still fit to throw a grenade. He was, but it burned like a motherfucker. While they had tourniquets and gauze soaked in quick-clotting chemicals, instant ice packs had apparently been considered non-essential. So had painkillers. Next time DJ would demand to carry both.

When they reached the fork, DJ expected Echo to simply take off, as seemed to be her usual M.O. It was frustrating, but he reminded himself that she was used to working solo and she'd more than proven that he could count on her anyway.

But she didn't. Instead, she stopped and examined him, looking uncharacteristically hesitant.

"How's your arm?" she asked at last.

"It hurts. But I can use it." He made a mock grenade throw, forcing himself not to wince. "Don't worry, Echo. Ty will never so much as glance in your direction. I'm on it."

"I know." A trickle of blood had dried along her cheek, like the track of a tear. It looked black in the moonlight. The color was leached from her eyes as well, leaving them gray as fog. The exposed skin of her face and throat and shoulders and arms glowed white.

DJ was beyond glad that he'd seen her climb the rock formation, or he'd be panicking to think of her going up against a man armed with a sniper rifle, wearing nothing but jeans and a tank top. But she could climb like a gecko and leap like a cat. She'd squared off with Guadalupe and walked away with nothing but that tiny cut. He had to trust her preference for mobility over protection.

She reached out to him, and for a surreal second he thought she was going to touch his cheek. Then her hand dropped low and she punched him lightly on the left shoulder.

"Don't do anything I wouldn't do," she said, and took off. The last thing DJ saw as she vanished around the corner was the pale glow of her tousled hair.

There was no way he could match both her speed and stealth while he was weighed down with a pack and weapons and body armor, so he opted for speed. If he wasn't in place when she signaled him to go with the flash-bangs, Echo just might decide to start climbing without waiting for the diversion.

But apart from Ty, the only enemies left were Amber and Match. DJ wasn't too worried about either of them. Amber's power only worked within grappling range, and if she did have a gun, he was running too fast to make an easy target. And Match wasn't dangerous to DJ at all: just an unusually intelligent wolf.

DJ shuddered. Match wasn't suffering, he supposed. Dr. Semple had said he didn't even remember being a man. But what was it like for the other werewolves to be in the pack sense with an animal? And what had it been like for Special Agent O'Donnell to feel his humanity slipping away?

DJ forced his mind away from those thoughts. They were distractions, like the pain in his arm. Non-essentials. Dead weight. He focused on the thud of his feet against the ground and the burn of air in his lungs and his senses spreading out like a net of trip-wires, and lost himself in the eternal present of combat.

He checked his location on the GPS, climbed nearly to the top of the ridge, inserted the ballistic hearing protection earplugs, and settled into a hollow to wait for his signal. DJ crouched silent and still, breathing steadily, all restlessness gone. He felt no pain, and his thoughts didn't wander. There was nothing on his mind but *wait*.

The buzzer in his pocket vibrated. In a single smooth movement, DJ activated the flash-bang, threw it as far as he could over the ridge, and put his forearm over his eyes. A second later, the crack sounded, shatteringly loud even with the earplugs.

He kept throwing flash-bangs until the buzzer went off again. Mission accomplished: Echo had taken out Ty. Echo was alive.

Echo was alive.

DJ sat back down in the hollow and leaned his forehead against the rough stone. All his senses came rushing back into his consciousness. His ears rang, his back was coated with a slippery film of sweat, and his arm throbbed with every beat of his heart.

He removed and re-packed the earplugs, took out the radio, and fumbled to call Echo. His right hand wasn't working too well, and between the pain and the aftermath of the adrenaline rush, he felt a little shaky. He'd almost be glad to get back to the lab. Dr. Semple could poke and prod him all she liked; he'd be asleep the instant he got horizontal. An examination table would do just fine.

"DJ here," he said. "What's your status?"

Echo's voice crackled over the radio. "Ty's tranquilized. I can't spot Amber or Match. Let's meet up at the fork and search for them."

"Sounds good. I'll be there."

Before DJ could sign off, Echo asked, "How's your arm?"

"Still hurts," DJ admitted. "And it's blown up like a fucking balloon. Guadalupe owes me big-time. DJ out."

He clicked off the radio, packed his gear, and hauled himself to his feet. This was the part that sucked, when the adrenaline had worn off but the job wasn't over yet. Once they made contact with the enemy, the adrenaline would come back like an old friend, and he'd be back in the zone. But until that moment, he'd be worn out and unfocused and wishing it was over.

When you start fixating on how tired you are, drink some water, DJ remembered Roy telling him. *You're probably dehydrated.*

DJ took out his canteen and drank. It did make him feel marginally better. It also made him wish Roy was with him. If Mr. Dowling had walked into Roy's room and said, "You and Torres are going on a mission, Farrell," Roy undoubtedly would have gotten off that fucking bed, put on his gear and SAW, and done his job. And then maybe he'd have gone back to bed, but that still would've been better than staring at the ceiling 24-7.

He drank again, wondering if he should suggest that Mr. Dowling put Roy to work, if Mr. Dowling would listen if he did, and whether that really would be an improvement or whether that crew of fucking sadists would run with the idea in a way that would make things even worse for Roy.

DJ felt a shove at the pack sense.

Match.

DJ's shields had been up, but he'd recognized that aggressive touch. His pain and weariness forgotten, DJ moved to intercept the wolf.

He edged behind a boulder. DJ still couldn't see Match, but the wolf had to be picking his way through rocky landscape.

Looking for me, DJ thought. *Well, not me specifically, just anyone to bite.*

Match pushed at the pack sense again. Even with his shields up, DJ got a suggestion of what the wolf sought.

He is *looking for me. Not me or Echo. Just me.*

DJ couldn't help being curious. But if he lowered his shields, he'd be overwhelmed, like he'd been in the cafeteria. He remembered that agonizing grief, that hopeless rage at a loss that could never be undone...

Could those feelings have come from Match? DJ had assumed afterward, based on what Echo had told him, that they'd belonged Emmett, who had lost his wife and daughter. Dr. Semple had said that Match didn't recall being human. But even if he didn't remember what he'd lost, maybe he remembered the loss itself.

There was only one way to find out.

DJ stepped out from behind the boulder. The black wolf was silhouetted against a stark monolith of gray stone. He didn't run or attack, but watched DJ with eyes as yellow as the moon.

Even your nerves *don't learn from experience,* DJ thought. *I must be out of my mind.*

He opened himself to the pack sense.

Grief and rage swept over him like a tsunami. But this time DJ was prepared. He stood fast in the emotional tide, letting it wash over him but not pull him under. He'd never experienced anything like it before. The pack sense allowed wolves to sense each other's emotions; it didn't transmit them like an infectious disease. Even with an incompetent alpha, the pack sense shouldn't be that powerful...

"I'm a fucking idiot," DJ said aloud.

Match's ears flattened at the sound of his voice. DJ shut up, but his thoughts raced. All the little mysteries he hadn't bothered to think about clicked into a unified whole.

Most werewolves only had their powers in their human form, but Match had no human form. DJ had assumed that meant he had no power. But he did. He could use the pack sense in ways that not even an alpha could. He could contact wolves who weren't in his pack. And he could transmit his own emotions with such force that wolves who *were* in his pack were driven out of their minds.

That's why the pack keeps going berserk, DJ thought. *It's not that Emmett can't control the pack sense. It's that he can't control Match.*

Emmett had to know what was going on. The entire pack had to know. And they'd said nothing. Mr. Dowling clearly had no idea, or he'd long since have killed Match...

...and that was undoubtedly why the pack had kept it a secret.

DJ remembered Justin's desperate grip on his hand. Justin's brown eyes, looking up at DJ with such trust that DJ would save him. The electronic squeals of those fucking machines, sending their useless alarms to alert everyone of what DJ already knew.

Justin was dead because the pack of made wolves had chosen to protect one of their own, at any cost.

DJ's own anger and sadness threatened to merge with the rage and grief in the pack sense. He pulled himself back. That was undoubtedly how the other wolves had gotten sucked into the whirlpool. But DJ wasn't part of Match's pack, and that gave him distance.

He reached out to Match, trying to build a wall between the wolf and his pain. An alpha could do that for any wolf in their pack, but all adult wolves could shield the pack pups. DJ gambled that being closer to a true wolf also meant being closer to a very young pup. Neither could speak in words.

The emotional hurricane died down, but an aching grief remained. It was true that Match didn't remember that he'd ever been human. But he knew that he'd lost everything he'd ever cared about, everything that made him who he was, all the way down to the knowledge of what it was that he'd lost.

From the memories Match was throwing at DJ, it seemed like the pack had tried and tried to remind him. But Match felt no connection to the images of the man whom DJ supposed had been Special Agent Richard O'Donnell, only bafflement and frustration at why the pack kept showing him irrelevant things instead of giving him back what he'd lost. He was certain that he'd know it if he saw it.

The joy of being a wolf was living completely in the present moment. Match was the first wolf DJ had ever met who didn't live in the present, and so lacked that joy. He was forever reaching back to a past and a self that he didn't remember, without even understanding what he was doing.

Along with the grief came a frustrated rage. He needed his pack but hated them, too, for keeping him from what he wanted most.

DJ sent him curiosity about what it was that he wanted.

Match replied with a sense of an infinite darkness, silent and peaceful and empty.

DJ pulled away from the pack sense. His head hurt, his chest hurt, his arm really fucking hurt, and part of him wished he hadn't asked. If he didn't know, then it wouldn't be his responsibility to do something about his knowledge.

If a member of the pack was wounded or sick beyond hope of recovery, with nothing in their future but a painful death, they had the right to ask their alpha for release. And the alpha had the responsibility to end their suffering.

Admittedly, Match wasn't dying. But he was suffering as much and as hopelessly as if it was the olden days and he'd been gored in the belly on a hunt.

DJ wasn't his alpha. But his alpha had refused him release. There were no pack traditions that covered the proper behavior for this situation, since it never fucking happened. But DJ could never respect himself again if he turned his back on Match. He was a wolf in pain. And he had no one else.

To be absolutely certain he hadn't misunderstood, DJ sent Match an image of himself putting his forearm around Match's throat and snapping his neck, and Match slumping lifeless to the sand.

Match sent him a firm negative. For a second, DJ was relieved. Then Match sent a competing image: DJ shifting, then tearing out Match's throat in a spray of blood.

"You're fucking kidding me," DJ muttered. "Seriously, you want the hunter's death?"

DJ didn't understand how Match could know that was the ancient tradition, when his fuck-up of an alpha had undoubtedly never instructed him and Match wouldn't remember it if he had. Some ancestral wolf memory, DJ supposed. In the unusual event that a modern alpha had a pack member ask for release, they'd plan some painless drug overdose, and the pack member would write a suicide note so the alpha wouldn't go to jail. That was the new way.

The hunter's death was the old way. Wolves killed deer by tearing out their throats, and fed the meat to their pups. The hunt was life, provided by the death of the deer. The hunter's death turned the prey's fate upon the hunters, to symbolize the final turning of the wheel from life to death. It had been considered the most meaningful and dignified way for a wolf to die. But it was an ancient ritual, no longer enacted in modern times.

Match shoved the image of the hunter's death at DJ, fierce and demanding, almost daring him to refuse. Then he lay down in the sand, rolled over, and presented DJ with his throat.

"All right," DJ said, or tried to. The words choked him, and Match couldn't understand them anyway.

DJ removed his rucksack, weapons, and helmet. Trying not to

think too hard about what he was about to do, he shifted.

Lechon felt much more confident that he was doing the right thing. Match was a wolf in need of help that only Lechon could provide. Lechon would give him the peace he deserved.

Lechon shielded himself from the pack sense so he wouldn't feel what he was about to do. Then he pounced on Match, got a good grip on his throat, and tore.

Hot blood spurted into Lechon's mouth, sprayed across his eyes, and drenched his fur. He shook his head, sending drops flying. The metallic, meaty smell overwhelmed Match's scent of sulfur and smoke. Match struggled instinctively, but could barely even lift his head. Blood soaked into the sandy earth beneath his body.

Lechon cautiously opened himself to the pack sense. He didn't feel any pain from Match. Shock had numbed him, so he only felt weak and cold. He knew that he was dying and that it was by his own choice, but he was frightened and lonely. He wanted his pack.

Lechon lay beside him, sharing his body heat and presence. No wolf should die alone. He nuzzled Match, then began to lick his face. Match's loneliness and fear eased with every swipe of Lechon's rough tongue. The pack sense faded as Match grew weaker, but before it slipped away completely, Lechon felt him drifting into a soft, warm, peaceful darkness.

Match shuddered, then stopped breathing. Lechon moved away from the wolf's body.

DJ crouched on the sand, his mouth and throat coated with sticky, coppery blood. He spat several times before he remembered his canteen, then grabbed it and rinsed his mouth. The canteen was nearly empty before the water ran clear. But DJ could still taste blood.

He scooped up a handful of earth and stuffed it into his mouth. It was bitter on his tongue, gritty against his teeth. The powdery texture threatened to choke him, and he quickly spat it out. But after he rinsed his mouth again, all he tasted was dirt.

Better than blood, he thought.

Then DJ remembered Echo, and the mission. He had to go find her. She must be wondering where he was. She might need his help.

He knew that, but he couldn't make his body obey. He was

shaking all over, curled into a ball with his forehead on his knees and his arms wrapped around his legs. His mind was stuck on a loop, circling from the taste of blood to the taste of dirt to the sensation of Match's flesh tearing in his teeth to the tickling of Match's fur beneath his tongue.

"DJ!" Echo shouted. "Look out!"

DJ dove forward and rolled. He looked back and saw Echo slam into a blonde woman, knocking her off her feet.

Amber. The last wolf. The one whose touch could kill.

DJ leaped up and aimed his dart gun at the struggling women. He hesitated momentarily, unable to get a clear shot at Amber, then realized that it didn't matter if Echo got tranquilized. It wouldn't hurt her, and Amber was the last enemy. DJ took his best shot.

A few seconds later, both women lay in a limp heap. DJ cautiously grabbed Amber by the back of her shirt and yanked her aside.

Echo was sprawled on the sand, her chest heaving as she desperately tried to breathe. Air whistled in and out of her throat. A blotchy rash was spreading across her face. In the seconds it took for DJ to grab an EpiPen and inject her through her jeans, her breathing got noticeably more labored.

Echo was conscious, her eyes focused on DJ beneath her rapidly swelling eyelids. She had to be so frightened. He took her hand. It felt clammy, and she didn't grab back.

"Hold on, Echo," DJ said. "The shot should start working any second now."

Wait a minute to see if they get better, inject them again if not, then rush them to a hospital, DJ had recited at the briefing.

Fuck that.

Echo could die if he waited, but DJ had never heard of anyone dying from an overdose of adrenaline. He injected her again, then lifted her over his shoulders and set off for the base at an all-out run.

He couldn't hear her breathing over his own, but he could just barely feel it. He didn't have enough breath of his own to encourage her, but he held her tight and hoped she'd take some comfort in that. DJ felt like he was running as fast as he could, but maybe he could go faster. He pushed his body till his lungs burned and a stitch knifed through his side, but it was worth it. He'd barely been running for ten minutes before he spotted the hidden entrance of the base.

"I'm all right." Echo sounded completely normal. "Put me down."

DJ slowed, unable to quite believe it. He wanted to ask if she was sure, but he couldn't get enough air to speak.

"Really," Echo said. "Stop running."

He skidded to a stop. Echo slithered out of his grip and leaped down, landing on her feet.

The rash and swelling had vanished, and she was breathing normally. It was as if he'd imagined the entire crisis. But though he didn't see any wounds, blood was smeared all over her clothes and skin. DJ didn't remember it being on her when he'd picked her up.

Nothing made sense or felt real. He couldn't trust his own eyes. And that meant he couldn't completely trust that Echo was all right.

"Was the blood there before?" DJ asked at last.

Echo looked perplexed, then her forehead creased in worry. "Yes, DJ. You were already covered in it when I found you. Is any of it yours?"

"No. I meant the blood on you."

Echo glanced down. "Oh. It got on me when you carried me, that's all."

"You were dying."

"The reaction wears off fast." Echo didn't even seem upset. "Of course, five minutes of not breathing is plenty to kill you if you don't have the antidote handy."

Amber had nearly been on top of him. Echo had risked her life for him as surely as if she'd taken a bullet meant for him.

A wave of dizziness swept over DJ. At first he thought it was relief, but black spots started to float across his field of vision. He hurriedly sat down and put his head between his knees. The last thing Echo needed was for him to pass out.

"DJ!" Echo knelt beside him. "You *are* hurt!"

"Just tired."

"Let me check."

She unstrapped his body armor, then ripped off his shirt. DJ wanted to tell her that he'd know if he'd been hit, but suddenly he wasn't so sure. He could barely feel her hands as she ran them over his head, then started prodding at his ribcage and belly.

"Does anything hurt when I touch it?" Echo asked.

"I can't tell."

Echo's hands went still, one flat on his stomach and one at his spine. "You need to go to the hospital."

"*You* need to go to the hospital. You're the one who nearly dropped dead ten minutes ago."

"We'll both go." She helped him to his feet and put her arm around his shoulders, supporting him.

There was nothing DJ wanted more than to lean on her, but he forced himself to step away. "I want to sleep in my own room. If you help me in, they'll think I'm in bad shape and keep me overnight."

"You *are* in bad shape."

"Only in here." He tapped his head. "Metaphorically speaking. I don't have a head injury. That I know of."

That didn't seem to reassure her. "DJ, what happened?"

"Let me tell you later, okay? Right now I think I'd better concentrate on keeping it together." He lifted his chin, straightened his back, and tried to look like he wasn't going to collapse at any second. "If I start acting weird, remind me that I'm still in combat. That should keep me going for a while."

"You won't need to keep it up for too long. If you're not hurt except for your arm, they'll treat that and take your report. Then you can go. A couple hours, max." Echo must have read in his expression that a couple hours was way too long. "Let's tag team them. I'll report while you're being treated. Maybe we can get it down to one hour."

"Okay."

DJ couldn't believe how unaffected she seemed, after she'd nearly died. She was so together, and he was coming apart. Maybe she had delayed reactions. Or maybe she was so used to almost dying that it didn't bother her any more. Come to think of it, he could've died when Guadalupe had nailed him, and that hadn't bothered him. It was only Match...

They walked for few more minutes, and then the doors of the base slid open and a bunch of medics and guards ran out, ready with stretchers and guns. DJ realized that they must have seen him and Echo on hidden cameras.

"Echo got tagged by Amber about fifteen minutes ago," DJ said. "I gave her two shots of adrenaline."

"DJ got tagged by Guadalupe," Echo said. "His right arm. The blood's not his. Check him for head injuries and internal injuries."

Mr. Dowling and Dr. Semple met them at the hospital. Echo sat on a bed and gave a crisp report while a doctor examined her and gave her a shot. Another doctor checked DJ over and told him he needed to get an MRI.

DJ remembered Echo's tag team suggestion. "Can I take a shower first? While she reports?"

"No," said Mr. Dowling.

"Yes," said Dr. Semple. "I'd prefer not to get blood all over my MRI."

To DJ's relief, Dr. Semple won that battle. He was escorted to a shower that, from the looks of it, was normally used for decontamination. But he wasn't fussy. He just had to get the blood off him. He washed it away, rinsed out his mouth with water, and then scrubbed it out with liquid soap. It didn't help. When he washed out the soap, he felt nauseated from the drop or two he'd accidentally swallowed, and he still tasted blood.

He got into the clean clothes they'd provided and walked back in. Spine straight. Still in combat. He could do this.

A medic led him to the MRI room. When DJ had gotten MRIs after he'd been blown up, they'd felt excruciatingly long. He wasn't claustrophobic, but it took all his willpower to lie still for an hour, not moving a single muscle. After he'd come out of the first few exhausted and drenched in sweat, the doctors sedated him for the rest.

It occurred to DJ to warn the medic, but if he was sedated they'd make him stay at the hospital. He decided that he'd prefer to be stressed. But once he was in the tube, the tremendous racket of the machine barely muffled by his earplugs, he had no impulse to squirm around. He lay still, feeling distant and numb. Barely any time at all seemed to pass before the medical technicians slid him out of the tube and told him he was done.

When he returned to the hospital room where Echo, Mr. Dowling, and Dr. Semple waited, Echo was done with her report.

"Just fill them in on what you did," Echo said. "I want a shower too."

Echo vanished as DJ began his report. A doctor gave him a shot of local anesthetic and confirmed that Guadalupe had torn out a piece of his biceps. With perfect timing, she stuck a huge needle in his arm and drained the trapped blood just as DJ got to his account of how that had happened.

Echo's shower set a speed record. She was back, in clean clothes and wet hair, about five minutes after she'd left. She listened as DJ told the story he'd decided on while he was in the shower.

"Match jumped me while I was a wolf," DJ said. "I'd shifted to see if I could scent anyone. I don't have my strength in wolf form, and he was on top of me before I could shift back. I had to kill him, or he'd have killed me."

Angry as he was at the pack, he couldn't rat them out for protecting Match. Ultimately, the fault lay with the fucking lab that had kidnapped Emmett, had been responsible for the deaths of his wife and daughter, and had made poor dying Agent O'Donnell an offer that he probably hadn't fully understood.

Roy hadn't fully understood DJ's offer, either. If DJ had taken the time to explain, Roy would have died. DJ had been so frantic at that thought that he'd broken the most important law of the pack.

DJ had been certain that any life was better than death. Now he had to admit that there were some exceptions.

The last video clip he'd seen of Roy had been just like a bunch of others. Roy lying in bed, staring at the ceiling, lonely and haunted. Despairing.

He isn't dying, DJ told himself fiercely. *And he isn't beyond hope of recovery. He isn't beyond* hope. *I just have to find him and tell him so.*

"Torres, you did what you had to do," Mr. Dowling said. "Anyway, Match is no great loss. Good work, you two. Good teamwork."

He asked Echo a question, but DJ's attention drifted. The doctor had said that his arm would heal quickly and he had no other injuries, but DJ felt feverish, hot and cold at once. His upper arm was numb, but his hands tingled. Both hands, so it couldn't be from the injury. Sitting still was making him feel trapped. Smothered. He had to move.

DJ got off the bed where he'd been sitting. He wanted to pace, but he had the feeling that if he started, he wouldn't be able to stop.

Sweat trickled down his back. "It's hot in here."

The words rang strangely in his ears. Every sound was simultaneously shrill and grating. Thoughts banged against his skull like a swarm of bees, each one demanding to be spoken, immediately. He was burning up, every nerve ending on fire. His clothes made his skin itch. His skin made his muscles itch. His muscles made his bones itch. He wanted to climb out of his body and run. The floor was sliding out from under his feet.

Oh, shit, DJ thought. *Here we go. I can't let them see what's happening. Dr. Semple will strap me to a table. And if I say one more word, they'll know.*

He clamped his jaw, shoved his fist against his mouth, and fixed his gaze on Echo. Her eyes were blue as water, her hair was white as snow, and her hands were strong as an avalanche. She could cool his fire. She could pick him up and carry him to safety. She could be the eye of his storm.

Help me, Echo, he thought, and prayed that she wouldn't need words to understand.

TWELVE

Echo

Hope

"It's hot in here," DJ remarked.

The hospital, like the rest of the base, was air-conditioned to within an inch of its life. Echo stared at him. DJ shut his mouth so fast that she heard his teeth click. His throat bobbed as he swallowed convulsively. He pressed his knuckles to his lips and said nothing. But his gaze met hers, imploring and desperate and trusting.

Echo realized that he was afraid to speak. More, she suspected that he was on the verge of a breakdown. She had to get him out of there before Dr. Semple figured it out too. Luckily, she and Mr. Dowling had turned away to confer with each other.

"I'm tired," Echo said. "The mission's done, and you got our report. I'm going to bed." Casually, she added, "Come on, Torres."

She turned and walked out before they could reply. Echo was crossing her fingers that Mr. Dowling and Dr. Semple were tired too, had gotten all they'd wanted from her and DJ, and wouldn't think hauling them back was worth the effort of making a fuss.

Sure enough, she made it out without being challenged. DJ followed her. Once the door slid shut, Echo put her hand under his elbow and steered him down the corridor. He was walking fast but jerkily, without his usual easy grace.

"Echo— I have to tell you—" His voice, too, was quick but off-rhythm.

"Don't talk," she muttered.

"But I—"

"You're still in combat. Keep it together."

That seemed to get through to him. He kept quiet until they reached their apartment and the door slid shut behind him. Echo looked around. To her annoyance, she found several new bugs.

"It's all—" DJ began.

"Still in combat," she reminded him, pointing at the walls. "I think you're dehydrated. Drink this."

She poured a glass of water and shoved it into his hands. To her relief, he obediently drank it as he paced, which at least kept his mouth occupied. She hurriedly swept the apartment and destroyed the bugs. By the time she was done, the glass was empty, though a fair amount of water had spilled down the front of his shirt.

"That'll teach you to drink and pace," Echo said.

He followed the direction of her gaze. "Couldn't keep my hands steady. Thanks for the water. I put a handful of dirt in my mouth."

"Did you really?"

"Had to get rid of the taste of blood." DJ scrubbed at his lips with the back of his hand. "Blood and dirt. I'm pretty sure I swallowed some of both. I'm lucky I have a strong stomach, or I'd probably be throwing up all night. I ripped Match's throat out with my teeth. I was licking his face when he died."

Echo tried to put her hand on his shoulder, but he was moving too fast, pacing in tight circles around the living room. "DJ, what happened? Was it really like you said?"

"No, that was bullshit." DJ noticed the empty glass in his hands and went to put it down on the counter. His hand moved too fast, and the glass shattered. "Fuck, sorry. I'll clean that up."

"Don't," Echo said, hastily moving him away from the sparkling fragments. "You really want to be messing with broken glass right now? I'll take care of it. You tell me what happened."

As she got some wet paper towels and cleaned up the glass, she listened to DJ's explanation. It was out of order and kept going off on tangents, but she knew enough of the context to follow it.

She'd known that even wounded and taken by surprise, DJ would have been able to subdue Match without killing him. She'd known, too, that he wouldn't have killed without a good reason. And she'd known something terrible had happened when she'd seen him crouched shaking on the bloody sand. But she hadn't imagined anything like the story he told.

He'd acted with honor and compassion, disregarding the cost to himself, for the sake of an enemy. And he'd made that decision all alone. It wouldn't have made any difference to the outcome, but she wished she'd been with him.

"So Justin..." Echo began.

"Collateral damage," said DJ, running his hand through his hair. It came away wet; he was sweating in the chilly room. "Match was pack. They were protecting him, but he didn't want their protection. They were trying to save his life, but he didn't want to be saved. I understand why they did it. But I don't know if I can ever forgive them. I held Justin's hand. I slapped his face when he was already dead."

"Oh, DJ..."

"I ripped Match's throat out with my teeth," DJ said again. "I was licking his face when he died."

"You did the right thing. I wouldn't have wanted to live like that, either."

"The closest I've ever been to anyone I killed was across the room, and it was a big room." DJ was speaking in quick bursts and breathing in between. "I'm a rifleman, you know, we fight from a distance. We train with bayonets but I don't think anyone's used them in combat since Vietnam. The maximum effective range of an M-16 is eight hundred meters if you're just trying to hit an area, and five hundred fifty meters for a specific target. For the SAW, it's thirty-six hundred meters. Or seven hundred for a specific target, but a machine gun is kind of inherently an area weapon. I wonder why we use meters to measure firing range, but feet and yards and miles for everything else. The lieutenant used to say—"

"DJ!" Echo said sharply.

He glanced at her, but didn't stop pacing. "What?"

"How fast is the ground moving right now?"

DJ tried to smile. "Pretty fast. Sorry. I know it's annoying, but I'll lose it if I stop. Seriously. I've never had a panic attack, but that would do it. If I even slow down, I feel like something terrible is about to happen."

"You don't have to stop."

"I ripped Match's throat out with my teeth." DJ spoke with the same incredulous horror as the other two times he'd said it, turning his disbelieving gaze to Echo as if he hoped she'd reassure him that he'd done no such thing. "I was licking his face when he died."

"I know, DJ. You said that before."

"Sorry. Sorry. I can't think straight."

Echo stepped up beside him, falling into the rhythm of his rapid footfalls. "Let's go to the gym. It's got more room to pace."

"Okay. Sounds good." DJ took a step toward the gym, then clutched at her wildly, still stumbling forward. "Shit. Hold on to me, will you? I just got really dizzy. I don't want to fall and hit my head. I think I'm breathing too fast."

"Then slow it down." Echo tried to hold him steady, but it was hard when he wouldn't stop moving. "Take a deep breath for the count of three. One… Two… Three."

He didn't even make it to two. "Can't do it. Makes me feel like I'm choking. Forget it, I can roll with it. I'll get off the carousel when the music stops."

Echo gave up on trying to talk him down. That clearly wasn't happening without a sedative. She moved in closer, putting her arm around his shoulders. His back was heaving as he panted, his body trembling.

"I'm holding you," Echo said. "I won't let you fall. Just come with me. You're going to knock over the furniture if you stay in here."

He let her lead him into the gym, talking in rapid-fire sentences and half-sentences. Echo walked with him, steadying him when he stumbled, as he went on and on about the duty of a wolf and how worried he was about Roy, the technical specs of an M-16 jumbled in with descriptions of the taste of blood and dirt.

He repeated sentences over and over again, word for word and with the same inflection every time. Occasionally he spoke in Tagalog, which Echo recognized because of his Gloc-9 playlist. After a while, she realized that he was repeating those sentences too. She stopped paying attention to what he was saying and simply stayed with him, keeping her arm tight around his shoulders.

They paced like that for over an hour. Then, without warning, he sagged against her. She caught him and held him up. He managed to regain his footing, though he still leaned heavily against her.

"Sorry." His voice was raw, but he sounded more like himself. "Ran out of gas. That was quick."

"Want to lie down?"

"Yeah, I think I'd better."

She helped him to his bed. He collapsed on to it, then grabbed at her when she started to straighten up.

"Don't go, Echo, please." He was shaking like he had a fever. "I'm fucked up, and I'm really scared."

Echo sat on the bed and held his hand. His grip was tight enough to hurt. She'd only meant to go to her own bed, but she realized that even that would have been too far for him. "What are you scared of?"

"I'm scared it won't stop." DJ swallowed. "That I'll feel like this forever."

"It's combat stress," Echo reminded him. "It wears off."

"Sometimes it doesn't. Sometimes you fall into a pit and you just keep falling."

"That won't happen to you. You're immune to PTSD."

"An evil mad scientist thinks *maybe* I'm immune," DJ corrected her. "I can't bank on that."

He seemed rational enough to be reasoned with, so Echo said, "You've felt like this before, right?"

"Yeah, a couple times."

"And it's always gone away on its own?"

DJ nodded, his trembling subsiding. "By the next morning."

"Then you'll be fine tomorrow."

"I hope so." DJ coughed, then rubbed at his throat. "I need to shut up occasionally. I keep wearing out my voice. I should carry cough drops."

"I don't know if there's any cough drops here, but I could get you some water."

"No, thanks." His mouth twisted wryly. "I'd rather have a sore throat while you're here with me than have you leave for thirty seconds to get water. It's a wolf thing, just go with it."

"Your call."

"God, I feel awful." DJ turned from side to side. It reminded Echo of how he'd struggled against the restraints when he'd had heat stroke, as if moving was painful but not moving was unbearable. "My jaw hurts. My arm hurts. The room's spinning so fast, I feel like I'm going to fly off the bed. And my thoughts are so fucking loud. I wish you were a wolf, then I could be one too and you could lie down beside me and chew on my ear."

Echo laughed, and was surprised that she could. "Does that feel good?"

He managed to smile. "It does if you're a wolf."

Don't say it, Echo told herself. *Holding his hand is plenty. Holding him is... irreversible. It's a not a step on a path that you can turn back from, it's throwing yourself off a cliff.*

"I'll lie beside you," Echo said, controlling her voice so she sounded casual. "If you want."

"You'd do that?" DJ's eyes widened in startled hope.

Echo lay down and put her arms around him. His body jerked as if he'd been shocked, every muscle snapping taut and quivering.

"Goddammit," DJ muttered. "I didn't mean to do that. I'm locked out of the control room. Everything's gone to some fucked-up autopilot. This is the worst it's ever been. I don't know how to turn it off."

"Let me try something." Echo pulled him close and began rubbing his back.

"Oh— You don't have to—"

"I want to."

"Okay." DJ curled into her, nestling his head into her shoulder. She could feel the rapid thrum of his heartbeat. At first his flesh was rock-hard, unyielding. But slowly she felt his tension ease.

"Thanks." His voice was softer, less agitated. "My family did that when I was in the hospital. I mean, when we weren't wolves."

Echo turned her head, which put her mouth right against his ear.

Teasingly, she asked, "Shall I chew on it?"

"Nah, that's okay. But if you want, I'll chew on yours."

Echo chuckled, wondering if he meant it. "I'll pass."

DJ re-settled himself, and then his strong arms wrapped around her and held her tight. His breath was warm against her throat, his hair velvety against her cheek. His scent of salt and flame filled the air. Echo breathed it in, imagining that they lay beside a campfire, under an open sky.

"How're you doing?" she asked.

"Better. I'm sorry I dragged you into my crazy world. It must've been exhausting. Just what you needed tonight, huh? You were in combat too."

"Not like you."

"Sure you were. You got hit. You could've died."

Echo rested her head on his shoulder, letting her eyes close. Everything was red behind the lids; she could turn off the lights, but getting up seemed an unimaginable effort. "I didn't kill anyone."

"Oh. Yeah, that makes a difference." His hand cupped the area between her shoulder blades, where she always felt most tense and had the hardest time working it loose. DJ kneaded the muscle until it softened beneath his fingers, and the dull ache went away.

"That feels good," Echo sighed. His touch was such a comfort to her that, for the first time that night, she realized how much she'd needed that.

"Any time."

He went on rubbing her back and shoulders, massaging the tight places until they relaxed. He even dug his thumbs into the base of her skull and gently rocked it from side to side until the tension released in her neck and face. It was only after he finished that it occurred to her that he easily could have snapped her spine with that grip. No matter how exhausted she was, her reflexes should have screamed out a warning. But she hadn't felt the slightest bit of alarm. And now her jaw didn't ache.

"Where'd you learn to do that?" Echo was so tired that her voice slurred.

"Used to have a girlfriend who was a physical therapist." His words too were half-articulated, hard to understand.

"What happened to her?"

She felt him shrug. "I deployed."

His hands moved from her head to her neck, searching for tightness, then to her shoulders and upper arms. She felt as if she was floating above the bed. When he came to her waist, she thought with vague regret that he was done, and now he'd take his hands away. Instead, he returned to the area between her shoulder blades, rubbing in slow, gentle circles until she drifted into sleep.

Echo usually woke up in an instant, with none of the lazy transition between dreams and waking that Charlie told her was the best part of sleep. But that morning she awoke in slow stages. First she was simply aware of being warm and relaxed and cozy. Then she recalled that she'd been on a mission the night before, though not what the mission had been, and spent some time dreamily contemplating how odd it was that she felt rested rather than drained and depressed.

Then she recalled the mission, and its aftermath. Only then did she register that she was in bed with DJ, with her arms wrapped around him and his around hers, pressed as close together as it was possible for two people to be. Even their legs were tangled up. His head rested on her shoulder, and she could feel his warm breath on the hollow of her throat.

She opened her eyes, careful not to move and wake him. He had to be exhausted. This close, she could see all sorts of details one normally didn't notice: the length of his eyelashes, the elegant sculpture of his collarbones, the strands of black hair growing out over his forehead. Echo hoped he wouldn't cut his hair. He'd look good with bangs. They'd call more attention to his beautiful dark eyes.

Either she'd moved or he'd somehow sensed that she was watching him, because DJ woke up.

"Hey." He smiled at her lazily, clearly still half-asleep, and lifted his hand to toy with a lock of her hair.

DJ's eyes focused and his hands twitched as he woke up completely. His expression shifted from dreamy contentment to tenderness to, abruptly, shock and dismay.

"Son of a bitch," he muttered. "I did it. I *already* did it. There's no take-backs now."

He rolled away from her and buried his face in the pillow.

Echo sat up and put her hand on his back, concerned. "You did the right thing. DJ, if I was in so much pain that I'd beg an enemy to kill me, I'd hope they'd have the compassion and the courage to do it."

DJ's shoulders shook under her hand. He didn't make a sound, but the pillow was probably muffling his sobs. Echo felt completely helpless. She sat there and rubbed his shoulders until the shaking stopped and he mumbled into the pillow, "Thanks, Echo. I think I'll take a shower."

Before she had a chance to reply, he leaped out of bed and bolted into the bathroom.

The water ran for a long time. But when he finally emerged, a towel wrapped around his waist, he gave her a small but genuine smile. "Sorry about that. I'm all right, really. Just a bit shaken up. I need to talk to the pack, though. Tell them why I did it."

"Be careful what you say. There's bugs everywhere." Reluctantly, Echo added, "I guess you could bring the pack here."

"I don't want them in here." DJ gingerly touched his arm. It was less swollen than it had been the night before, but a wide black band wrapped around his upper arm. More bruising extended over his shoulder and past his elbow in shades of blue and purple. "I'll be discreet. Not DJ-discreet, actual discreet. Shower's yours."

Echo also took a long time in the shower, thinking about the made wolves and the mission, about mercy killing and doing the right thing and the glistening drops that had clung to DJ's muscular chest when he'd stepped out of the shower. Water poured over her in an endless stream as she recalled the smile that lit up his face when she liked a song he played, what it had felt like to wake up in his arms, and how he'd stood in the lab with his fist pressed to his mouth, radiating absolute trust that she would rescue him.

When she'd been suffocating from Amber's touch, she'd felt no more fear than if it had been a particularly unpleasant training exercise. Her lungs had screamed at her to panic. But her mind had promised her that DJ wouldn't let her die.

When she returned to the bedroom, music was booming from the tiny iPod speakers. Unusually, it was a song she'd known before she'd met DJ, "Jesus Walks." She sat on the bed beside him to listen. The background chant had a military cadence, and she wondered if that was what he liked about the song.

When the last notes faded away, she remarked, "I didn't know you listened to Kanye West."

"Oh, sure. Mainstream doesn't mean bad. But I wanted to play that as… a tribute, I guess." He jumped up before she could ask him what he meant. "Let's get some coffee."

They met Charlie at her apartment, and filled her in on the mission. Echo hadn't meant to tell her about DJ's breakdown, or at least not in front of him, but DJ said, "I started to come unglued at the hospital, but Echo hustled me out of there so I could have my meltdown in private. She stood by me and took care of me while I was pretty much out of my mind— and that was after she'd been in combat all night and had to be treated for anaphylactic shock. Your sister is the best."

Echo avoided Charlie's eyes. The plot to attach her and DJ had worked, Echo supposed, but it made no difference. Charlie had already outlived her predicted lifespan. She could have five years left— she could have ten years! When Charlie died, DJ would be long since gone.

"She's the best of the best," said Charlie.

Echo was certain that Charlie knew exactly what she'd been thinking, but she didn't know what Charlie felt about it. Lots of different things, probably. Let one feeling in, and you ended up with hundreds banging down your door.

Let yourself truly feel what it meant to take a life, and you ended up knocked down like a house of cards.

She stole a glance at DJ. He was swinging his legs and pulling threads out of the sofa cushions, but that was just his usual overflowing energy, not the desperate agitation of the night before. He'd managed to stack his cards back up. She hoped he'd be more careful next time. Or maybe she could coach him on how not to feel.

DJ picked up Charlie's book. "What's this?"

"*The Devil Duke's Deception*," Charlie replied.

Echo pushed her thoughts aside and examined the book. The cover displayed a heaving-bosomed woman with a death grip on the ankle of a sneering man on a rearing horse. "She's going to yank him off his horse."

"Right into her arms!" Charlie agreed.

DJ inspected the wild-eyed horse. "That is not a happy animal. I hope he runs away and finds some nice mare for a happily ever after."

"That'll be the sequel," Echo suggested. "*The Happy Horse's Homecoming.*"

Charlie glanced at her watch. "We need to get going if we want to catch the pack. They're never in the cafeteria after ten."

In the cafeteria, the pack was finishing their breakfast in dead silence. Emmett had a bandage taped to his head. Guadalupe glanced up, and her gaze fixed on DJ. Simultaneously and without exchanging a word, the others looked up too.

Echo was standing so close to DJ that she heard the tiny crack as he forced his tensed shoulders down.

"You want us to wait at a table?" Charlie asked. "Or come along?"

DJ looked from Charlie to Echo, who hadn't offered because it had never occurred to her *not* to go with him. "Come along, if you don't mind. I could use the moral support."

The pack never stopped watching him, unblinking and hostile, as they approached the table. Out of the corner of her eye, Echo saw that the entire cafeteria was riveted. News traveled fast around Wildfire Base.

"There's something I want to tell you." DJ deliberately glanced around, reminding them of the ever-present bugs. "I was in the pack sense with Match."

All of the pack but Emmett were former soldiers or law enforcement, trained to underreact. There were no dramatic gasps or exclamations. But their quickly-suppressed expressions of guilt and anger told Echo that they understood exactly what had gone down.

"So I know how he felt when he died," DJ went on. "I want you to know that he didn't die afraid or alone or in pain. The way I did it—" He gritted his teeth, then continued, "I know it looked brutal. It— It *was* brutal. But in the old days, it was how a wolf would have wanted to die. You can ask Emmett. It's called the hunter's death."

Guadalupe broke the ensuing silence by inquiring, "How's your arm?"

"It hurts," DJ replied. "But there's no permanent damage."

As calmly as if she was discussing the weather, Guadalupe said, "I should've gone for a head shot."

Echo barely stopped herself from taking a swing at her. Instead, she slammed her fist down on the table. Plates jumped, and Amber's glass of orange juice tipped over. "I will fucking kill anyone who hurts my partner. You all got a pass last time because you were out of your minds. But anything you do in the future, I'll assume that you meant it."

"Thanks, Echo," DJ said, looking pleased but unsurprised. Turning back to the pack, he added, "That goes for me too, of course. But about Match... I killed a member of your pack. As a pack, you all tried to kill me, and I was wounded. Wolf justice says we owe each other heart's blood. That means we have the right to ask something of each other. Isn't that so, Emmett?"

Emmett scowled, but nodded.

"You all take your time and think about what you want to ask of me," DJ went on. "But I want the same thing from all of you. Dr. Semple recorded what happened to Justin in the hospital. I want you to sit down and watch that video, from when Justin arrived to when she pronounced the time of death. Set aside a day. It took seven hours."

Echo stole a glance at Charlie. Her sister's lips were pressed together, bloodless and white.

"What happens if we refuse?" Push asked at last. "Do we duel?"

DJ shook his head. "If you refuse my request, then I refuse yours. That's all. And I'm making it individual, not everyone in or everyone out. Any one of you who watches that video gets to ask me for something."

Amber spoke for the first time, her blue eyes cold. "Can I ask you to cut your own throat?"

"No major physical harm to himself," Emmett said automatically. "Minor is allowed, like a beating or a shallow knife cut. No permanent marks on the face, neck, or hands. No harm of any kind to others. No sexual coercion, no bond coercion. No requests likely to cause him to go to jail or ruin him financially or break up a relationship. Anything else is up for grabs. This isn't about destroying his life. It's a chance to get reparations or make him feel some measure of the pain he caused."

The pack stared at Emmett.

"There's a lot you haven't told us, isn't there?" Ty remarked. His voice was casual, but he watched Emmett as if he was peering through a sniper scope.

"This is born wolf stuff," Emmett said defensively. "You're made wolves. I didn't think it applied."

"Wolves are wolves," DJ said.

"I'll do it." Ty spoke more to his pack than to DJ when he went on, "I'll let you know what I want from you when I figure that out. But I think you're right. That video is something we should see. Match was our responsibility."

The rest of the pack was silent.

"All right," DJ said. "Offer's on the table. Let me know what you decide. There's no time limit."

He went to the table where they'd left their breakfast trays, Echo and Charlie following. DJ sank into a chair and downed his triple espresso in a single gulp. Echo pushed the extra one she'd ordered into his hand, and he drained that too.

"That's sweet of you, Echo, but he's going to be bouncing off the walls," Charlie remarked.

"No, he won't," Echo said.

DJ spun a fork in his left hand. "Thanks for being there, Charlie. Thanks for standing up for me, Echo. And for the coffee. I'm tempted to get another, but after a certain point it does start revving me up. That's what happened with the No-Doz. I took the equivalent of ten espressos, and the sky started dripping down on to my helmet. I think I've had enough excitement for the day."

To Echo's relief, the pack rose in a body and left the cafeteria. Now that she wasn't waiting for one of them to try to kill her or DJ, she drenched her waffles and bacon in maple syrup. Once the first bite of salt-sweet-starchy hit her mouth, she became ravenous.

DJ, who had also been watching the pack, stopped twirling his fork and fell on his steak and eggs like a starving wolf.

Charlie picked up a strawberry, examined it carefully, then began to eat it in tiny, bird-like bites. Echo forced herself not to nag Charlie to get some protein, stare disapprovingly at her "breakfast" of five strawberries and half a slice of plain toast, or quiz her about the state of her digestion. Charlie hated all that, and Echo didn't want to get in a fight with her sister in front of DJ.

"How's Kevin?" Echo asked. Boyfriends were always a safe topic.

"Oh, we broke up." Charlie didn't sound particularly upset. "He was getting too possessive."

"I thought you liked possessive," said Echo.

"I like possessive *gestures*." Charlie finished her strawberry, nibbling carefully around the cap. "I don't like being interrogated about everyone I've ever dated, with a nasty judgy look in his beady little eyes."

"What's a possessive gesture?" DJ asked.

"Glaring at men who are looking at me. Stepping between me and other men. Putting his hand on my hip in a way that signals, 'You're *mine*.' That sort of thing." Charlie examined a second strawberry, found some invisible flaw in it, and set it aside.

Echo suppressed a snicker at DJ's perplexed look. She was willing to bet he'd never made a possessive gesture in his life.

"But Josh in accounting has been looking at me in a flirty way. Echo, you know Josh—" Charlie began, then interrupted herself. "No, you probably don't. He's black, very tall, with silver-rimmed glasses and lovely sharp cheekbones. And he has an *air* about him. I sense dominant tendencies. He seems like the kind of man who owns a box of silk scarves and velvet blindfolds. Elegant instruments of bondage."

"Wow," DJ muttered, looking pole-axed.

Echo snickered. "DJ, you have a sister too. Didn't she ever talk to you about guys?"

"No." DJ grinned at her. "Five talks about women. She's told me some wild stories. But I don't recall her using the phrase 'elegant instruments of bondage.'"

"No one but Charlie would ever use that phrase," said Echo.

Charlie took a sip of tea, unperturbed. "Just you wait. I've got my eye on Josh. I give him two weeks, max, before he's unlocking his box for me."

"That sounds like..." DJ began. "I don't even know what that sounds like. I'm getting another steak, anyone want anything?"

"Hazelnut cappuccino," said Echo.

Charlie shook her head, and DJ fled with his plate.

"You scared him off," Echo said, though she couldn't help being amused.

"I cheered him up," Charlie corrected her. Her dreamy gaze sharpened. "Was he exaggerating about the meltdown?"

"No." Echo swished her last piece of bacon through the maple syrup. "And I don't blame him. 'Brutal' didn't begin to cover it. He was literally drenched in blood. It was dripping off his hair. And—" Echo thought about how to phrase it for the benefit of the bugs. "Even if you're killing in a fight, even if it's not cold blood, it can be hard."

Charlie, who had lived with the bugs all her life, understood as easily as if Echo had said, *It wasn't a fight.*

"You kill in cold blood," Charlie pointed out.

"I'm used to it." Echo frowned. "Working here will be hard on him. I didn't think about it before. I wish I could say I'd do the cold blood work so he doesn't have to, but I'm not sure how possible that'll be."

"He'll get used to it," Charlie said callously. "You did."

A spark of anger flared in Echo's chest. "Don't be mean. You didn't see how messed-up he was last night."

"I've seen how messed-up *you* used to get. How about how hard it is for *you?*"

Echo didn't know how to answer that. "Charlie…"

"Let someone else take some of the burden, for a change," Charlie went on. "So he was a wreck last night. He seems fine now. He's strong. Lean on him."

"I can't get used to leaning on him," Echo hissed, dropping her voice.

She didn't say it, but *he won't be around long* didn't have to be spoken.

Charlie took a nibble of toast and a sip of tea before she replied. "Give him a chance. He might last longer than you expect."

He might never escape.

Echo rubbed at her shoulders, which had suddenly started aching. "I hope not." For the bugs, she added, "I never wanted a partner."

DJ returned with his steak and Echo's cappuccino. He sat down, glancing warily at Charlie. "Awfully quiet around here. Don't let me wreck your girl talk."

"Boys can be included," Charlie said magnanimously. "DJ, have you ever tried bondage?"

He nearly choked on a bite of steak.

"You don't have to answer that," Echo said. "Charlie, stop torturing him. Are you sure you're a sub? You're acting like a sadist."

As Echo had hoped, that sent Charlie into lecture mode. "Domination and submission aren't the same thing as sadism and masochism. You could be a submissive sadist. Or a dominant masochist. You see…"

Echo drank her cappuccino while DJ ate his steak and asked questions. It seemed like he was perfectly happy to talk about sex in the abstract, so long as it wasn't his own sex life under the microscope.

She let the conversation drift over her head and focused on the sweetness and nuttiness and heat of her drink. She didn't want to listen to DJ discussing sex when she could never have it with him, she didn't want to get used to leaning on a support that would soon be gone, she didn't want him to be wrecked by being forced to do her job, and she especially didn't want him trapped here forever.

As far as she knew, no one had ever escaped Wildfire Base alive. But that didn't mean it wasn't possible. If anyone could do it, DJ could.

A messenger approached their table. "Mr. Dowling wants to see Echo and Torres in his office."

Echo gulped the last of her coffee, DJ stuffed a giant chunk of steak in his mouth, and they both stood up.

"Bye!" Charlie called, but their mouths were too full to answer.

In Mr. Dowling's office, DJ's gaze flickered all over the place. She was sure he was memorizing the layout and inventory, all the way down to the pencil jar.

"I'll make this brief," Mr. Dowling said. "Torres, I know about your deal with the made wolves, and I don't see any reason to interfere with your…" He gave a condescending sniff. "…customs. They've been warned not to take any revenge beyond what you offered them."

Echo renewed her vow to watch out for the pack. Guadalupe and Amber in particular. Just their luck that the most deadly of the werewolves were also the most pissed off.

"As I said last night, good work," Mr. Dowling continued. "Congratulations, Torres, you're done with training. You two are officially partners."

Both DJ and Echo stared blankly at him. Echo had no idea what feelings DJ was concealing, but she was flooded with anxiety that they'd immediately be sent to assassinate someone in cold blood and hope that being able to go on missions would lead to DJ escaping. But as soon as she had that hope, she missed him so intensely that it made her chest hurt. How absurd was that? He was standing right there beside her.

Mr. Dowling seemed mildly disappointed by their lack of reaction. "Torres, you're injured. And both of you could use some R&R."

He tossed them a car key and a pair of credit cards. "Take a break. Drive to Las Vegas. I'm giving you three days."

"I can leave the base?" DJ exclaimed.

"What did I just say?" said Mr. Dowling. "Take off. You know what happens if you don't come back."

From the rage that flashed across DJ's face, Echo half-expected him to vault over the desk and grab Mr. Dowling by the throat. Then it smoothed out, replaced by an icy calm.

"Speaking of Roy, you should make him get out of bed and exercise," DJ suggested. "Give him some light work. Have him interact with people. He thinks he's in a military hospital, so have someone put on a uniform and give him some orders. He won't refuse. He'll be useful to you if he gets better, and he's not getting any better with nothing to do but be depressed and lonely."

"I'll take it under advisement," Mr. Dowling said. And that was all DJ could get out of him.

DJ practically flew down the corridors. They stopped at Charlie's apartment to let her know, but she wasn't there.

"Probably opening Josh's box," Echo said, to watch DJ squirm, and left her a note.

At their apartment, DJ flung some clothes in a bag and carefully wrapped his iPod, then paced around, waiting impatiently for Echo to finish packing.

"Don't say anything private in the car," she warned him. "You'd have to tear it apart to get at the bugs."

"No problem." He sat on his bed, then moved to her bed, then belly-flopped on the floor with his feet on his bed. "Come on, how many tank tops do you need? Buy new ones in Vegas!"

His enthusiasm was contagious. They ran together to the vehicle bay, dodging guards and lab techs and paper-pushers.

"Shotgun!" Echo called, and tossed DJ the car keys.

Five minutes later, they were flooring it through the desert. Echo was dubious at first about DJ's pedal-to-the-metal driving, then saw that he had the skills to compensate. She settled back and relaxed as he kept up a delighted stream of commentary over the landscape and the sunlight and his most memorable trips to Las Vegas.

"I'd just come home from my first deployment," DJ said, gunning the car over an enormous pothole and nearly sending it into orbit. "Five years ago. I'd turned twenty-one in Afghanistan, so it was also a belated birthday trip. Needless to say, I got so drunk that I don't remember much of it. I was with some of the guys from my unit, some of my old friends from San Diego, Five, and some people we sort of collected along the way, I don't really know who they were. I think one of them might have stolen Alec's gold watch. Or he might have lost it in a drunken bet that he doesn't remember. This time I won't drink so much. We all spent a lot of time throwing up, except for Five. You're going to laugh, but that's her power."

"Not throwing up?"

"I think it's actually immunity to poison. Obviously, she can't test that. But she never gets hung-over, she's never had food poisoning, and she's traveled all over the world without so much as a stomach upset, even though she drinks the water unless it actually has stuff floating in it."

DJ swerved to avoid a roadrunner. Thoughtfully, he added, "Though a lot of water-transmitted diseases are parasites or bacteria, and poisons can't be alive, right? So really her power is the ability to eat or drink anything without getting sick."

"The power of iron stomach," Echo said. "That's a good one, actually. What are the rest of your family's powers?"

"Dad dreams of random people's lives. It's cooler than it sounds, because they're all in other countries. I'm sure their lives seem ordinary to them, but I used to love sitting down for breakfast and hearing about an hour in the life of a yak herder or a Zen monk or a kindergartener in Hungary."

"Or a child soldier," Echo said, and immediately regretted it. Why couldn't she be more like DJ, and enjoy a happy moment without looking for the dark side?

But DJ didn't seem perturbed. "Well, that's the funny thing. When I got older I asked Dad if he was censoring them, to leave out the depressing ones. He said no. Apparently his power only draws him to peaceful lives."

"What about your mom?"

"Strength, like me. That's a coincidence; powers don't run in families. Grandma Steel has super-fast reflexes, and Nutmeg has a photographic memory. He can recall books word for word. He aced the bar exam."

DJ chattered on until they reached Las Vegas, where he promptly pulled into a strip mall and withdrew some cash, then drove to a different strip mall and beckoned her out of the car.

"I'm buying a disposable cell phone," he explained. "I want to call Five."

"Are you crazy?" Echo whispered, glancing around the parking lot. "Her phone's probably tapped."

"Can't be," he whispered back. "She buys a new disposable one every month or so. We use them for werewolf-related phone calls when I'm deployed."

"Don't tell her where the base is," Echo warned him. "If your family decides to launch a rescue mission, they'll probably get Roy killed."

"Yeah, I know. I wouldn't put it past them to try, but they're civilians with zero training. They'd probably get themselves killed too."

DJ bought his phone. In the parking lot, he said, "I'll call from the hotel. Let's go to a cool one."

"Is a giant black pyramid that shoots a beam of light to the mother ship every night cool enough for you?"

DJ grinned. "My first choice would be the mother ship itself, but sure. Let's go to the Luxor."

Echo booked the rooms at the Luxor, since DJ was busy prowling around the lobby and gawking at everything. They rode up the side of the pyramid in a slantwise elevator, which DJ was delighted to learn was called an inclinator. It was only when they entered their room that Echo realized that she'd automatically booked one similar to the apartment they shared, a suite with two beds. She easily could have gotten two singles.

But DJ didn't mention it. Instead, he ran around touching everything and admiring the view, then threw himself down on a bed and dialed his cell phone.

"Do you want some privacy?" Echo asked.

"Doesn't matter." His face lit up with joy. "Five! I'm calling from a disposable phone. You won't believe where I am. Guess!"

There was a pause, then he said, "No, I haven't escaped. Yet. Sorry, I should have said that first. They let me leave the base, but I have to come back. Now guess where I am!"

Looking at Echo and grinning, DJ said, "Nope! I'm not locked up in a dog kennel. Thank you very much, Five, that's very flattering."

He again met Echo's eyes, letting her in on the joke. "No. I am not in Paraguay to assassinate the president with a fork. Make a real guess."

DJ listened, then rolled over on to his back. "And no. I'm not in DC to put a hit on a senator. Come on, Five, you know I wouldn't do that."

There was a long pause. "Give up? Okay, here comes. I swear I'm not making this up. I'm on an all expenses paid vacation in Las Vegas, courtesy of the evil scientists!" As DJ cracked up, Echo couldn't help laughing too.

He gave his sister the run-down on absolutely everything. It was like the way Echo and Charlie talked. Like the way she and Brava and Della and Althea used to talk, leaving nothing out. DJ told his sister about Roy and asked her to see if she could dig up any info on where he might be held. He told her about Match and his breakdown, and the promise he'd made to the pack. And he told her one lie: that he'd flown in.

But Echo realized that he was leaving something out: her. He told Five that he had a partner and that she was with him, and credited her with saving his life. But he disclosed absolutely nothing else: not that she was a clone, not that she had a sister, not even that they were roommates.

When he finally hung up, Echo said, "You didn't tell her about me."

"I thought you might not want me to. Should I have?"

"No." On impulse, she added, "Let's not tell anyone what we do this weekend. Not Five. Not even Charlie. Just once, I'd like to have something that's private."

"What happens in Vegas stays in Vegas," DJ promised her. "Now let's go exploring!"

For the first half of the day she let DJ lead her around Las Vegas as the fancy took him, to casinos and dancing fountains and the Pinball Hall of Fame. But by the afternoon, she got tired of being pulled every which way and started taking him places, to a dessert bar with a floor-to-ceiling chocolate fountain, to a volcano that erupted every hour outside of the Mirage hotel, and finally to a quiet bar where she convinced him to try her chocolate martini.

DJ made a face, said it tasted like a melted Hershey bar, and, with a mischievous glance at Echo, asked the bartender to fix him something manly. Either the bartender had a sense of humor or everyone had a different idea of what manly meant, because DJ was handed an elegant concoction of red shading into gold, adorned with a curling strip of orange peel and a maraschino cherry.

"Classic Manhattan," said the bartender.

DJ took a sip, seemed to approve, and set it beside Echo's martini for comparison. "Mine's prettier."

They'd had the place to themselves when they'd arrived, but several more customers came in and sat down at the bar. Without even having to look at each other, Echo and DJ grabbed their cocktails and moved to the empty back room.

"Do you go to Las Vegas a lot, Echo?" DJ asked, sipping his Manhattan.

"I used to." She could have stopped there, but she went on, "This is the first time I've wandered around the Strip for fun since Brava died. She was a bit like you, actually."

"I like her already. How?"

"Funny. A little hyper. Really physical. We used to spar together, and she loved dancing. She liked to dress up in steampunk outfits, with ruffled skirts and fitted leather coats, and go to clubs and flirt— with men and women. She colored her hair every couple months and wore nail polish that matched. Hot pink, leaf green, silver. When she died, it was sapphire blue." Echo made herself look him in the eyes, refusing to let feelings get the better of her. "She never gave up."

She expected him to change the subject. This was supposed to be their fun time, their relax-and-forget time. DJ had certainly thrown himself into the fun.

"You want to make a toast?" DJ too seemed to be forcing himself to meet her gaze, and his eyes were very bright. "Raise a glass to the people we lost, who died too young?"

Echo nearly spilled her martini. "Seriously?"

He nodded, not breaking eye contact. "I'll tell you something about mine. You tell me something about yours, like you did with Brava. And then there'll be one more person in the world who'll remember them."

Echo used her bio-control to ensure that her hand didn't tremble, lifted her glass, and clinked it against his. She couldn't believe DJ had talked her into toasting her sisters. It was as if she was under an enchantment.

"To my sister Brava," Echo said, and they drank to Brava.

DJ raised his Manhattan. "To Frank Alvarado. He was a squad leader who lost two men on a patrol. It wasn't his fault, but they died under his command. It broke him. He was jumping out of his skin all the time, he couldn't sleep, and he started drinking. They finally had to ship him home. To get treatment, they said. I don't know whether it didn't work or he didn't show up or what, but two months later he drank a bottle of whiskey and drove his motorcycle off a cliff."

"Do you think it was suicide?"

"Who knows?" DJ swirled his drink into a sunset-colored whirlpool. "If it was an accident, it was the sort you have when you don't care if you live or die. I don't know what anyone could have done differently, but I can't help feeling like somehow, we let him down."

He clinked his glass against hers, and they drank to Alvarado.

"To my sister Della," Echo said. "She was seventeen when she died. It was completely unexpected. She went to sleep one night and she never woke up. Della was a sweetheart. Like Charlie, but less sneaky."

"Charlie's sneaky?"

Echo had barely had three sips, but she felt like she was already drunk. The sort of drunk she didn't get, where you'd say anything. "Maybe sneaky's the wrong word. Charlie understands people. She can get them to do things without them ever realizing she's the reason they did it. If she thinks you're an asshole, she'll plant an idea in your head that'll convince you to do something stupid, and next thing you know, you're fired or your girlfriend dumped you. If she likes you and you're down, she'll know exactly what to say to make you feel better."

DJ cocked his head at her. "So this morning, she thought I needed distracting, huh?"

Echo nodded. "Della was like that, too. But not so calculating. She liked listening to people's stories and trying to solve their problems. She'd have made a good therapist."

No one was within earshot. Still, she lowered her voice. "She'd have made a fucking terrible assassin, so maybe it's just as well she didn't live long enough for them to send her on missions. She'd probably have drunk a bottle of whiskey and driven her motorcycle off a cliff."

She stopped abruptly, tears stinging her eyes despite her bio-control, and clinked her glass against DJ's. Echo blinked hard as they drank to Della.

"To Jose Suarez," said DJ. He swallowed before he could go on. "The thing about Suarez— God, this is the thing about Alvarado too, it's like a theme— is that what sticks in my mind isn't who he was, it's how he died. He was shot in the head in the same ambush where I was burned. If I'd been killed, I'd hate to have the thing people remember about me be that I was blown up by an IED."

DJ stopped for so long that Echo said, "What was he like?"

"Well, he was nineteen. And he was a bit like me when I was that age. Enthusiastic. Eager to please. A Scottie dog. He was thrilled to bits to be a Marine, and he absolutely loved it. Had a family he adored, half of them in Mexico, half in New Mexico. Roy was from New Mexico too, and they both said it was a weird, weird state. Suarez used to live next door to a guy with an alien landing pad on his roof. He picked up a rock once and said he was going to give it to his neighbor and claim it was from the secret Marine mission to Jupiter."

DJ lifted his glass. "I hope someone mailed that rock to his family with a note telling them what to do with it. Suarez would have gotten a kick out of pulling a prank from beyond the grave."

He touched his glass to hers, and they drank to Suarez.

"To my sister Althea," Echo said, holding up her martini. "But it's like you said about Suarez. I remember her dying better than I remember her. She was sick off and on her entire life. Whenever she was well enough, she was in the gym practicing martial arts. When she was in the hospital, she watched sports and travel shows on TV. She hated knowing that she'd been made to go on adventures— that was what they called it when we were kids— but she'd never be strong enough. I think that bothered her more than knowing that she'd die young."

"How old was she when she died?" DJ asked.

"We were twelve." Echo failed to prevent a tear from slipping out. "Goddammit."

DJ touched her face, but not to catch the tear. His finger drew a line down her other cheek, marking the path of the tear she hadn't shed. "She sounds worth crying over. All your sisters do. I'm sorry I'll never get to meet them."

Another tear met his finger as Echo touched her glass to DJ's. Then his hand fell away as they drank to Althea.

"Okay, I've got one more," DJ said. "He's the guy I was thinking of when I started this. But I realized I'd start crying if I said his name. So I thought, well, I'll drink to Alvarado first, I've talked about him before and I know I can do it, and by that time I'll have pulled myself together. But it wasn't happening. So I thought, well, I'll drink to Suarez next, and by then I'll have pulled myself together."

"No such luck, huh?"

DJ shook his head and smiled a little, but his lips were quivering. "And now I'm thinking, if I do cry, who the fuck cares?"

He leaned in close and spoke softly. "Wolves cry. There's no point refusing to show an emotion that everyone can feel in the pack sense anyway. Never crying is a one-body thing. Marines don't cry, so I don't cry in front of Marines. But you don't care, do you, Echo?"

"Of course not. I just cried in front of you."

DJ lifted his glass. "To Justin Graham."

He choked up more and more as he went on. "I didn't know him well. Just for seven hours. But he was brave and determined and he deserved a whole lot better than he got. Every time I listen to Kanye West or Eminem, I'll think of him."

DJ clinked his glass to hers, so hard that she was surprised it didn't break, and tossed back his drink. Echo finished her martini as well, drinking the last strong, sweet drops to Justin.

Echo's tears had dried up, but DJ put his face in his hands and sobbed, noisy and unashamed. Echo knew how much he was comforted by touch, so she put her arms around him. He leaned into her, and his hot tears ran down the bare skin of her shoulder.

"I tried so hard to save him." DJ's words were ragged. She could feel his lips moving against her body. "I gave him everything I had, and he fucking died anyway. I've always believed I could do anything if I just tried hard enough and didn't give up. Either that's not true or I fucked up, and I don't know which is worse."

Echo lowered her head to touch it to his. His hair was soft against her forehead. "You didn't fuck up. It was impossible. I've always known there were things I couldn't change, no matter how hard I tried."

"Yeah. I can see how you'd feel that way. I might have become a totally different person if Nutmeg had died."

"I don't know about that," Echo replied. "I can't imagine you being anyone but you."

"Thanks," DJ mumbled. "I think."

His tears stopped, but he didn't move away. His head rested against her shoulder as if they'd been made to fit together, like a magazine clicks into a pistol grip. She tightened her arms around him and hoped he'd stay where he was, at least for another minute or so. This was the only way she'd ever get to touch him for more than a second's worth of playful scuffling.

Echo's wistfulness flamed into anger. Why couldn't he see her as anything but a good friend? Why did he have to go? Why couldn't Echo be like Charlie, and find appealing qualities in men who were actually available? Why did her sisters have to die? Why did Alvarado and Suarez and Justin have to die? Why did the only person in the world who loved her have to be dying? Why didn't she get to have a future? Why was everything in her life always so utterly and completely fucked up?

DJ straightened up, forcing her to let him go, and scrubbed at his face with a cocktail napkin. "Thanks, Echo. You're a good friend. Like Charlie said, you're the best of the best."

Echo suppressed a hysterical laugh by sheer force of will. "Any time."

The moon had risen by the time they left the bar, but was washed out by the street lights and neon signs. The Luxor's beam was lit, a pillar of white light piercing the sky.

"Do you know why it's flickering?" Echo asked.

DJ shook his head.

"Bats," said Echo. "Thousands of bats. The light draws moths, and the bats come to eat them. And then owls come to eat the bats. It's an entire ecosystem in mid-air, powered by thirty-nine xenon lamps and millions of tourist dollars."

"Cool," DJ replied absently, but was uncharacteristically quiet as they walked down the brightly lit streets, worn out by emotion or lost in thought.

The cool night breeze carried away Echo's anger and grief, replacing them with restlessness. She wanted to move every part of her body, all at once and as fast as she could. She wanted to get in the car and floor it out of town. She wanted to run until she sprouted wings and flew, until she broke the sound barrier, until she plummeted off the edge of the world.

She wondered if that was how DJ felt all the time.

I drank too much, she told herself, though it made no sense. She'd had one cocktail after a full meal. That shouldn't affect her at all.

I thought about my sisters. That had to be it.

By the time they got to their suite, she couldn't stand it any more. Everything was moving in slow motion. She wanted to kick the world and make it speed up. She'd never be able to sleep like this. She had to burn off some of her excess energy.

"Want to spar with me?" she asked.

DJ turned, his red-rimmed eyes snapping into focus. "Here?"

"We'll have room if we move the furniture."

"Sure." He easily hefted a heavy armchair. "This'll be fun. I'd been meaning to ask."

DJ helped her move the living room furniture into the kitchen and bedroom, leaving a large bare space. He took off his shoes and socks, then shifted rapidly from foot to foot, bouncing like a lightweight boxer.

Belatedly, she checked his arm. The swelling was gone, but a black patch still covered half his biceps. "How's your arm?"

He rotated it. "Fine, so long as you don't hit or grab me there."

"Don't worry, you delicate flower," she teased. "I'll be careful not to bruise your petals."

"Thanks. You're very considerate, for a gopher shifter."

"A gopher?"

"They're the bane of my mom's rose garden. Anywhere you don't want me to hit or grab you?"

"*I* don't have any weak spots," Echo retorted.

She too was moving back and forth, getting her rhythm and observing him. From the one fight they'd had, she knew he could match or surpass her strength if he got her in a hold. He wasn't as quick as her, though, or as agile. She'd have to dart in and out, and not allow him to grab her. He'd have the advantage if they went to the floor.

"Ready?" he called.

He'd been watching her too, no doubt making the same calculations.

Echo leaped over his head.

She heard him half-laugh, half-gasp in surprise. Then her feet slammed down on the carpet behind him. Immediately, she lashed out in a reverse crescent kick. But he wasn't there any more. He'd dived forward and rolled.

DJ sprang to his feet. Once again, they faced each other across the room.

"Good one," he said.

She smiled. "There's lots more where that came from."

"Yeah?" He smiled back. "Let's see."

His gaze flicked upward, no doubt calculating how high he'd need to jump to grab her in mid-air. She crouched slightly, as if poised to leap again, and he instantly did the same. But she rushed him instead.

He side-stepped, faster than she'd expected, and swung out his leg to sweep her ankles out from under her. She jumped, letting his foot slice through empty air, and slid in with a jab. DJ deflected it and raised his fist as if to punch back. As Echo moved to block the punch, he attacked with a roundhouse kick, slapping her side lightly with the back of his foot.

"Point," he called.

As DJ's foot returned to the floor, he instantly lashed out with his other leg. Echo dropped down, squatting on one leg and extending her other nearly flat to the floor. His kick flew over her head, and she grabbed the ankle of his standing leg and yanked. DJ went down, twisting in mid-air to control his fall. The instant he landed, Echo's knife-hand strike sliced down and stopped a finger's width from his throat.

"Point," said Echo.

His gaze traveled past the hand at his throat, along Echo's outstretched body. "That's a beautiful stance. It's from kung fu, right?"

Echo nodded, holding it for his inspection. "I wouldn't use it if I was fighting for real. But it's fun for sparring. What've you trained in?"

"Karate, when I was a teenager. Marine hand-to-hand combat. Another round?"

"Sure. I'm hardly warmed up."

They both squared off again. Echo slid in, attacking with a backfist to his face. Looking startled, DJ flung up his right arm in a block. If she completed the movement, her fist would slam into his bruise. She forced herself to stop, nearly stumbling with the effort. Taking advantage of her distraction, DJ darted behind her and locked his forearm around her throat.

"Point." He laughed as he stepped away. "I knew you wouldn't bruise my petals."

"Oh, you tricky bastard," said Echo, but she was laughing too. "Watch out. I won't be so considerate if you try that again."

And then they were fighting too fast for fakes or pre-planned moves, reacting purely on instinct and the necessity of the moment.

There was no attacker or defender, only two people moving together, sometimes tapping fast but lightly, sometimes slipping out of the way.

Sweat slid down Echo's face, and a drop stung her eyes. Her breath burned in her lungs. DJ too was sweating, his black hair shining, the smooth brown skin of his face and arms glistening. They were both kicking less and striking more, too tired to lift their heavy legs so high. They didn't stop to count points, or even announce them. Neither had enough breath to speak. She could hear him panting, no softer or louder than her own gasps.

They fell into a rhythm, strike and block, strike and deflect, strike and slide. It was more like a dance than a fight. She knew what he'd do before he did it. He too seemed to know her moves a split second in advance. They were reading each other's bodies so easily and well that it felt as if they were reading each other's minds.

When DJ lunged in with his hand open, Echo knew it was a grab disguised as a strike. She could have slid out of range to evade it, or slapped it aside. Instead, she let his hand wrap around her wrist, and grabbed his in turn. Two feet shot out, two ankles were swept, and they fell together to the floor.

She expected him to immediately try to pin her. She knew she was fast enough to pin him first. But she didn't. And he didn't. They lay together, side by side and inches apart, in a silence that said more than words. His warmth and his fire-and-salt scent rose up in a dizzying fog. She wanted to kiss him more than she wanted to breathe.

Echo looked into DJ's guileless eyes and knew he wanted her too, as surely as she'd known that his open-hand strike was really a grab. As surely as she knew that he was waiting for her decision.

Holding him was throwing myself off a cliff, she thought. *Kissing him would be walking into a fire. This is the most reckless thing I'll ever do.*

She reached out and stroked his cheek. Her hand was trembling. His skin was hot and slick with sweat.

"You're not going to regret this, are you? Tell me you won't regret it." DJ's scratchy voice was deeper, rough as sandpaper. He was trembling too, like a runner waiting for the starting pistol. "There's still time for take-backs. We can pretend it never happened. I'll take a cold shower. Go for a run. Have another drink. We can listen to—"

"Shut up," Echo said, and kissed him.

His chest shuddered against hers. Then he was kissing her back, hot and passionate, his hands clenching into fists, then opening to grip her shoulders. She wrapped her arms tight around him. His muscles shifted under her hands, sliding beneath the damp cloth of his shirt. She could smell not only his smoky natural scent, but his sweat and hers and the lemony aroma of the shampoo they shared.

They were hardly doing anything, just kissing and holding each other, but Echo could barely breathe. Her head was spinning, and they weren't even undressed yet. His lips were so soft. He was clutching her like she'd fallen off a cliff and he was holding her in mid-air.

She remembered the terror in his eyes as he'd leaned over her, blood dripping from his hair and splashing on her skin, and jammed a needle into her thigh. She remembered his fake-casual shrug as he'd admitted that he'd let himself be tortured to protect Roy. But most of all, she remembered his brilliant smile, his laughter, and the trust that shone in his eyes every time he looked at her.

Echo broke off the kiss. DJ didn't pull her back in, but lay where he was, stroking her shoulders and watching her with that impossible, unwarranted, absolute trust.

Her hands were shaking, and she knew he could feel it. He'd seen her cry, and rather than trying to dry her tears, he'd told her that her sisters were worth crying for. He'd offered her everything and held nothing back.

He loved her. She knew it without him having to say anything. It was written in the yearning lines of his body, in the brightness of his eyes, and in his silence.

He loved her, but he wouldn't sacrifice Roy's life to stay with her, any more than she would sacrifice Charlie's. And she couldn't have loved him if he would.

"I love you," she said. "This is going to break my heart. But I don't care any more. Let it break."

"I think mine already did," DJ replied softly. Then he laid his hand on her cheek and smiled his wry, yes-I-know-it-looks-hopeless-but-I'm-not-giving-up-yet smile. "I don't care either, honestly. I've never been in love before and it's so much more than I ever imagined. *You're* so much more than I ever imagined. If this was all we got— if the hammer came down right now, before we even had a chance to make love— I'd still think it was worth it."

Echo swallowed, holding back tears. She'd sensed how he felt, but hearing the words, as he'd said, was so much more. "I've never been in love either. I thought it would feel different, too."

"Different how?"

She had to think about it. "More *I want you no matter what*, less *I want you to be happy*."

"You can make me happy right now," DJ said cheerfully. He tugged at the strap of her tank top. "Can I take it off?"

"If you let me take off yours."

"Rip it off, if you like."

Echo's melancholy brightened into amusement. "Do you have a thing for women tearing off your clothes?"

Unabashed, he replied, "I never thought of it before, but it was really hot when you ripped up my shirt on the mission last night. Do it again?"

Echo laughed. Then she put her hands on his collar and yanked. His shirt tore straight down the front and back, coming off in two pieces. She balled them up and tossed them across the room, then pushed him down on his back. Echo crouched over him and started to lean down to kiss him, but he put up a hand to stop her.

"My turn." He pulled off her tank top, then unsnapped her bra and took it off.

Echo had never given any particular thought to her breasts, but the sight of them did seem to make DJ happy. "Well? What do you think?"

"They're exactly as perfect as I imagined." He reached up and caressed them, now cupping them in his hands, now rubbing at her nipples until they hardened to his touch.

Echo's breath came quickly. Electric tingles ran through her at every movement of his hands, at every shift of his body, at every beat of her heart. She let it all happen, not controlling or even monitoring it.

She settled down atop him. They both still had their jeans on, but she could feel how hard he was beneath her. And she could feel her own gathering heat. Echo began to rock against him. She felt his breath catch, and heard his gasp. He matched her movement, and her hands clenched over the bulging muscles of his shoulders. Every nerve was alight with desire.

Echo had experienced those sensations before, but they were completely different when they had *feelings* attached. She wasn't only trying to please herself, she wanted to give DJ pleasure. He wasn't a warm body interchangeable with any other warm body, he was *DJ*, who had bled on her and cried on her and made her willing to feel. It was as if she was having sex for the very first time, with all the thrill of a new experience but minus the nervousness and uncertainty as to how it all worked.

DJ caught her by the shoulders and rolled her over, so they were on their sides again. He undid her jeans, then stopped with his fingertips on the delicate skin just below her belly. "Can I?"

"Go for it." Echo's focus had already narrowed in to that tiny patch of flesh where his fingers touched.

He slipped his hand lower, stroking downward with excruciating slowness. Her whole body had stiffened in anticipation when he finally slid a finger between her wet folds. She sucked in a ragged breath, then another. With every stroke of his finger, she seemed to float further above the floor, suspended weightless in a hammock of rippling heat waves and electric currents, the intensity building and building until it broke in a burst of pleasure and white light.

When Echo came back to herself, she was gasping and trembling, with her face buried in DJ's shoulder. She was abruptly conscious of being a person and having a body and being with DJ. For a second there, she'd forgotten absolutely everything. She'd *been* the light.

"That was fast," he remarked. "Or maybe I'm just that good."

Echo caught her breath, then chuckled. "I had a couple weeks of foreplay."

DJ laughed as well. "I know what you mean. Well, I don't want to stop and run down to the corner store, so when you're ready, you want to show me what you can do with *your* hands?"

Echo was still floating on a dreamy cloud of contentment, so it took her a moment to interpret that. "I have condoms in my purse, if you don't mind me stopping and running to the bedroom."

He grinned. "Run!"

She reluctantly extracted herself from his arms, leaped over the table and sofa that blocked the doorway, and rummaged in her purse.

"Got them!" Echo called, and returned with the strip.

He reached up for it. She let it dangle until it was almost within his grasp, then snatched it away. His fingers closed on air.

"We're not even undressed yet."

"Don't let me stop you." DJ glanced curiously at the condoms. "Did you know this was going to happen?"

"No. They live in my purse. I don't date like Charlie does, but sometimes I pick up men for one-night stands. One-hour stands, really. I don't spend the night."

She didn't expect him to judge her, but she heard the wary note that crept into her voice. Once she'd overheard a security guard telling a new hire he should have a go at Charlie, the "base mattress." Echo broke his nose, his jaw, three ribs, and both his arms before the rookie tranquilized her. Echo was reprimanded, the guard was fired, and that was the last unkind word she ever heard about Charlie.

DJ must have caught some hint of her thoughts, because he said, "I hope you don't disapprove, but I'm not a virgin either."

Echo smiled, relaxing. She stripped off her jeans and underwear, slowly, enjoying watching him watch her. His throat bobbed as he swallowed.

"After all this time being roommates, I can't believe this is really happening," he said. "I thought you weren't into me like that."

"I thought *you* weren't into *me*," she returned. The air-conditioned currents were cool on her bare skin, making her nipples harden again. "So, *are* you into bondage?"

She watched, amused, as his expression shifted from where'd-that-come-from to no-actually-it-does-make-sense-in-this-context to okay-sure-if-you-like. "Not especially, but if you want to tie me up…"

"I notice you didn't offer to tie *me* up," Echo remarked.

"I assumed you'd want to do the tying. But I could do it. If you like. Wait a second." He pointed at her accusingly. "This is for the mission report you're giving to Charlie later, isn't it?"

"I won't tell her the details if you don't want me to. But yeah," Echo confessed. "I can't not tell her we had sex, and after that conversation this morning, I had to ask. I've never tried any of that stuff myself. What about you?"

"Once I dated a woman who wanted me to tie her up. And once I dated a woman who wanted to tie me up. So..." He shrugged.

"You're such a pushover," Echo said, laughing. "You'd do absolutely anything if I asked you to, wouldn't you?"

"Yes," he said, his expression suddenly serious. "Yes, I would."

Echo could see that he meant it. But it made her feel protective rather than powerful. He was so strong physically, but he'd put himself completely in her hands. She'd have to be very careful not to hurt him.

Trying for a lighter tone, she asked, "Which did you like better? Tying, or being tied?"

"My problem both ways was that there was too much planning and thinking involved. Especially when I did the tying. It felt like I was commanding a mission. One of my favorite things about sex is *not* thinking." He took off his belt and started to undo his jeans.

"Want me to rip them off?" Echo asked.

"No, thanks. I like these jeans." He stripped them off, then lay back with his hands clasped behind his head.

Echo took the opportunity to admire the view. Her attention was first drawn to his impressive hard-on, then to the arching bones of his pelvis and the graceful hollows above his hips. She hadn't realized how far his burn scar extended. The shiny, rippled scar tissue spilled over his ribcage and belly and down his hip, as if someone had splashed him with boiling water.

"Will it hurt if I touch it?" Echo asked.

"No, of course not—" DJ began, then laughed. "Oh. You meant my scar. No— well— Maybe this part." He indicated the red furrow over his ribs.

"Did that happen later?"

"No, it's the same injury." DJ was eyeing her warily, as if he saw something in her that she wasn't aware of. "The burn cracked wide open, down to the bone. The doctors couldn't close it. It has to heal from the bottom up. It'll fill in eventually."

"You almost died, didn't you?"

"Yeah." DJ reached down, caught her hand, and pressed two of her fingers beneath his jaw, so she could feel his pulse. "But I didn't. It's all right now. I'm all right. Come on…"

He tugged her up to lie beside him, caressing and kissing her until she forgot about the fragility of the human body, and only felt the life coursing through her veins and his. She tasted the salt of his sweat and ran her tongue over the smoothness of his collarbones and the roughness of the stubble along his jaw. He nibbled at her ear, making her laugh, and slid lower to taste her, making her gasp.

"Tell me if I go too hard," he said, raising his face. "Or too soft. Too fast. Wrong place. Whatever."

"I'll give you coordinates," Echo suggested. "Clitoris, latitude forty-eight degrees north, longitude twenty degrees east."

"Thanks, that's very helpful," remarked DJ, and bent his head to her again.

Echo rarely let men go down on her, and never for very long. There was something about the position, not to mention the proximity of teeth, that made it feel too risky. Or too intimate. But it was like when DJ had put his thumbs at the base of her skull: it didn't feel dangerous when it was him. He stretched up one hand to clasp hers. Echo gripped his hand and closed her eyes.

"Too soft," she said once, but otherwise she let her body's responses guide him. His tongue was as deft as his fingers had been. She floated on waves of sensation. It was intimate but not invasive, hot and shivery and satisfying.

"Can you come just from me being in you?" he asked at last. "Or should I use my hands?"

"Use your hands," Echo said dreamily. She was already halfway there. "You've got good hands."

When he pushed inside her, they were lying side by side, like they had at the start. Her eyes were closed, her lips locked on his. They rocked together, her arms clasped around him, one of his hands caressing her back and one wedged between their bodies, stroking her clitoris. The heat of passion flowed through her, pushing her up and up until she was trembling on the brink, and then she was falling, falling, throwing her head back to cry out her ecstasy.

When she opened her eyes, DJ was still moving inside her, watching her with love and trust and tenderness.

"I love you," DJ whispered, the words tumbling into each other as he thrust faster and faster. "I love you so much. I'm so glad I met you. I've never known anyone like you. I never knew there *could* be anyone like you. I can't believe how lucky I am. I—"

The flow of words broke off as he came, his hands clenching tight and his face alight with joy.

While they'd been making love, all outside sounds had faded out. But as they lay together on the floor, Echo slowly became aware of the hum of the air conditioning and the faint roar of traffic outside. DJ traced lazy patterns on her skin, intricate spirals like the inside of a seashell. It reminded her of how he'd played with her hair while he'd still been half-asleep.

"What really happened this morning, when you woke up?" Echo asked. "I thought you were traumatized over having killed Match. But that wasn't it, was it?"

"I am traumatized," DJ replied, his expressing briefly clouding over. Then he shook himself and went on, "But you're right, that wasn't it. I woke up holding you, and I remembered how fucking awesome you were, on the mission and afterward. And you looked so beautiful and it felt so good to have you in my arms. I thought I was falling in love with you, and I told myself to stop it. And then I realized that it was too late. I was already in love."

"And then you burst into tears?"

"Nope." DJ grinned. "I thought, *DJ Torres, this is just your luck. Find the absolute perfect woman for you, and* of course *she's an enslaved one-body assassin trapped in a place where she can't leave and you can't stay.* I wasn't crying. I was laughing."

Echo suspected that it had been the sort of hysterical laughter that was halfway to tears. "I know how you feel."

He abruptly sat up. Echo recognized the look on his face. She'd seen it when he'd won a fight by discoursing on the platypus, when he'd made his repeated attempts to escape from the Humvee, and when he'd told her he loved her. It was the expression of a man about to close his eyes and throw himself off a cliff, trusting that someone would be waiting at the bottom to break his fall.

"Let's not break our hearts." DJ took her hands in both of his, pressing them together as if he was swearing a solemn vow. "I'll never ask you to leave Charlie behind. But I don't want to leave you behind, either. Let's plan on you and me and Charlie and Roy all getting out. I don't know how yet. But I do know that if you decide in advance that something's impossible, then it definitely won't happen."

"It *is* impossible," Echo said.

"I know," DJ replied. "Let's do it anyway."

He settled back down and kissed her before she could contradict him. As she kissed him back, his ridiculous suggestion seemed to float in the air above them, gathering strength with every second that it went unanswered.

It occurred to Echo that DJ was wrong. Thinking that something was impossible didn't mean it couldn't happen. Not long ago, she wouldn't have thought falling in love was possible.

She wouldn't have thought *DJ* was possible. But here he was, with his soft lips, his warm skin, his scratchy voice, his clever hands, his banter, his music, his restless energy, his sweetness and his ruthlessness, his happiness and his pain, his impossible love for her, his outrageous trust in her, and his absolutely lunatic determination.

His contagiously lunatic determination.

As Echo pulled him close to her, she was filled with the most terrifying emotion of all, the only feeling more dangerous than love.

Hope.

Author's Note

Thank you for reading *Prisoner*. I hope you enjoyed it. *Partner* will come out next. Echo and DJ's story will conclude in book three, *Packmate*. Don't worry, they will get their happily ever after. Eventually.

Echo's Wolf is part of the "Werewolf Marines" series. The other book is *Laura's Wolf*, which is about Roy Farrell. It doesn't matter which you read first.

Please consider reviewing this book, even if you only write a few lines. I appreciate all reviews, whether positive or negative.

The Rifleman's Creed was written by Major General William H. Rupertus. *Watership Down* (the rabbit book) was written by Richard Adams.

Thank you to the readers of *Laura's Wolf* who wanted to see more of DJ. Thank you to Victoria Janssen, the inspiration for DJ's musical taste, for introducing me to Sniper, Dessa, and Gloc-9. Thank you to Sherwood Smith, for helping me brainstorm the mission in this book and several of the missions in *Partner*. Thank you to Chilla Varkulya, for cheerleading, cheer, and inspiration to keep writing.

I work as a therapist, specializing in the treatment of post-traumatic stress disorder (PTSD). "Lia Silver" is a pen name used to separate my writing career from my therapy career. When I'm not working, reading, or writing, I enjoy cooking, hiking, horseback riding, martial arts, and cuddling my cats. My email is liasilvershifter@yahoo.com.

Notes on Dyslexia, PTSD, and Combat Stress

A Note on Dyslexia

I based DJ's dyslexia on pure alexia, in which a person can write but not read what they've written. That's normally caused by brain damage, such as from a stroke or an injury, rather than being something one is born with. I did this for plot purposes. Dyslexia is fairly common, and DJ needed a version rare and intriguing enough to pique Dr. Semple's interest.

Dyslexia is a catch-all term for any sort of neurologically-based difficulty with reading. A person with dyslexia might read quickly, but see words shimmer or move on the page. They might read with good comprehension but very slowly. Or they might struggle to read a single sentence. Because dyslexia can mean so many things, different people will be helped by different interventions.

Dyslexia has nothing to do with intelligence, though if it's not diagnosed, it can cause people to be told or to believe that they're stupid or lazy. People with dyslexia are often extremely intelligent and creative. A few of the many famous people with dyslexia are talk show hosts Jay Leno and Whoopi Goldberg, directors Steven Spielberg and Steve McQueen, environmental activist Erin Brockovich, and writer Octavia Butler.

A Note on PTSD and Combat Stress

Laura's Wolf contains a detailed afterword on PTSD, which is my specialty as a therapist. Regarding the depiction of PTSD in this book, for the purposes of the story the characters view it as less treatable than it actually is. In fact, it's very treatable and definitely does not have to last forever or ruin your life. If you read *Laura's Wolf*, you'll see how Roy copes with it once he gets out of the lab.

What the characters call combat stress is also known as an

acute stress reaction. It also happens to civilians who've undergone trauma. It means that their usual coping mechanisms have been temporarily overwhelmed. It's a normal response to extremely traumatic events, and usually goes away within hours or days. It doesn't mean that they'll get PTSD. The main difference between PTSD and an acute stress reaction is that PTSD typically doesn't go away without treatment. The symptoms may also be different.

Acute stress reactions look different in different people. Some people do get very agitated and talk or pace compulsively, but it's more likely for them to seem calm but spaced-out— slowed down rather than revved up. Repeating the same sentences or describing the same images over and over is common, though. They may forget what was said to them within seconds of hearing it. Afterward, they often recall only the most general outline of what happened.

Regarding Dr. Semple's theories on PTSD, it's true that the US military has done an enormous amount of research on attempting both to prevent PTSD and to identify which soldiers might be resistant against it and which might be susceptible. These efforts have produced limited results. A previous history of trauma, such as child abuse, makes a person somewhat more likely to get PTSD from subsequent trauma, such as combat. Strong social support and good training make people somewhat less likely to get PTSD. However, these are relatively minor factors. If you didn't let anyone with previous trauma serve in combat, you would still see lots of combat-related PTSD (and have a much smaller pool of soldiers to draw upon).

The real predictor is not who a person is, but what sort of trauma they encounter. The more intimate, deliberate, and long-lasting the trauma, the more likely it is to give any person PTSD. Rape, child abuse, and combat are all very likely to cause PTSD, because they are traumas caused by the deliberate actions of other human beings. Natural disasters and accidents sometimes cause PTSD, but much more rarely.

Efforts to select only PTSD-resistant soldiers for combat are probably doomed to failure. It's not the vulnerability of individual soldiers that causes PTSD, but the nature of war. So while Dr.

Semple's theories on DJ's possible immunity to PTSD may or may not be true in the context of the story, take them with a grain of salt in terms of their application to real life. In the real world, probably no one is immune.

Sneak Preview Chapter
Laura's Wolf
(Werewolf Marines)

One
Roy

Caged Wolf

Roy Farrell paced in circles around his cell.

He tried to tell himself that it was a private hospital room, not a jail cell or a cage. But he wasn't convinced.

If it's locked from the outside, it's a cell, he thought.

When he'd first woken up stateside after his helicopter had been shot down in Afghanistan, a doctor had told him that he was in a military hospital for wounded soldiers with "unique issues."

Roy hadn't taken it in at the time— he was too busy trying not to pass out or throw up. The glare of the overhead lights felt like red-hot knives stabbing into his eyes, the hum of the machines filled his head until he couldn't think straight, the chemical smells nauseated him, and all of it together made his heart speed up like he was in the middle of a firefight.

Once he'd managed to tell them what was wrong, he'd been moved into a darkened, quiet room and repeatedly asked if he'd injured his head (maybe), or had a history of migraines (no), or had been exposed to chemical weapons (not that he knew of).

His wounds healed, but his senses remained stuck on overdrive. They gave him all sorts of medications, none of which did anything but make him sick or knock him out. They tried gradual exposure to various stimuli, as the doctors called everything that bothered him, which did nothing but create a depressingly long list of ordinary things that now hurt like hell. They gave him test after test, with results that were always inconclusive. At least, that was what they told him.

Finally, a woman came in and informed him that she was going to be his therapist. He'd assumed she meant physical therapist, and waited hopefully for her to give him some exercises. Instead, she asked him to imagine a bright light and tell her what emotion that made him feel.

That was when Roy figured out that "unique issues" was the polite way of saying "broken and crazy."

But what military hospital— what psych ward, even?— wouldn't allow him any contact whatsoever with the outside world? And what hospital of any kind never let the patients so much as see each other?

Roy finally told the main doctor, Dr. White, that he refused to cooperate with any more tests until they put him in touch with his commanding officer.

"You're not ready for that yet," Dr. White had said.

When Roy shouldered him aside and started to walk out, the doctor pressed a button on the little black box that all the personnel in this place carried. It never even touched him, but Roy dropped to the floor, unable to do more than twitch like a gaffed fish. Two guards dumped him on the bed, where he lay paralyzed for hours.

High-tech straitjacket, Roy thought. Some bureaucrat had undoubtedly written up the whole incident, with a note like, "Violent outburst – not safe for release."

The room seemed to get smaller every day. Pent-up anger and frustration surged through Roy. He wanted to punch the walls. But they were solid concrete— he'd checked, quietly, when his candles had burned out— and the last thing he needed was a set of broken knuckles.

He dropped to the floor and started doing push-ups, concentrating on speed and perfect form, trying to drive all other thoughts from his mind.

Sweat soaked his shirt and dripped from his face, making a tiny pool on the floor. His muscles burned, but he kept up his pace. Pain was information. This pain told him that he wasn't yet up to his usual strength. He'd stop when it told him that he'd tear a muscle if he kept going.

He paused when he heard a knock. Before he could ask who was there, the door opened. Roy shielded his eyes against the glare of the corridor until the doctor closed the door again, leaving them in the flickering candle light.

In the low light, Roy could recognize the man: Dr. White, who had last visited him a week or so ago. It was hard to track time in this place. Roy didn't know how long it had been since he'd last seen sunlight.

But he would have known the doctor even if he'd been blindfolded, by the man's smell of burning rubber. Everyone had their own distinctive scent now, beneath whatever cologne they wore or antiseptic they used to clean their hands. His therapist washed her hair with lavender-scented shampoo, but her scent beneath that was hot and pungent, like fresh-laid asphalt. The guy who brought his meal trays smelled like green apples.

Roy hadn't mentioned that aspect of his newly-heightened senses. The human odors weren't unpleasant, even when he couldn't bear their real-world equivalents, and he didn't want to get sucked into yet another tedious round of pointless tests.

He got up and wiped the sweat from his face, eyeing Dr. White warily. The doctor had the little black box in his right hand, with the business end aimed at Roy. Of course.

"Hello, Roy," Dr. White said. "How are you?"

"Fine."

"How's your appetite?"

"Fine."

"How have you been sleeping?"

"Fine."

The doctor gave him a skeptical stare, eyebrows raised. "Really."

"*Fine*," Roy repeated. He was done providing symptoms for

them to dissect.

"I have some news for you. Take a seat." Dr. White indicated the bed, then sat down on the chair nearby.

Roy reluctantly sat. The bed creaked under his weight. "What is it?"

"It's for the best, really. I hope you'll be able to adjust your expectations and take a more realistic look at your prospects. After all…"

Roy clamped down on the temptation to demand that Dr. White spit it out. If he made the doctor think he was going to get violent, he'd probably get shocked again. His only hope was to stay calm and appear cooperative.

Dr. White finally ran out of platitudes. "You've been given a medical discharge."

Roy told himself that he'd known this was coming. Of course he'd been discharged. He couldn't even handle an ordinary hospital ward, and he wasn't getting any better. He'd be useless on the battlefield.

It still felt like his heart had been ripped out of his chest, leaving an empty hole the size of Montana. He'd never wanted to be anything but a Marine. He'd never *been* anything but a Marine. If that was taken from him, what did he have left?

In the back of his mind, he heard a wolf howl in answer. Roy kept his expression blank. If there was one thing he'd learned all the way back in boot camp, it was self-control.

"How do you feel?" asked Dr. White.

Roy wondered if he was imagining a greedy tone in the doctor's voice, as if the man was sadistically eager to hear exactly how crushed Roy felt.

"I've been expecting this," Roy said calmly. "I know that I have a disability. I hope it will get better with time and therapy, but I understand that I have to accept…" What was that depressing phrase the therapist kept using? "…the new me."

"That's good to hear," Dr. White said.

Roy didn't want to be the one to break the ensuing silence. He couldn't sound *too* accepting, or the doctor would get suspicious. Or was silence also suspicious?

He wished this was a problem he could solve by shooting or punching his way out. He'd never been good at mind games. But he had to win one now, or he might never get free of this place.

"So, what's next for me?" Roy asked.

"What would you like to be next?" Dr. White inquired. Now there was a man who was good at mind games.

Roy tried not to sound overly eager. "I think I'm ready to be an outpatient now. I'd like to get outside."

Dr. White shook his head. "You're nowhere near recovered enough to leave the hospital. Besides, we need to run more tests."

"You've run tests on me every day for..." Roy had no idea how long he'd been locked up. Months, probably. "For ages. You've had me lifting weights and running laps! I'm in good shape. I'll wear dark glasses. I'll be fine."

"We need to keep you here for your own safety. Unless..."

"Unless what?"

"Unless you tell us what you really are," said Dr. White. "Or better yet, show us."

Roy kept his facial muscles still, concealing his alarm. But his suspicions were confirmed: they did know his secret. Or knew that it was a possibility, at least. "I don't know what you're talking about."

"Oh, I think you do."

"I don't." Roy tried to look perplexed, but displaying the wrong emotion was a lot harder than keeping a stone face. He could tell he was doing a lousy job of it.

Behind whatever strange expression he'd shown the doctor, his mind was racing. If Dr. White already knew— if the entire hospital knew— then they'd never had any intention of letting him go. They'd keep him trapped forever to experiment on, like a lab rat.

Everything he'd gone through already— the tests, the pretense that he was crazy, the medications— was probably an experiment. Maybe he'd just completed test number 99, "How will the subject react to a strong hint that we know he's a werewolf?"

An icy rage seeped into him, burning like frostbite. He didn't know whether these people were a top-secret government black ops branch or some private organization or organized criminals or even agents from another country. But whoever they were, they were holding him against his will. They were the enemy.

A captured Marine has a duty to escape.

Dr. White was nearly Roy's size, moved like a man who knew how to fight, and had his black box poised and ready. He was expecting Roy to try to hit him or try to run. But maybe he wasn't expecting Roy to try something a little less direct.

Roy mentally crossed his fingers that Dr. White really was a doctor. Or that if he wasn't, he'd at least taken the same first aid course that Roy had, complete with the drill on the signs of a heart attack. Though Roy would normally be much too young for that, there was so much wrong with him already that anything bad ought to seem possible.

He hunched over, wincing. "Can we talk later?"

Pain in the chest, left arm, or jaw.

Chest seemed too obvious. He rubbed his left shoulder, squeezed the muscle of his upper arm, and winced.

A quick flicker of alarm passed over Dr. White's face, followed by suspicion. Then his expression smoothed into exaggerated calm. "What are you feeling right now?"

"Frustrated. Angry." Then, as if he was reluctantly admitting it, Roy added, "Sad."

The doctor looked irritated. "I meant physically."

Denial.

"Nothing. I'm fine." Roy rubbed his shoulder again, as if he didn't notice that he was doing it.

He heard Dr. White's breathing speed up. If he listened hard, he could even hear the quickening thump of the man's heartbeat. He'd never told the people here that he could do that, and he was glad of that now.

Dr. White took a step forward. "This isn't the time to tough it out. Are you feeling sick?"

Nausea.

"I'm not *sick*. Maybe I ate something that didn't agree with me."

"Are you nauseated?"

"A little." Roy deliberately recalled the last time he'd thrown up, in vivid detail, until he started feeling sick for real. He hoped it would show on his face.

"Only a little?" Dr. White frowned, but Roy was glad. Clearly, something had shown.

"Uh…" *Cold sweat breaking out on his face. Jumping up and bolting to the bathroom. Realizing that he wouldn't even make it to the toilet, and leaning over the sink.* "I'm sorry, I really don't feel good. I better go to the bathroom."

Roy stood up, then swayed as if he was dizzy.

"Sit down," said Dr. White.

Roy lowered his head, watching the doctor's feet to see if he'd come closer and try to steady Roy before he could fall. To his disappointment, the shiny black shoes didn't move. Roy sat down on the bed, heavily enough to make the frame shake.

"Does your left arm hurt?" asked the doctor.

"Yeah. I think I overdid it with the push-ups. I guess I pulled a muscle."

"Let me take your pulse." Dr. White switched the black box to his left hand and came closer. "Give me your wrist."

Roy held out his hand. As Dr. White reached out for it, Roy grabbed the doctor's right wrist and slammed the side of his hand into the doctor's left wrist. The black box flew across the room and hit the wall with a loud crack.

Before the doctor could yell, Roy jerked him forward and punched him in the jaw. Dr. White dropped as if he'd been zapped by his own little black box. Roy caught him and heaved him on to the bed.

He hastily pulled off the doctor's shoes, pants, and white coat, then kicked off his own slippers and scrambled out of his hospital-issue thin cotton pants. He yanked on the doctor's shoes and buttoned his white coat over Roy's own shirt. The pants were too short and the shoes were painfully tight. But he was lucky that Dr. White was a big guy too, or Roy wouldn't have been able to get into them at all.

He put on the stethoscope and took the ID card out of Dr. White's back pocket, then picked up the black box. It was cracked and probably useless, but at least he could carry it as a prop.

Try to look confident and doctor-like, he strode out of the room. The bright lights jabbed needles of pain into his eyes and straight through his skull; he was forced to walk with his face lowered and his eyes half-closed. The sickening chemical smell of the air was stronger in the corridor, but beneath it, he could smell a light, fresh scent: outside. He followed it down the corridors, using Dr. White's ID to get through the locked doors.

He passed a few hurrying people in scrubs. Roy's heart hammered, but they didn't give him a second glance. His headache went from bad to excruciating, threatening to become disabling. But the scent of outside was getting stronger. It smelled like hope.

He waved Dr. White's ID through another sensor. It took him three tries, his hands were shaking so badly. Then door slid open, and Roy came face-to-face with a pair of security guards.

The men were armed with both black boxes and dart guns, like you'd use to tranquilize a wild animal. That went a long way to confirm what they knew or guessed about Roy.

Forcing himself not to hurry, he started to walk past.

"Hey!" One guard tried to grab his arm.

Roy punched him in the stomach, doubling him over, and snatched his dart gun. In one smooth movement, he swung around and slammed the gun's butt into the second guard's shoulder. The man dropped his dart gun with a cry of pain. But before Roy could stop him, he hit a red button on the wall.

Brilliant lights began to flash. A siren went off. Pain exploded in Roy's head. His knees banged into the floor, the dart gun falling from his hand.

Clenching his jaw, Roy forced himself to his feet. He couldn't get his eyes to open. He staggered, dizzy and blind, barely able to think through the agony. He felt like he was about to pass out. Even if he managed to stay conscious, he couldn't fight. One way or another, he'd be captured and dragged back to his cell.

He only had one chance left: to transform into a wolf.

He'd sworn that he wouldn't try it here. He didn't know if it would help. He didn't even know if it was possible. He'd only become a wolf once before, in Afghanistan.

A captured Marine has a duty to escape. Whatever they do to me— whatever I've become— I'm still a Marine.

In his mind, a wolf howled.

He'd done it before. He could do it again. Roy had been avoiding the memory, but now he sought it, trying to recall every detail.

Tearing pain in my chest. Blood in my mouth. DJ's fingers digging into my shoulders. His hoarse voice shouting my name. DJ's face and the sky and the wrecked helicopter in the distance, all fading out. Hot sand under my back.

And then...

Hot sun on my fur. Four paws scrabbling in the sand. Scents everywhere, rich and distinct: me and DJ and blood and sand and weeds and metal and oil and...

Roy reached inside himself, searching for the part of him that was wild and free and would rather die than be caged.

He found his wolf.

The overwhelming dizziness eased. The sirens and flashing lights were still agonizing, but his wolf body was that crucial bit stronger, better equipped to cope with pain. He was lower to the ground, in a world without colors, but with scents as bright and clear as neon lights.

A man was raising a dart gun. Roy instinctively jumped to avoid the dart, his ears swiveling to catch the hiss and thwack as it buried itself in the wall behind him. He leaped at the man and slammed him down. The dart gun skittered across the floor.

He could smell the sharpness of the guard's fear. It would be so easy to bend his head and rip out his enemy's throat...

The fresh scent of open air was ahead of him. Roy released his prey and bounded ahead, racing through the closing door.

Freedom!

He was outside. It was night. People were shouting and running toward him.

An electric fence let out a low crackle and a smell of ozone. Roy tore toward it. He had no idea if he could jump high enough to clear it, but he'd rather die than be locked up forever. And now that he'd revealed what he was, they'd never let him go.

A dart hissed past his ear as he gathered his strength and leaped as high as he could. He cleared the fence and landed hard on the other side.

The shock of impact, in that unfamiliar body, sent him tumbling head over paws. When he finally fetched up in a heap, darts were hitting the ground all around him.

Lucky I rolled, he thought.

He gathered himself and leaped forward again. This time he landed smoothly. A forest was before him, dark and welcoming. He raced through it until all sounds and scents of pursuit were gone, and then he kept on running for the sheer joy of it.

In his wolf's body, in this natural environment without electric lights or chemical smells or crowds of humans, he finally felt at ease. For the first time since he'd been wounded, his body was working as it should, strong and swift and without pain. Even as simple a movement as his paws striking the earth was a pleasure. It felt so much better to be a wolf than it did to be a human.

That thought gave him pause. What if he liked being a wolf so much that he stopped wanting to be a man?

He reached into himself, remembering the weight of his rucksack on his back, joking with his buddies, firing his SAW…

Roy stumbled, off-balance on two feet, and grabbed at a tree to stop from falling. He took a deep breath, focused on the rough texture of the bark under his fingers, and settled into his man's body.

To his relief, the doctor's clothes had come with him. To his greater relief, the moonlight didn't hurt his eyes. The sounds and smells of the forest were distinct and noticeable, but not overwhelming. If he'd only been allowed into a natural environment earlier, he could have saved himself a whole lot of misery.

Remembering the tumble he'd taken, he checked himself for injuries. His knees and shoulders were bruised, and he'd strained his left wrist: nothing serious. Roy walked on, setting a brisk pace and taking care not to leave a trail.

For the first time, he examined the forest with a man's mind, recognizing the landscape of huge gray boulders and enormously tall trees with corrugated, cinnamon-colored bark. He'd only been to northern California once, years ago, but he'd never forgotten the redwoods.

He wasn't concerned about being alone in the wilderness with no supplies or weapons. He'd roughed it before. Weapons could be improvised, and food could be hunted or gathered.

The scents of rich earth and moss rose up with every footstep. Owls hooted, crickets chirped, and small animals rustled in the bushes. The moist dirt underfoot told him that water wouldn't be a problem. He didn't even need to make traps— as a wolf, he ought to be able to catch rabbits, maybe a deer.

His biggest concern, apart from pursuit, was the temperature. His breath condensed in puffs of mist, and the boulders were patched with frost. He didn't feel cold, but that was probably because he'd exerted himself enough to work up a sweat. But as a wolf, he had a thick fur coat. If it got too cold, he'd change. He'd never heard of wolves getting hypothermia.

Wilderness survival was easy. But figuring out what he should do once he was out of the woods was much more complicated. It could have been months since his helicopter had been shot down. What did his team think had happened to him?

Even if they're all still in-country, they'd never be okay with not hearing from me at all, Roy thought. *They probably got told that I'm dead or MIA.*

He hated to think how DJ must feel about that. It would just about kill Roy if he thought he'd done everything he'd could to save DJ and then learned that he'd died in the hospital, alone.

But now that Roy had revealed what he was, his captors would be after him for sure. They could have his entire unit's phones and email tapped, waiting for Roy to contact one of them. He couldn't risk getting in touch with anyone he knew until he learned more. He needed to find some safe place to lay low.

An odd feeling tugged at his mind, an inexplicable urge: *That way.*

That way didn't look any different from any other way. But if he'd learned one thing in his years as a Marine, it was that funny little feelings were worth paying attention to.

Funny little feelings could mean that you'd noticed tiny clues, without even noticing that you'd noticed them, that meant that there was a bomb in the road, or that the innocent-looking civilian wasn't innocent and wasn't a civilian, or that the wild-eyed man trying to charge the roadblock *was* an innocent civilian who was trying to get help for his sick wife.

He'd travel faster as a wolf. And with no supplies of any kind, he'd probably sleep safer and enjoy eating raw rabbit more as a wolf, too.

Roy found his wolf. And loped off through the redwoods, heading *that way.*